SQUELCHED

Robinne Weiss

Published by Sandfly Books

Copyright 2020 Robinne Weiss

ISBN-13: 978-0-473-50769-5

Cover design by Mibl Art

This book is also available in electronic formats.

Discover my other books and stories on my website:
https://robinneweiss.com

For my son, who refused read this one
until it was published.

1

Nico

Nico stood beside the freshly filled grave willing himself not to cry. No one else at the funeral had, and he wasn't going to be the one to show weakness, even if it was his father in the dark mahogany box down there. A hand landed heavily on his shoulder, and he jumped, cursing himself for his inattention. No one should be able to sneak up on Nico Michaelson.

"He was the best we've had in years. Tragic." Luther hardly sounded cut up. Nico could hear the barely-suppressed glee in the voice of the man who had stepped into his father's job before they'd even retrieved his body. The worst of it was, his dad would have admired Luther for that move. He would have expected Nico to do the same, if he'd been in a position to do so.

"You have the talent, boy, but if you don't have the ambition, you'll go nowhere. And we need people like you at the top—people with real power." Dad's eyes had bored into him, intense and commanding, but behind the steel was a swell of pride. *Pride in me,* Nico had thought.

And he would make Dad proud now. He straightened under Luther's hand. "Tomorrow's meeting is still on, I assume?"

"You know, no one expects you to—"

Nico turned to face Luther. "I'll be there." Then he

nodded, thinking he probably shouldn't have cut Luther off. "Thank you for being here today."

⸺❧⸺

Years had passed since his father's death, but Nico hadn't forgotten Dad's lessons. He'd risen fast within the Division, and now he had his eyes on the Assistant Director for International Operations position. Surely the old cow currently occupying it would retire soon. Then he'd be one step below Luther. Ready to take over the minute Luther stepped away from his desk, just as Luther had done to his father.

Not that he'd do anything to make that happen. Luther ran the Division with discipline and precision, and he took care of his own. Nico admired that. Someday, he'd run the Division like that himself. Same as his dad had done.

But if he was going to take over, he needed to prove his worth. He shook his head to dispel the daydreams and focused on the task at hand.

Disguised as an appliance repairman, he knocked on the apartment door. He knew she wasn't home, so he didn't wait for an answer, but sprung the lock instead. He smiled as he heard the solid click of the deadbolt sliding back. With a quick a glance at the other apartment doors, he let himself in.

2

Tory

Tory scanned the bookshelf in her living room for a second time. "Waters, Watson, Winter—where is Wilde?" She had promised to loan *The Picture of Dorian Gray* to her friend Jess. How could it not be in its place? She frowned and widened her search, running a finger along the shelf. Ah! There it was, slipped between Vanderbilt and Vincent. Her frown deepened. It wasn't like her to misshelve a book. She'd have to go through and check her whole collection over the weekend to make sure everything else was correctly shelved.

Now, though, she needed to get to work. She slipped the book into her bag along with her lunch and zipped it up. At the sound of the zip, Puck came trotting into the room, tail up, and wound around her ankles, greeting her with a loud *meow*.

"Ready for work?" Tory ran through her mental checklist as she clipped Puck's leash on. Breakfast dishes were clean and dry and put away, the kitchen counter was wiped down, her bed was made, she'd put the trash out, and fed the cat. She nodded, shrugged on her jacket, and grabbed her umbrella—autumn in Pennsylvania could be wet, and even though it looked nice out this morning, you never knew what it might be like by afternoon.

Puck meowed again and batted at his leash, dragging along the floor.

Tory bent down and picked up the end. "Yes, we're going."

When she'd first adopted Puck and started taking him with her everywhere, she'd gotten strange stares. Occasionally, she'd been kicked out of restaurants. But after a while, everyone who came into contact with her during her normal weekly routine got used to the sleek, talkative Siamese that followed her like a shadow. He had, in fact, become quite a fixture in the Laurel Glen Public Library where Tory worked.

⸺◦◦◦◦⸺

At precisely 8:30 a.m., Tory swiped her card and let herself into the library. She was surprised to see the lights already on in the old brick building.

"Morning Jess," she called to the short purple-haired woman who sat behind the checkout desk. "You're here early."

Jess stabbed at the keys, her brows knitted into a singularity. She hit return, huffed, and flung herself back in the chair.

"Something's wrong," Tory guessed. She shrugged off her coat, and Puck leapt to the desk to say good morning.

Jess sighed and reached out to pet the cat. "Morning Tory. Hey, Puck. How's it going, dude?" The cat's tail thrashed, and he purred loudly as he leaned into Jess's scratches.

"Jess, what's wrong?" Tory pulled out a chair and sat next to her friend.

Jess finally looked at Tory. Her eyes were bloodshot, her mascara smudged. She'd penciled her eyebrows into black slashes, and her sharply-defined red lips were more savage than seduction. "Three guesses."

Tory laughed. "Michael."

Jess raised her index finger. "Got it in one." She

blinked rapidly as her eyes filled with tears.

"What this time? Or should I ask *who* this time? Jess, I know I've said it before, but—"

Jess raised her hand. "No need to say it again. When I caught him in *my* apartment last night in bed with *my* sister, I kicked him out on his ass."

"Your *sister*?" Tory raised her eyebrows.

"Yeah." Jess sniffed and dabbed at her eyes before squaring her shoulders and growling, "And I booted her out too."

"About time. Good for you." Jess's sister had been squatting in her apartment like a toad, mooching off her for months after losing her job. As far as Tory could tell, she had settled in for good.

Jess hung her head. "Yeah. Good for me, I guess."

"I'm sorry, Jess. I know it feels awful now, but I'm sure it's for the best. Is there anything I can do for you?"

Jess huffed. "Not unless you'd like to commit murder." She took in a shaky breath. "No. I'll be fine." She forced a smile, more a bearing of fangs than a show of mirth. "Now we can be single together."

Tory put a hand on Jess's shoulder. "If you need to take the day off, I'm sure I can manage without you. Go home, get some rest—it looks like you didn't sleep last night. I brought you the book you wanted. You could curl up on the couch and read all day."

Jess shook her head. "No. The distraction will be good for me. And, hey, the day can only get better, right?" She fingered a spiky lock of her hair. "Maybe I'll dye my hair tonight."

"What color this time?" Tory asked with a smile. Jess rarely had the same hair color for more than a few weeks at a time. Her response to stress was to dye her hair.

Jess tossed her head. "I don't know. Maybe green."

Tory laughed. "For jealousy?"

"And because Michael hates green."

The Laurel Glen Public Library was a quiet place, even for a library. Its creaking floors, cramped spaces, and small windows encouraged library patrons to drive ten miles to the modern, spacious, light and airy Johnsonburg Library, which sported a coffee shop, free Wi-Fi, study rooms, power outlets at every table, a preschool, and conference facilities.

But Laurel Glen had Puck.

When Tory was hired by the library, she insisted as part of her contract that she be allowed to bring Puck to work with her. At first the director balked, but applicants for the position had been few because Johnsonburg Library was about to open. Nobody wanted to work at Laurel Glen if they could instead work at Johnsonburg. And then, while they were still negotiating with her, the library staff discovered a nest of mice tucked into a cozy little niche between a rare copy of *Wood's Natural History* and a signed edition of *The Lord of the Rings* in a basement storage room. The mice had gnawed into the covers of both books and used the resulting fluff as nesting material. Puck was welcomed after that.

Puck greeted the first visitor of the day with a loud *meow*.

"Good morning Mr. O'Brien!" Tory smiled as the elderly man patted Puck's head. "It's good to see you again. We missed you last week. Are you feeling better?"

"Yes. Thank you my dear. And thanks for calling last week when I didn't show up. My daughter was thrilled a young lass was looking after me."

Tory laughed. She loved Mr. O'Brien's lingering accent and the mischievous twinkle in his eye. He must have been the stereotypical Irish rogue when he was young. "Did you tell her it was just the librarian, reminding you of overdue books?" In truth, the computer system sent out

6

automatic letters for overdue books, but Tory had noticed Mr. O'Brien's absence—he always visited the library on Tuesday—and thought she should call instead. You never knew with elderly people living alone. What if they fell and broke a leg, and no one noticed until the smell started bothering the neighbors? She shuddered at the thought and did her best to keep tabs on her regulars.

Puck had obviously missed Mr. O'Brien too. He hopped to the floor and reared up on his hind legs, patting the man's pocket, and issuing a querying *meow*. Mr. O'Brien chuckled. "Yes, I brought your treat, you cheeky bastard." He reached a hand into his pocket and pulled out a couple of fish-shaped cat treats. "Say hello." He held a treat high in the air.

Puck meowed, teetering on hind legs, eyeing the treat.

"Now jump!" Puck sprang up, neatly picking the treat from Mr. O'Brien's fingers. "Ah! Good boy!" He bent and held out the remaining treats for Puck. When the cat finished, Mr. O'Brien gave him another scratch on the head. "Come on. Let's go find us a good murder mystery." He shuffled further into the library, with Puck padding behind, tail up, the tip waving like a flag.

Library patrons loved Puck. He strolled the library at liberty, greeting people he liked and snubbing those he didn't in true cat fashion, with a rear end in the face. He curled up with children in the bean bag chairs in the picture book section and rubbed against little old ladies' ankles among the romance novels. He glided along the tops of bookshelves and lounged on windowsills. He often sat, sphinx-like, on the librarians' desk, blinking at patrons as they checked out books. Tory imagined him asking them riddles, and then leaving dead mice in their library books if they answered incorrectly.

"Nice cat." The man surprised Tory, coming up quietly behind her as she re-shelved books with Puck riding on her shoulders. She turned to face him, and he surprised her again—he was young. Most of Laurel Glen's patrons were either elderly, preferring the cozy comfort of a traditional library, or children who came to the library to play with Puck. This curly-haired man couldn't have been much older than thirty. Puck's tail went up and he leapt deftly to the man's shoulder.

"Oh! Sorry about that," Tory cried. "He has no respect for personal space." She reached out to snatch him away.

"No, it's okay," the man replied. He stepped away from Tory's outstretched arms.

Tory hesitated, and then drew her arms back. "Can I help you with anything? Are you looking for something in particular?" Laurel Glen Library housed most of the county's older volumes—out-of-date, musty copies of everything from cookbooks to crime novels. People outside Laurel Glen's normal demographic who turned up were often searching for a specific book, referred here by the online catalogue.

"Ah … yeah. I'm looking for—" he glanced around at the shelves and ran a hand through his hair "—for a copy of *Middlemarch* by George Eliot."

Tory tried not to raise her eyebrows. It was unusual for anyone to ask for George Eliot's work, and those who *did* ask were generally women. Not that Eliot's books didn't deserve a wider audience, in Tory's mind. They beat the socks off the more popular and far more vapid Jane Austen books. "George Eliot's books are shelved over here." She turned and walked down the aisle and around the corner into the next aisle, trusting the man to follow. Puck hopped off the man's shoulder and trotted at Tory's heels.

"Here it is." She pulled the book from the shelf and held it out to him. He swallowed and blinked at the book for a moment, and then cautiously reached out, snatching it as though he was afraid Tory would bite him.

"Thanks." The man nodded and then turned and disappeared into the next aisle.

Tory shrugged. "Am I that scary?" she asked Puck. He answered by scratching his ear, and then bounded off toward the children's section.

———

At ten-thirty, Tory pushed her empty cart back to the desk where Jess was helping Mrs. Martin, a retired schoolteacher, load a stack of books into her bag.

Tory glanced at the titles. "Lots of knitting planned?"

Mrs. Martin looked up with a smile. "Yes. There's another grandchild on the way."

"Congratulations!" Tory parked her cart. She held the door for Mrs. Martin and wished her a good day. Then she turned back to Jess. "Coffee?"

"I need a large today," Jess replied. She rubbed her face. "Maybe two larges."

Tory smiled. "Coming right up." She picked up her purse and headed out the door to Espressions of Interest, the café across the street from the library.

Tory opened the door of the café, and the owner's voice boomed out. "There's Tory! It must be ten-thirty."

She smiled at the big dreadlocked blond. "Good morning, Leroy. The usual for me today, but Jess wants a large."

Leroy nodded and started to make the coffees. "Where's the feline this morning? I saved him a little chicken."

Espressions of Interest was one of the few

restaurants that didn't mind Puck's presence, though she had been shooed out the door once when the health inspector was there. "He's cavorting with a couple of preschoolers at the library." Tory laughed. "Last I checked, they had every single cat book off the shelves."

Leroy chuckled.

Tory paid for her drinks and accepted Puck's chicken, wrapped in a square of butcher paper. "You spoil him, you know?"

Leroy laughed. "Tell him I missed him."

When Tory returned to the library with Puck's treat, Jess raised her eyebrows. "That's three weeks now Leroy's been saving food for your cat every day. He must seriously be in love with you."

Tory scoffed and waved a hand. "He just likes cats, that's all."

"Uh-huh. Ten bucks says he asks you out before the week is over."

Tory snorted. "He'll ask Puck out, not me."

"Speak of the devil."

Puck trotted toward the desk ahead of the children he'd been sitting with. Their mother trailed behind. When he heard the crinkling of butcher paper, he bounded forward. Tory set the meat on the floor for him, and Jess checked out the children's books.

"Tory!" cried one of the children—Natalie or Natasha—she had a hard time telling the twins apart. "Puck can read!"

Tory crouched down beside the girls. "Really? What's his favorite book?"

"*The Cat in the Hat!*"

Tory smiled. "No surprise there. He's just as troublesome as the Cat in the Hat sometimes." She ruffled the girl's hair and stood.

When the children left, Tory strolled with her

coffee to the children's area and re-shelved the books they'd scattered. As she approached the desk again, the phone rang. Jess answered.

"Laurel Glen Public Library, Jess speaking ... Hi Margo." She raised her eyebrows at Tory. Margo was the director of the county library system. She treated Laurel Glen with the sort of disdain Puck reserved for dogs. "We're good. Things are going well here ... A quiet day, yes ..." There was a long pause, and Jess frowned. "What?" She pressed her lips together sending her savage look into overdrive. "I see ... When? ... Yes ... I understand ... Yes, we'll do that ... Thank you." Jess put down the receiver and swore. She looked up at Tory, leaning over the desk now. "They're closing us down."

3

⸰⸭⸰

Nico

Nico sat in the Espressions of Interest café, feigning interest
in his book. He checked the time—10:44—something was
wrong. The woman was always here by 10:32. Maybe this job
was finally going to become more interesting.

He laughed to himself. Yeah, right. He'd been on
this assignment for a month now, and the woman he was
tailing hadn't altered her weekly routine by more than a
minute. He wasn't even really tailing her anymore; he was
simply showing up where he knew she would be arriving
soon. It was too much to hope she was doing something of
interest to the Division.

Oh, she was powerful—he agreed with his boss
there. He didn't dare get too close to her; no one knew what
she was capable of. But she was so *boring*.

In his head, Nico had been composing the report
he was going to submit to the Division. *Subject appears not
to recognize her own nature. She has no imagination and, provided
she is left alone, I am confident she will never use her power in any
conscious way. Her habits are so predictable, it would be simple to limit
her contact with Users, thus rendering her innocuous.*

Innocuous. Except she would kill him with boredom
if he was stuck tailing her for much longer. He checked the
time again—10:45. This was the most interesting thing to
happen in four weeks. He should try to locate her. He'd

catch hell back at the office if he lost her. He knocked back the last of his coffee and was about to rise when she stepped through the door. He pulled out his book and ducked his head, pretending to read.

"Tory! You're late today." Leroy wagged a finger at the woman.

She looked tired. "Yes, it's been a difficult week." She brightened. "But I brought Puck with me."

"Ah! My little feline friend." He reached out to pet the cat perched on the woman's shoulders. What sort of cat rode around on people's shoulders? Puck purred and playfully batted Leroy's hand. "I expect I can find a little something for you, Puck." He stepped into the back and returned with a lump of meat on a sheet of butcher paper. He handed it to Tory, and the cat pounced on it as she set it on the floor for him. That had to break half a dozen health and safety rules.

Leroy's gaze turned back to Tory. "It must be something bad to make you fifteen minutes late for your coffee."

Tory nodded. "They're closing the library as of the end of the month."

"Oh no! And what about you and Jess?"

"We're out of a job." The woman's face scrunched up, twisting the scar on her left cheek. Nico shuddered inwardly. That scar gave her a sinister look, even half-hidden with makeup; it was like an evil clown smile, bright and shiny against her dark complexion. It apparently didn't faze Leroy, though, because he took Tory's hand in his.

"Oh, Tory. I'm so sorry. Look, today's coffee is on me, for both of you. The usual?"

The woman sniffed and blinked. "That's sweet of you, Leroy, but there's no need. We'll both manage. It's just … well, you know, it means looking for a new job, probably a new apartment …" She sighed. "It totally makes sense for

13

the county to close Laurel Glen Library. It's an anachronism. Doesn't even have Wi-Fi. But ... well ... it's my job, and I like it."

Leroy handed over two coffees, stubbornly refusing to accept payment for them. Tory thanked him and turned, looking for Puck. It was only then Nico noticed the cat rubbing around his ankles.

The woman set down her coffees and swooped to pick up the cat. Nico scooted his chair back from her. "I'm sorry, sir. He's a little too friendly sometimes." Her eyes rose to his face. "Oh!" She smiled. "You were at the library on Tuesday. Are you enjoying *Middlemarch*?"

Nico forgot to breathe and felt his pulse race. He wasn't supposed to catch the attention of the person he was tailing. He should have known she'd recognize him—he wasn't a *regular*, and her life was nothing but regulars. He also should have been able to smoothly recover, but she was so close, it made his lungs burn and scattered his thoughts. "I ... um ... yeah, it's good." He lifted the book from the table in a sort of salute. "Thanks for asking."

She smiled and nodded, then hoisted the cat onto her shoulder, picked up her coffees, and left the café.

—⸺∞⸺—

That evening, Nico phoned his boss after sending in his written report for the week. He hoped James would take him off the assignment.

He was disappointed.

"Keep following her. This change in employment might reveal something. We know she's been in contact with that Russian agent—one of the ones we think tried to rig the election. She might contact him again."

Nico tried to keep his voice reasonable, tried not to whine. "As far as I've seen, that Russia 'contact' was all one-sided, initiated by the Russian. Since I've been keeping tabs on her, she hasn't responded to him at all. Honestly, the woman isn't a threat to anyone, provided we stay away from her. She's nothing. All she's done for the past month is go to work, walk her cat in the park, and visit used bookstores on the weekends."

"And what about Arthur Grayson? She walked into his bookstore, and Arthur was dead before he knew what hit him. Even oblivious to her power, she's a threat."

"Arthur's death was an unfortunate accident. The woman doesn't travel far. She has a routine. All we have to do is stay out of her way. The less we have to do with her, the less likely she is to find out what she is and use it against us."

"Her father is a known anti-government agitator, and he knows what she is."

"But she's never met him!"

"We *assume* she's never met him, because he's alive. That doesn't mean she hasn't ever communicated with him. We can't assume she hasn't been influenced by his thinking. And if she learns about her power, if she can control it? Well, I don't even want to think about the damage she could do."

Nico sighed. "James, I'm begging you. Don't make me follow her anymore. I'm the best in the Division, you know that. Why am I stuck on this effing assignment? Can't you put Clark or Davis on this job? It's a waste of my time, a waste of my talent."

"You're on this job precisely *because* you're the best in the Division. The Director of the FBI has taken a great deal of interest in this woman. He wants to know everything about her skills, her nature and her sympathies. We can't mess this up. Clark is too old—you know as well as I do she'd snuff him out as soon as he was within ten feet of her. And I've put Davis on the Russia investigation."

"You put *Davis* on the Russia job?" Nico's voice

rose. "You promised *me* that posting. I've been studying goddamn Russian for months!" That posting was supposed to earn him a step up within the Division. How could James have taken it from him?

Nico could imagine James on the other end of the line closing his eyes and pinching the bridge of his nose, like he always did when trying to hold his temper. "You have your orders, Nico. You can take them, or you can quit. You choose."

Nico huffed. Quitting wasn't an option, and James knew it. He tried to swallow his outrage. "How long do I have to keep following her?"

"Until I tell you to stop." James hung up.

Nico slouched in his chair. "Fuck."

4

⟨∞⟩

Tory

In two weeks Tory would be out of a job. She paced her apartment, a knot cinched tight inside her stomach. Twenty-eight, single, and facing unemployment—if that wasn't failure, she didn't know what was. She looked around her living room at her couch and mismatched armchair, cast-offs from her mom that she loved because they were familiar from her childhood. She had a plain wooden coffee table and a floor lamp she'd picked up on sale at Walmart when she first moved in. And there was the floor-to-ceiling shelf unit filled with her favorite books, all properly labeled and shelved using the Dewey Decimal System.

Everything was exactly as she liked it, and it reminded her of her childhood home and her mother's used bookstore. Jess would call it boring, but the thought she might lose the comfort of her familiar apartment made Tory jittery and unable to sit down.

Her thoughts leapt to finances. She had a fair bit of money saved up—she wasn't a big spender, and she gave herself a strict budget on the weekends when she scoured used book stores for interesting reads. She wondered how long she could pay the rent without a job.

And what if she couldn't find a job? What if the only job she could find was far away, or wouldn't allow her to bring Puck to work? What if choosing a career as a librarian had been a big mistake? Everyone talked about libraries as an endangered species—funding cuts, e-books, a population that got more and more of its reading material online every year. What if she had to choose another career? What else could she possibly do? What skills did she really have? She knew the Dewey Decimal System and the Library of Congress Classification by heart. She could ferret out information on just about anything on the internet or in print. She was good at organizing things. She had a hard time imagining what other career would require those skills.

And she didn't *want* another career, anyway. She flopped onto the couch beside Puck. "What should I do when I grow up?"

Meow!

"Yeah, I figured that's what you'd say." Puck reached out and pawed her leg until she scratched him behind the ear. "Sometimes I think my only worth is as an ear scratcher for you."

The phone rang. It was Jess. "I'm guessing you're sitting on the couch moping about losing your job," she accused Tory.

Tory laughed, the knot in her stomach loosening slightly. "And you?"

"I have a plan. And I've got a bottle of expensive French wine Michael bought for my sister, which I confiscated before I kicked him out. You got two glasses? I'll be over in five."

Tory smiled as she hung up the phone. She and Jess had roomed together at university, first by luck of the draw in freshman dormitory assignments, and later by design. Jess was everything Tory wasn't—messy, loud, bossy, creative, decisive. They should have hated each other, but somehow, stumbling through that first year away from home, confused, lonely, and flexing their new adulthood, they'd bonded. Tory was thrilled to be working with her, after Jess aborted her career as a journalist.

When Jess arrived, she plonked the bottle down on the coffee table and kicked back in Tory's armchair. Tory poured the wine into their glasses. "So. What's your plan?" She handed a glass to Jess.

"Road trip."

Tory curled up on the couch. "Road trip? Where to?"

Jess shrugged. "Who cares? But it's the perfect thing to do. We're both out of a job; we're both unencumbered by the male sex. We should take off for a couple of weeks, see some of the country. I've always wanted to visit Florida; we could go to Disneyland! I don't know. See Cape Canaveral. We could stop in D.C. and go to the Smithsonian. I don't care. I just want to go somewhere, have an adventure."

"And what would I do with Puck? I can't leave him at a cattery for two weeks."

"Bring him with us."

Tory frowned. Puck enjoyed car rides, but she'd never taken him on a long trip.

In fact, she'd never taken a long trip. Not once in twenty-eight years. The farthest she'd ever gone from her hometown had been two hours' drive to university. Lack of money, lack of time, lack of imagination—there had always been an excuse to stay home.

Money wasn't a problem for now. And in two weeks, she'd have plenty of time off. But she struggled to imagine a trip to nowhere in particular. She shook her head. "I don't know."

"What do you mean, you don't know? It's a great plan. Just us and Puck and the road!"

"I feel like I should be looking for a job, not going on a trip."

Jess waved a hand. "A couple of weeks won't matter. There will still be jobs when we get back. And who knows?

Maybe we'll both find work along the way. There are libraries all across the country. No reason we have to stay here."

No reason except that Tory didn't want to move. She didn't want anything to change. Part of her hoped that if she didn't do anything, life would simply go back to normal. She envied Jess's ability to just roll with the punches. She sighed. "Traveling without any destination or goal in mind? I don't know, Jess. It sounds ..." Tory laughed. "It's like something a college freshman would do."

"Exactly!"

Tory shook her head. "I'm not sure."

Jess sipped her wine, studying Tory. "What would it take to convince you?"

Tory shrugged.

"What if we had a goal? Is there somewhere you've always wanted to go? Something you've always wanted to see?"

Something she'd always wanted to see? *Someone.*

"My dad."

"Huh?"

"My dad. He vanished the day I was born."

Jess frowned. "Vanished as in disappeared, or vanished as in left your mom?"

Tory shrugged. "I'm not sure. He's not dead. He secretly gave me money for university."

"But you've never met him?"

Tory shook her head. "I don't even know his name, or what he looks like. Mom blacked out all the pictures with him in them."

Jess scoffed. "Sounds like he's not worth searching for."

Maybe not, but she was surprised at how strong the desire was, now that she'd thought about it.

The following day, Jess and Tory began packing up books and equipment destined to be scattered to the other county libraries. Library visitation spiked for a week or so as people came in to say goodbye, and then dropped to almost nothing.

"We're so sorry you're closing," Natasha and Natalie's mom said on Tuesday. "It's such a shame."

"We drew pictures of Puck for you!" The girls handed Tory wrinkled drawings of a gray cat lounging on a pile of books.

Tory knelt and marveled at the drawings. "These are lovely! Thank you, girls!"

"We don't want to go to the new library," said one of them with a pout.

Tory smiled. "The new library is very nice. It's got a huge children's section with lots of cushy chairs and games, and even a book cave."

The girls' eyes went wide at the thought. Tory sighed inwardly. They *would* love the new library. Everyone would, once they got used to it. But closing Laurel Glen still felt like burying a friend.

"Will we see Puck at one of the other libraries?" an elderly woman, Mrs. Johnson, asked hopefully on her usual Wednesday visit.

Tory smiled. "Probably not."

"I'm sorry. I'm sure you'll find another job soon." She patted Tory's hand and smiled. "Or maybe a husband, eh?"

Tory squashed her irritation at the assumption that a woman's life was a choice between marriage or work. Maybe it had been for Mrs. Johnson. "Maybe." *Doubtful.*

Jess grinned after the old woman as she shuffled out the door. Then she turned to Tory. "There's always Leroy, you know, if you don't get a job."

Tory rolled her eyes. "Will you back off about Leroy? Just because he asked me out this morning—"

"I can't believe you said no!"

"I'm busy. I'm going to my mother's place this weekend."

"So will you say yes next week when he asks?"

"Jess."

"Okay, okay. I'll lay off. I just want to see you happy. A little romance would go a long way, you know." She wrapped an arm around Tory's shoulder and squeezed.

Tory smiled. "I know." She hugged Jess back. Her friend meant well, but sometimes Tory thought they lived in parallel universes. Jess almost always had a boyfriend and was madly in love with every one, until he invariably turned out to be a jerk. Tory dated now and again, but rarely got beyond the first date with anyone. She enjoyed them, for the most part, but sparks simply didn't fly between her and any of the men she'd dated. She was beginning to think there was something wrong with her. Surely she should have fallen in love at least once by her age.

Jess finished filling a box, taped it shut, and labeled it *Fiction: AAR – ABI*. She shoved it aside, and then scrutinized Tory as she packed another box. "Maybe you're gay."

Tory sighed. She knew Jess wouldn't be able to let it go. "I considered that a few years ago. Briefly."

"And?"

Tory chuckled. "I'm not gay." Her one 'date' with a woman had been a complete disaster. She had been up-front with Lily about her uncertain sexuality, and Lily had been cool with that. But every advance Lily made was met by an involuntary withdrawal by Tory. Lily finally gave up, saying "I don't know *what* you are, but you're definitely not gay."

"So what's wrong with Leroy? He's good-looking, friendly, likes your cat."

"Sounds like *you* should date him, Jess."

"*I* am off men for the moment. Besides, he hasn't asked *me* out."

"Well, maybe I'll say yes next week."

Jess made a satisfied grunt.

"But don't expect anything to come of it."

On the weekend, Tory drove up to Oakfield to visit her mother. She lived in a little gabled house nestled amongst similar houses around the corner from the bookstore she owned. Tory had grown up in the house, and she still called it home. It had hardly changed since she'd left ten years ago, and Tory enjoyed her usual rituals upon arrival. After greeting her mother, she carried her overnight bag upstairs to her old bedroom. She peeked out her little dormer window into the postage-stamp back yard to check on her favorite tree—blazing yellow now with autumn color.

On her way back downstairs, she stopped at each photograph hung in the stairwell: Mom's high school graduation photo, in which she wore those horrible horn-rimmed glasses; Mom smiling in front of her bookstore the day it opened; Mom's wedding photo, with her father's face carefully inked out; Tory as a baby chewing on her first picture book; her as a child, curled up in a corner of the bookstore, reading; and a montage of her graduations from high school, undergraduate, and graduate school. So much for those graduations—all that education and she was still losing her job.

She made her way into the warmth of the kitchen, where her mother waited with a steaming mug of coffee. Puck was already curled up on her lap, purring at the attention she lavished on him.

"Have you decided what you'll do?" her mother asked. "You know, you're welcome to move back home and help out at the store until you find something."

Tory poured herself a cup of coffee and sat across the table from her mother. She took a sip and considered how to start this conversation. "Thanks, Mom. I actually thought I might take a little time off."

"Oh?"

Tory continued. "Jess and I were considering taking a road trip. You know, see the country a bit. I've never even been out of the state." She took a deep breath. "I thought I might look for Dad."

Her mother swallowed and set her mug carefully on the table. "Why would you look for your father? He abandoned you the minute you were born." Her mother's rage simmered in her clipped words, even after twenty-eight years.

"But he didn't abandon me. Why did he set up that bank account for me, with all that money in it to pay for my college tuition?"

Her mother huffed. "Guilt finally got to him, I suppose, after leaving me to raise you on my own. He left me while I was still in the hospital with you! What kind of father does that? I had to bring you home in a taxi, by myself. He's a selfish asshole who realized at the last minute that a baby would cramp his style, so he left."

"Maybe there's some other explanation. Maybe—"

"There's no other explanation. He explained it himself." Her mother rose and disappeared to her bedroom, emerging a moment later holding a small wooden box. She lifted the lid and pulled out a scrap of paper that looked like it had been crumpled and smoothed out again many times. She thrust the paper at Tory. "His explanation. He left it with the ward nurse. Didn't even have the guts to hand it to me."

Tory carefully unfolded the paper.

My Dear Donna,

I am sorry, my love. I cannot stay or I will lose myself. As dear as she is, this child will be the death of me. There is a book I must find, and then I may return.

Love,
Vic

Tory finished reading and looked up, a frown on her face. "Dad left to—"

"To look for a book. Yes. Because a book was obviously more important than raising his daughter." Her mother slammed her fist on the table, sloshing coffee out of her cup.

"And the book?"

Her mother waved her hand as though swishing away a pesky fly. "I assume it's the one written on the back of that sheet—*Magical Anomalies of the New World*. I've looked for it. The full name is *Magical Anomalies of the New World: 1640 to 1840*. Written by Esther Godwit. What kind of name is that? As far as I can tell, all twelve copies ever printed were destroyed by church leaders in a witchcraft purge in 1846. The book no longer exists, and your father is never coming back. Not that I expected him to." She picked up her coffee and glared over the rim as she took a slurp.

Tory re-read the note. Her father had signed it *Vic*. Short for Victor? She knew better than to ask her mother. Not right now, at least. "Can I keep this?"

Her mother waved her hand again. "Be my guest. I memorized it years ago. I only kept it to show you, figuring I'd have to talk you out of trying to find him someday." She jabbed a finger at the paper. "There's the kind of man he is—chose a book over his own daughter. Forget him." She held out the box. "Here, take this too. It was a gift from your father. Used to play music when you lifted the lid. Stopped working after you were born. I thought it was a fitting place to put his damned note."

Tory took the box and carefully placed the paper back inside it. They drank their coffee in silence for a few minutes. Tory wanted to ask more about her father, but anger poured off her mother in hot waves. Her mother finished her drink. She stood and set the dirty cup in the sink. Gripping the edge of the sink without turning, she said, "Your idea of a road trip with Jess sounds like a lot of fun. But don't go looking for your father, Tory. If he had wanted to be part of your life, he would have stayed."

5

Nico

Nico watched from his hideout in the shrubbery as Tory and Jess loaded bags and cat into Tory's car. Who takes a cat on a road trip? Nico muttered, "Davis is on his way to Russia to investigate international espionage, and I'm following the crazy cat lady."

"Is that everything?" Tory asked.

"That's the lot." Jess slammed the hatch.

"I suppose we're ready, then."

Jess let out a whoop, but Nico didn't stick around to watch them get into the car. He was scuttling down the side street to his own vehicle.

He pulled out onto the street, discreetly letting another car pass before tailing the blue Ford Escort.

In the past two weeks, Nico had spent seventy-two hours listening to Tory and Jess pack up the contents of the library through the bug he'd placed on the underside of the checkout desk. He'd spent fifty-six hours listening to her talk to her cat in her apartment through the bug he'd tucked behind the bookshelf. He'd spent twenty hours following her on foot to and from work and in the park where she walked the cat every day. And he'd spent four hours shadowing her and Leroy on a date. At least on the date he got to see a movie. Otherwise, it had been one hundred and fifty-two hours of unrelieved boredom.

He'd monitored her phone calls and her e-mail. He'd followed her on Facebook through a false account. He'd watched her Twitter feed. He even subjected himself to the irritation of LinkedIn to check her professional profile and activity there. She was as boring online as she was in real life.

The woman was perhaps the most uninteresting person Nico had ever had the misfortune of tailing.

And worst of all, he had to do it without his usual tools. He had to rely on false moustaches (the adhesive gave him a terrible rash), wigs (who would have thought they were so itchy?), and padded clothing (hot and uncomfortable) for disguise. He couldn't *push* her gaze off him without her knowing. He couldn't make her forget the black sedan with tinted windows that appeared everywhere she did. It was like walking down the street naked. It turned his ordinary swagger into a mincing scurry at the indignity, the impotence of his situation.

Oh, he'd tried his usual disguises. He'd tested her. He had entered the library one day looking like a wrinkled octogenarian. She stripped the disguise off him before he even reached the aisle where she was shelving books, and she didn't even know she was doing it. He shuddered to think what sort of monster she would become if she found out what she was. The FBI was right to be concerned about her. Luckily, her discovering her power was about as likely as bipartisan support for a healthcare bill in Congress. Finding out on her own was nearly impossible, and anyone who could tell her wouldn't stick around to do it. Not even her father had done that.

If Tory made contact with him, of course, he might tell her. But would she believe his story? Not likely, coming from the man who had abandoned her when she was an infant. It would challenge everything Tory believed about herself.

Nico wasn't particularly worried that she would find him, anyway. She'd searched the internet for men named Vic, but with little to go on except his nickname, she was unlikely to track him down. And if she saw a picture of him online, would she guess that a man who looked no older than thirty-seven could be her father? She'd probably dismiss him without ever making contact. No. Tory wouldn't find her father.

He mused as he followed the Escort onto the freeway. It was no surprise Tory had never met her father. He couldn't have raised her, anyway. It probably would have killed him to try—the man was in his late eighties, old enough to be her grandfather. Nico chuckled at the thought that Tory's mom probably had no idea he was so old—the man looked fifty years younger than his true age.

Nico knew more about Tory's father than she did. Victor Hughes, Professor of Archaeology at Boston University was regularly monitored under the FBI's 'Salem' program. He had a strong anti-government stance and had been arrested in the late 1960s for participation in an anti-war demonstration that turned violent. Nico wondered how much Tory's mother knew about Victor's past, and what had possessed Victor to marry a Normal who he'd have to lie to for the rest of his life.

His thoughts were interrupted when the Escort exited the freeway ahead of him.

"Bathroom break already?" he muttered.

6

⎯⎯⎯⎯

Tory

"This is our exit." Jess peered at the map on her phone. "Turn left at the end of the ramp, and then go two and a half miles to Beacon Street, where you'll turn right. Beacon Books is four blocks down on the left."

Tory signaled and pulled onto the exit ramp. A gas station and a McDonald's flanked the end of the ramp. All the usual other fast food dives lined the street near the freeway entrance. They could have been in any town in America—until they turned onto Beacon Street and stepped back in time. Tory smiled as she took in the Victorian-era houses and store fronts.

"*Beacon Street historic district,*" Jess read as they passed an ornate sign.

"It's gorgeous!"

Jess pointed. "There it is—Beacon Books. Wow! That sign is brilliant!"

Tory struggled to parallel-park across the street, thankful the only witness was Jess. When she'd finally tucked her car into the space, she looked at the store. It had big bay windows in a yellow, wood-sided facade. Worn sandstone steps led to a heavy wooden door hung with a notice that declared the store open. She craned her neck to see the hanging panel affixed to a bracket above the entrance. "What about the sign?"

"You can't see it from here." They were looking at it straight on edge. "Get out and look—it was glowing and moving."

Puck raised his head from where he lay curled on the back seat. *Meow!*

"Come on, Puck." Tory reached in and lifted the floppy warm cat off the seat. She clipped his leash on, but kept him in her arms as she stepped out onto the quiet street. Jess joined her, and they waited for a black sedan to pass. Then she angled across the street to get a better view of the sign. She frowned. "It doesn't even say the name of the store. Are you sure we have the right place?"

Jess peered up. "Aw! It's not working now. As we were driving up, the image of the lighthouse lit up, and the little beam of light coming from the lighthouse swung around to the other side of the sign and lit up the name, Beacon Books. It was so cool!"

"Well, it's just a picture of a lighthouse now." Tory shrugged, disappointed she'd missed out. They made their way to the door and stepped inside.

The store appeared deserted. There was no one behind the counter, so they wandered the aisles. Tory let Puck down to trot alongside them.

"Wow. Lots of books on hunting and fishing," Jess remarked.

"And cookbooks. Look. Here's one just on chocolate!" Tory slipped the book off the shelf and opened it to a photograph of a chocolate cake, decorated with chocolate curls and gold leaf. "Wow! I want to make that one."

Jess peered over Tory's shoulder. "You don't even cook."

"Maybe I should learn. I'm unemployed now, I have time on my hands." She shut the book and put it back on the shelf.

"Oh, here's my section!" Jess exclaimed from the next aisle.

"Romance?" Tory guessed.

Jess laughed. "And I thought there were a lot of hunting and fishing books."

"I'll leave you to them." Tory didn't have much interest in reading romances, but Jess couldn't get enough of them. When a new one came into the library, she would read it first, before entering it into the system for patrons to check out.

Puck rounded the shelf ahead of Tory and hissed. Tory hurried to catch up, and saw a gray-haired woman entering the shop through a door behind the counter. "Oh!" The woman gave a start. "My goodness! I didn't hear you come in." She glanced at the door. "Is my doorbell not working?"

"Sorry to startle you. I didn't hear a bell when we walked in." Tory hooked a thumb toward the door. "I think your sign is broken too."

Puck growled low in his throat. The woman frowned. "You've brought a cat into my shop?"

Tory stepped toward the counter. "He's well-behaved ... usually ..." She glanced back at Puck, who was resisting her tug on his leash. His fur was standing on end, making him look like a bottle brush. "I wonder if you can help me. I'm looking for a particular book." She'd written the name of the book on a piece of paper, and now placed it on the counter. "It's an old book, and apparently quite rare." She looked up at the woman. "Are you okay?" The woman's eyes were wide and she pressed herself against the back wall.

"I'm afraid I have to ask you to leave." She swallowed. "I can't help you."

Tory paused. "I'm sorry, is there a problem with Puck? He's well-behaved, and we won't be long. I'm just looking for this one book, you see."

The woman's eyes darted between Tory, Puck and the door. "Just leave. Get out of my shop. I ... I have to close for a while. Family issues."

Jess came up from behind, a pair of novels in her hand. "Oh. Can I pay for these first?"

The woman shook her head. "No. Please. Just take them."

"But I'm happy to pay." Jess smiled helpfully.

"No. Take them and go. Please." She waved her hands, as if shooing them away.

Tory and Jess shared a bewildered look. Jess shrugged. "Thanks." They left the store, and Tory heard the woman bolt the door as they reached the car.

Tory settled in behind the wheel and pulled out onto the street. "That was weird."

"Yeah. Really weird," replied Jess. "I can't believe she wouldn't let me pay."

"She looked terrified."

"Yeah. Of *you*."

"Me?" Tory shook her head. "I don't know. She acted fine until I showed her the title of that book. I think it was the book that did it."

"A book title terrified her?" Jess laughed.

Tory laughed. "I don't know. Why would *I* scare her? But my father was looking for that book, and Mom said all the copies were supposedly burned. *Someone* thought the book was dangerous."

"Yeah, in the eighteen hundreds when people still believed in witchcraft and in women who'd sold their souls to the devil in exchange for sex, or whatever." She laughed. "Nah. My guess is there *is* a copy of the book left. It must have been stolen or something—probably worth a fortune if all the copies were supposedly burnt. She must have thought you were an undercover cop, looking for the thief. Maybe she knows who stole it." Her eyes widened. "Maybe *she's* the thief!"

Tory raised her eyebrows. "So you think we should go back and question her?"

"Maybe we should. We could make fake police badges and act all official and everything."

"Sure. What could go wrong?" Tory chuckled. "You should write crime novels, Jess. You've got a great imagination."

Jess sighed dramatically. "You never take me seriously."

"You're rarely serious."

"Well, I'm serious now when I say you've just missed the freeway entrance."

"Shit." Tory turned around to the accompaniment of Jess's laughter.

As they accelerated onto the highway, Jess suddenly sat up straight. "Tory! What if your *dad* is the thief?"

"Jess, we don't even know the book was stolen. We don't even know if it exists."

"Yeah, but your dad was looking for the book."

"Twenty-eight years ago. Maybe he found it then. Bought it legitimately. It could have been stolen *from* him, not *by* him." She thought for a moment. "If he'd found it, he'd have come back though. That's what he said in his note."

"What *is* that book? And what sort of man is your dad, to have wanted an old book so desperately he left his wife and infant daughter to look for it?"

"You mean, other than a jerk?" Tory shook her head. "Maybe Mom was right. Maybe I shouldn't go looking for him."

"No. I think you need to find him. I've been doing some research, and I think your dad is at the root of all your troubles with men."

Tory laughed. "My troubles with men? Jess, there are no men in my life. I have no troubles with men."

"That's exactly what I mean." She pulled out her phone and began tapping furiously. "See, I was on this psychology website yesterday, and it was saying … here it is … *Children of parents who have divorced or separated sometimes find it difficult to trust their partners. Some even avoid establishing close relationships entirely, for fear of being abandoned.* That's you! You never let a guy get close to you, and it's because of your father."

Tory shook her head. "No. That's not it. I hardly ever even thought of my father growing up. Remember, I've never met him. I never thought of myself as abandoned." She paused, thinking about how her mother always cut off questions about her father, saying he wasn't worth talking about. "Okay, maybe I did a little."

"Aha! You see?"

"But I don't try to keep men at a distance." Tory laughed. "And if anyone's experience makes me think twice before entering a serious relationship with a guy, it's *yours*, not my mom's."

"Hey, just because Michael was a dick—"

"And Evan before him, and Bruce and—what was that guy's name—the one who stole your car, dressed in your clothes, robbed a bank and then tried to frame you for it?"

"That would be Daniel. Asshole. He wrecked the car too."

"Yeah. I don't need to invoke my dad to find reasons to keep men at arm's length. And honestly Jess, I don't *try* to keep them away. I just …" Tory shrugged.

Jess toyed with her necklace. "He was really sweet, Daniel. He brought me flowers every Friday."

Tory huffed. "Flowers he stole from that little kiosk on Queen Street. I can't believe you can say anything good about him."

"Because you've never been in love. That's your problem, Tory, a serious lack of love."

"Well, I'm sure someday I'll find the right guy," Tory said, though she wasn't convinced it would ever happen. "But you're wrong. I don't lack love. I've got Puck."

The cat sat up and stretched with a questioning *meow*.

Jess scoffed. "If you say so."

7

Nico

Nico found the bookstore owner shaking and clutching a cup of coffee. He flashed his badge.

"Nico Michaelson. FBI." Her eyes went wide and he continued. "*Our* division." He winked and snapped his fingers. A steaming coffee appeared in his hand. "Mind if I join you?"

Her shoulders relaxed, and she let out a long breath. "Well, I'm thankful you're here, but you're too late. That … thing is already gone. What was it? She looked human, but—"

"Oh, she's human … sort of." Nico took a sip of coffee and grimaced. Maybe he should have simply asked her for a cup rather than showing off.

The woman frowned. "She's not … was she a … a *Squelcher*? It was like she sucked away my breath. I could barely think. Frankly, I was worried for my life."

Nico nodded. "She's a Squelcher. And you were right to be worried; she's proven deadly in the past."

"But aren't Squelchers just stories? Imaginary monsters? My mother always told me they were like the bogey-man—made up to get little kids to behave."

"Maybe some of them are, but this one is real alright." Nico started to take another sip, but thought better of it.

"But why did she come here? Why to *my* bookstore?"

"That's what I was hoping to find out from you. Did she just come in and browse, or was she looking for something in particular?"

"She was looking for a book." The woman chewed on her thumbnail. "One I'd never heard of before—*Magical Anomalies of the New World?* Something like that."

Nico noted down the title. "And did she say why she was interested in the book?"

The woman huffed. "I didn't give her a chance. I wanted her out of here as quickly as possible. Her friend had some romances she wanted to buy; I assumed the friend was like her and shoved them both out the door." She frowned. "There aren't two of them, are there?"

"No. The friend is an Insig. Only thing unusual about her is her hair."

The woman shook her head. "Kids these days! I had a fellow in last week with so many piercings he looked like the victim of a jewelry store explosion."

Nico laughed. "Is there anything more you can tell me? Anything that you noticed about her?"

"She had a cat ... or something that looked like a cat. Do Squelchers have familiars?"

"Yes, I know about the cat. She takes it with her everywhere." He shrugged. "Must be a Squelcher thing." The woman had nothing more to add, so Nico nodded. "Thank you. I appreciate this information." He snapped his fingers and his coffee disappeared.

He turned to leave, but the woman put a hand on his arm, a look of terror on her face. "Do you think she'll be back?"

"I can't say for sure, but I doubt it. We're keeping an eye on her. We don't think she means any harm. Not at this point, at least."

"But she ruined my sign and my doorbell, and—"

she shuddered and pressed a hand to her heart, "—I felt this pain in my chest."

"We think she doesn't know what she is."

The woman's eyes went wide. "How can she not know?"

Nico shrugged. "Who would stick around to tell her?" He pulled a business card from his pocket and handed it to her. "If you have any concerns or you learn anything more about this book, let me know."

The woman nodded. Nico turned to go, and then stopped. He looked back at the woman. "You don't happen to have anything by George Eliot, do you?"

She looked surprised, but then smiled. "Of course I do. Such an excellent writer! She really was ahead of her time. Shame she had to write under a pen name to be taken seriously." She bustled to a shelf near the back of the store and pointed to a section crammed with Penguin Classics. Nico picked out a copy of *Silas Marner*, paid for it, and left. At least he'd have reading material for the evenings.

Tory and Jess were long gone by the time he pulled back onto the highway, but he was able to track them with the tiny radio transmitter he'd stuck onto the underside of the car's rear bumper.

About five-thirty, he found the Escort parked at a small hotel on the edge of downtown State College. He pulled into a parking space and turned the car off. He leaned back in his seat and shut his eyes. He hated driving. It was ridiculous, his boss making him travel like this. Driving half the day was a waste of his time when he could get there almost instantly instead.

"I'm not going to risk you falling from the sky or vanishing entirely because you got too close to her," James had argued.

"Yeah, but if I know where she is—"

"And if you don't, we could lose you. Nope. I'm

firm on this. You'll have to do it like all the normal FBI agents do."

Nico took a deep breath and opened his eyes. He grabbed his bag and the book he'd bought, and stepped into the hotel lobby.

"Have you got a room with a balcony?" It might be useful to have an exit that wasn't the front door.

As he waited for the front desk clerk to print the paperwork, he heard familiar voices coming down the stairs into the lobby. He ducked his head, hoping they would pass by without noticing him. No such luck. He heard a light thud on the carpeted floor, and then Puck was winding himself around Nico's ankles.

Meow!

"Go on. Go away." Nico gently nudged the cat with his foot.

Then Tory was there, and Nico struggled against the oppressive feeling she delivered like a heavy weight on his chest.

"Sorry, sir. He really is friendly." She bent and picked the cat up. "Oh! I see you're reading George Eliot." She pointed to the book resting on top of his bag, then she looked at Nico and smiled. "Oh! You came to the library for *Middlemarch* a few weeks ago." She laughed. "What a coincidence, seeing you here. I take it you enjoyed *Middlemarch*, if you're reading another of her books. Personally, *Silas Marner* is my favorite one of hers."

Nico could barely breathe this close to Tory. Her presence pressed his lungs and strangled his voice. He blinked at her. His heart pounded in his ears, screaming at him to run away, but he was backed against the counter, and Jess had come up beside Tory, blocking any chance to move.

Jess smiled. "I remember you. What brings you to State College? Did you go to university here?" She didn't wait for him to answer. "We did. We're back to enjoy our old stomping grounds for a couple of days, you know?"

Nico struggled to order his thoughts. "No. I ... I'm visiting ... family," he replied breathlessly.

"Oh. Well, have a good visit. Maybe we'll see you around town." Jess raised her hand in a farewell, and she and Tory, with Puck in arms, headed out the door.

Nico took a deep breath. Okay, maybe it *was* best he was traveling by car. He usually had a good sense of where people were around him—he could sense Insigs and Users even without seeing them. He hadn't quite noticed before how invisible Tory was to his senses. Until she was on top of him, of course, when she punched him in the gut.

"Sir?" The clerk had been trying to get his attention. He turned back to find the man failing to suppress a smirk. "Don't worry. I'd be tongue-tied too, if a woman like that showed interest in me." He let out an appreciative whistle.

"What?" Nico had felt assaulted by Tory. "A woman like *that*? Not my type."

"Whatever you say, sir." The man's smirk grew. "Here's your key. Room two fifteen. Up the stairs and to the left."

"Thank you." Nico took the key, hoisted his bag onto his shoulder, and climbed the stairs.

Two minutes later, he slipped over his balcony railing and dropped quietly to the ground. Tory's car still sat in the parking lot. The women had gone on foot. He cursed himself for not keeping his head when he ran into them inside. He could have wheedled information out of them and learned where they were headed. He started walking toward downtown. His first thought was to catch up to the women, but he couldn't see the point of it. Tory had no idea what she could do, and she wasn't going to learn anything here. He was following a woman who was no threat to anyone except by accident. He'd spent all day driving and he was exhausted. Maybe he'd take the evening off.

His steps slowed. He stopped outside a bar with a sign advertising a double-mushroom cheeseburger. A burger and a beer. That was exactly what he needed. And maybe some fries to go with it. He forgot about Tory and stepped inside.

One beer became three, and an hour later when a man fizzing with power sat down next to him, he was just drunk enough to strike up a conversation.

"Wouldn't have expected to run into one of our kind here," he said in a low voice.

The man raised an eyebrow. "Our kind?"

Nico shifted so his shoulder blocked the view from the rest of the bar; he wasn't *that* drunk. Then he opened his left hand to reveal a small flame dancing just above his palm. He snapped his hand shut, snuffing the flame out. "Our kind."

The stranger shrugged. "Big university. Bit of a funky town. There are a fair few of us here, from what I've seen." The young woman at the bar took the stranger's order. He smiled warmly at her and asked how her studies were going.

"You know her?" Nico asked after she'd moved away.

The stranger shrugged. "A little. She reminds me of my daughter. Guess I look out for her a bit, since I can't look after my own."

Nico raised his eyebrows, the alcohol making him curious. "Divorced?"

"Separated. But not my choice, really." The man's gaze focused on something Nico couldn't see. "I still love both of them—wife and daughter."

Nico swigged his beer. "Wife and kids are just trouble, if you ask me." He thought of his own parents. Living together, but so separate they could have been on different continents.

The young woman returned with the stranger's beer, and he took a long drink from it. He set the glass down with a sigh. "You from out of town?"

Nico nodded and took another swallow from his glass. "You?"

"From Boston. But I'm on sabbatical at Penn State."

"You a professor?"

The man took a swig of his own beer and nodded. "What about you?"

"FBI."

The man's eyebrows rose, and Nico savored the instant respect his job gave him. "And what would an FBI agent be doing in State College?"

"That would be classified." Nico laughed as the man nodded in understanding. "Not really. Actually, I probably should let you know for your own safety." There was an unspoken rule in his division—Users were to be protected at all costs.

"Hm?"

Nico looked around to make sure no one was listening. Then he leaned in toward the man. "There's a Squelcher in town."

"Really? Squelchers are the stuff of legends. You sure it's real?" His eyes darted around the room and he took another swallow of beer.

Nico laughed. "I wish it weren't. But it's no joke. This one doesn't know what she is, but it didn't stop her from accidentally killing a User a few months back. FBI's been keeping tabs on her since." He finished his beer in one gulp and grimaced. "That's my job."

"Why're you watching her if she doesn't even know about her power?"

"We think she might find out. Her father's a User. Of course, he knows exactly what she is, and he's a pretty anti-government sort of guy, you know? She's never met him." He snorted a laugh. "Can you imagine if your wife gave birth to a monster like that? It's no surprise he hit the road when she was born. But she's on a road trip right now to find him. She pulled into town a couple of hours ago."

The man choked on his beer. Nico sat up straight and thumped him on the back until he stopped coughing.

"She thinks her father's here? In State College?" the man wheezed.

"Nah." Nico waved at the bartender and indicated refills for both him and the man. "She's got no idea where he is. Doesn't even have his full name."

"I see. And so what is your job, exactly?"

"Damned if I know. Follow her. Learn what she's capable of. Find out what she knows. Find out whether she shares her father's political views. Determine if she's a threat to the U.S. government." He laughed. "She's not. I can tell you that. Most boring assignment I've ever been on—she's a *librarian*." He rolled his eyes.

"And if she were a threat? What then?"

"Eliminate her." Nico made like he was shooting a gun.

The man frowned. "Eliminate her?"

"Yeah. Wish I'd done more firearms training." He shuddered. "I don't like the idea of getting close to her to do it. She's creepy, if you ask me. Not natural. Feels like she's stomping on your chest if you get too near."

"Excuse me. I need to go. Nice meeting you." The man rose abruptly and left, leaving his untouched beer behind.

Nico blinked at the beer glass, bubbles streaming upward like his surfacing thoughts.

He groaned and rubbed his face. *Fuck.* Professor in Boston. Looked to be in his late thirties. Separated from his wife. It was the beard that had put him off—all the pictures of Victor Hughes were of a clean-shaven man, but he'd obviously recently grown a beard.

He raised his glass to down the remainder of his beer, thought better of it, and set the glass down with a clunk. He was going to have a big enough headache in the morning explaining the situation to his boss. He didn't need a hangover too.

———

By morning, Nico had formulated a less self-incriminating explanation of how he happened upon Victor Hughes. He'd overheard a few conversations, put two and two together, and realized Hughes was in town. He'd tracked him to the bar and engaged in conversation to gauge whether he knew his daughter's whereabouts. Maybe he'd erred in telling him a Squelcher was in town, but there was no guarantee Victor would make the connection with his daughter.

Nico took a deep breath, called his boss and gave his slightly fictionalized report.

"I don't like it," was James' reply.

"Come on. Victor has stayed away from her for decades. Surely he'll take extra care to keep away from her if he knows she's looking for him. Besides," he lied, "they're both just passing through town. The chance of them meeting here is slim to none."

"Still, I don't like it. Too much opportunity for her to meet him, learn what she is, and be influenced by his politics. I don't like the idea of that monster working to bring down the U.S. government."

"That's pretty far-fetched, isn't it?"

"Look. I need to talk to the head honchos about this. Stick to her like glue. Do whatever you need to do to prevent her from meeting her father. I'll call you back later. We may need to get rid of her."

8

⊷

Tory

"There are four used book stores in the area," Tory said, peering at her phone over breakfast the next day. "One of them is new since we were at school here, and their website claims they specialize in rare books."

"That's promising," Jess replied through a mouthful of waffles. "But before we go on a wild goose chase, have you thought to check the Penn State Library? There are all those historic books in the special collections."

"Yeah. But not all of the special collections are searchable online. We'll have to go in and talk to one of the librarians. That'll be tomorrow's work."

"Man, you're a slave driver, Tory. When I suggested a road trip, I was thinking we'd have fun, see the sights, pick up guys in bars—not spend our days doing research. May as well be at work."

Tory set down her coffee cup. "Yeah well, since we're unemployed at the moment, being at work isn't an option." Jess had finished her meal, and Tory shrugged on her jacket. "And who knows? Maybe the Penn State Library is hiring."

Jess grabbed her purse and stood. "Or maybe we'll find some cute guys in the library. Probably a better place than a bar to find a date, anyway. Higher quality options to choose from."

Tory laughed. "It's a plan. You look for a man, I'll look for a book."

Two of the book stores and the library were within walking distance of their hotel. They took Puck with them, his harness jingling as he trotted beside them down the sidewalk. At the first store, Jess pointed to a sign taped to the window. "*Dog Parking: No dogs allowed in store,*" she read.

"They're probably not keen on cats inside then." Tory tied Puck's leash to the hook provided, and then scratched his head. "Try to behave. Don't bite any dogs. We won't be long."

Puck responded with a meow that Tory was certain meant *Me? Misbehave? Never!* She pushed open the door and breathed deeply. "I love the smell of old books."

"I thought you liked the smell of new books," Jess replied.

"I do." Tory shrugged. "I guess I just like the smell of books."

They started down the nearest aisle, scanning the shelves for anything promising. After four aisles, Jess commented, "Not many older books are there?"

Tory frowned. "All novels and textbooks." She pulled a dog-eared copy of *Harry Potter and the Goblet of Fire* off a shelf, sighed, and pushed it back in. "Wouldn't it be great if I could just summon the book—*Accio book!*"

"It would be quicker, but probably you should ask the guy at the counter instead." They rounded the corner and the checkout came into view. Jess held out an arm to stop Tory. "Or maybe *I'll* ask him. Is he hot or what?"

Tory rolled her eyes. "Jess, he can't be older than eighteen."

Jess smiled. "I'm only a decade over eighteen. What's the problem?"

Tory strode forward before Jess embarrassed either of them by flirting with the guy. "Excuse me. I'm looking for a specific book." She pushed the slip of paper with the name on it across the counter. "It's quite old. You don't happen to have it do you?"

The man glanced at the title with a frown. "I doubt it, but let me ask the boss." He disappeared through a doorway behind the counter and returned a minute later following a tall woman whose tight ponytail and retro glasses gave her a decidedly bookish air. She smiled at Tory.

"Hi. I'm Elaine." She held out the slip of paper to Tory. "I'm afraid I don't have this book. I rarely deal in these old, valuable sorts of things."

"Oh." Tory took the slip of paper.

"But I had to come and see who was asking for it. You're the second person in two weeks to be looking for that same book."

Tory's heart gave a skip. "Really?"

"I'm beginning to think *I* should be hunting the thing down, if it's in this sort of demand."

"Who was the other person, if you don't mind my asking?" Tory struggled to keep her voice light as her breathing grew shallow and her heart beat faster.

"Well, I don't think he's found the book, if that's why you want to know. He said he's been searching for it for years."

Tory swallowed. Her voice shook a little. "Who was it? Maybe we can combine forces."

"Some professor up at the university." Elaine opened a drawer and rummaged around in it. "He left his card in case I happened to come across the book ... Ah, here it is." She scanned the card. "Oh, he's not from Penn State, though." She read the card. "*Dr. Victor Hughes, Professor of Archaeology, Boston University.*"

"Victor Hughes?" Tory's hands shook. This *had* to be her father. "He's from Boston. But he was here?" Here, in this very book store, only two weeks ago? And he was still looking for the book?

Elaine shrugged. "I didn't ask why or anything."

Tory didn't ask for the man's contact details. With a name and university affiliation, she was confident she could find him. Besides, she was afraid she'd burst into tears if she had to ask, or blurt out her whole life story. She didn't trust herself to speak coherently.

"Oh, well. Thanks for your help." Tory nodded to Elaine, and then looked around for Jess, desperate to tell her what she'd discovered.

She found her in the reference section, making eyes at the young employee as he pointed her toward a book on motorcycle maintenance.

Tory strode purposefully toward the pair. "Jess, time to go." She wasn't going to blurt out her news in the store.

"But Jason was helping me find a book to tell me how to fix my motorcycle."

Tory rolled her eyes. "You don't *own* a motorcycle, Jess. Come on. We need to go."

Jess flashed a parting smile at Jason and followed Tory out the door.

They stepped onto the street to see Puck winding around the legs of three young women in miniskirts. "He's as big a flirt as you are," Tory muttered.

Jess laughed. "Three at once? I'm not half the flirt he is."

"C'mon Puck." Tory smiled at the women, and then tugged on the cat's leash. He trotted along beside them.

"I take it they didn't have your book?" Jess asked.

"No, but I think I got his name." Tory struggled to keep her voice down.

"It was Jason. And I would have managed a date with him if you hadn't rudely interrupted."

"No, not *his* name. My dad's."

"What?"

"The owner of the bookstore said a man had been in last week looking for the same book—Victor Hughes, professor at Boston University."

"Victor ... Vic." Jess shook her head. "It must be a coincidence. Your dad was looking for that book twenty-eight years ago. Surely he's not *still* after it."

"Maybe he is. He never came back, which means he never found it."

"He never came back could easily mean he never had any intention of coming back, Tory. Or maybe he meant to return, but found another woman instead. Or maybe he—"

"It's him. I know it. There can't possibly be two Vics out there searching for the same obscure book."

Jess was silent for a few minutes as they continued down the street. "What are you going to do?"

Tory laughed. "What any good librarian would do— research him."

"Whew! I was worried I'd have to talk you out of calling him up right away."

Tory glanced at the sign overhead. "Here we are. Bookstore number two." She pulled the door open. "Though if Victor Hughes has been here before me, I doubt we'll find the book."

The moment they stepped into the store, a huge *Autumnal Books* display near the entrance collapsed with a loud crack. Books tumbled like dominoes. A large pumpkin hit the floor and exploded in a spray of seeds and chunks of wet flesh. A pair of smaller gourds bounced and rolled toward the door. Colorful leaves fluttered in the air. Puck shot back out the closing door, ripping his leash from Tory's startled hand. Jess gave a squeak, and customers throughout the store turned toward the commotion. A middle-aged woman came running from the back of the store and stopped several paces from the ruined display. Her eyes darted from the display to Tory and Jess, then back to the display.

Tory raised her hands. "We didn't touch it. We just walked in the door."

The woman's gaze landed on Tory and her eyes narrowed. "No. I'm sure you didn't touch it. You wouldn't have had to." She rubbed her chest. "What do you want, coming here?"

Tory laughed nervously and waved a hand around. "A book? This is a bookstore, right?"

"Just a book?" The woman swallowed. "What book?"

Tory blinked at the woman. Awfully brusque for a salesperson. Maybe she thought Tory and Jess had knocked the display over. She pulled the slip of paper from her pocket and stepped forward, holding it out to the woman.

The woman recoiled at first, folding her arms across her chest. Then she took a deep breath and reached out, snatching the paper from Tory's fingers and darting back. Her eyes scanned the paper. "No. I don't have it."

"Did you ever have it? Has someone else come looking for it?" Tory couldn't help stepping forward eagerly.

The woman stumbled back. "I never had it. Never even heard about it until last week." She shoved the paper back at Tory. "Now get out so I can clean up the mess you made."

"We didn't do anything. It fell on its own."

"Out!"

Jess tugged at Tory's sleeve. "Come on. She doesn't have the book."

Tory let herself be pulled out the door. Only then did it register that Puck was gone.

"Puck!" Her stomach clenched. She scanned the street. Surely he wouldn't have gone far in a strange place. Of course, frightened, he might have run anywhere or be hiding somewhere. Or he could have been hit by a car on the busy street. "Puck!"

She grabbed the sleeve of a passing pedestrian. "Have you seen a cat? Siamese. Gray. Dragging a blue leash behind him." The man shook his head and walked on. The sidewalk was bustling, and Tory craned to see up and down the street around all the people. Her heart raced. Where could he be?

"You go left, I'll go right," Jess suggested. "We'll find him. Meet back here in ten minutes, regardless."

Tory nodded and they split up. Tory pushed impatiently through the crowds, jostling people out of her way. She apologized, but she still got irritated looks.

"Sorry, my cat is lost. Gray. With a blue leash. Have you seen him?" she asked anyone who would listen. When she reached the corner, she let out a sigh of relief. There he was, across the street, twining around a man's ankles while he scratched Puck's head. Her terror fled, leaving irritation in its wake. "Puck!" she said under her breath. She waited impatiently for the light to change, and then jogged across the street.

"I'm sorry, sir." She saw he had hold of Puck's leash. "Thank you for—" The man straightened. "Oh! It's you again!" She recognized the man from the library—the man she thought of as *Middlemarch* man.

Meow! Puck put his front paws on the man's leg, begging for more attention.

The man looked down at the cat. "He certainly is friendly."

"I'm sorry he keeps bothering you. Funny we should run into each other again, isn't it?"

The man looked up again. "Ah. Yeah." He held Puck's leash out. "Here."

"Oh! There you are!" Jess came up behind Tory at a jog. "Someone said she'd seen Puck this way." Her smile widened. "Hello again. We really need to stop meeting this way. We might start to think you're stalking us." She batted her eyes, and Tory shook her head. The man started to stammer something, but Jess held out a hand toward him. "I'm Jess, and this is Tory. You've met Puck."

"Um, hi." The man shook Jess's hand. In response to her raised, expectant eyebrows, he replied, "Oh, Nico. I'm Nico. Nice to meet you."

"Nico, it's nice to meet you too. And since we keep running into you anyway, would you like to join us for a drink this evening?"

Nico took a step back, and Tory shook her head. The poor man looked terrified of Jess's advances. "Jess, we've only just met him. Maybe you should back off. Look, you're making him nervous." She turned to Nico. "Sorry about Jess. She's harmless, really."

"I was only asking him out for a drink with us. How else will we get to know each other?" She turned back to Nico. "So, what do you say? Eight o'clock at that Liberty place round the corner?"

"I, um ..." Nico shook his head and took another step back. "Sorry, family thing tonight."

"Oh, right. I forgot you were here visiting family. No problem." Jess smiled. "Maybe some other night. We're in town until Thursday. We're in room three seventeen." She winked.

"Sure. I ... ah ... I should go." He gave an awkward wave. "Nice meeting you two."

9

Nico

For the hundredth time, Nico cursed this job and the ridiculous methods he had to use. Disguises were one of his fortes—he taught new recruits all the nuances of making yourself invisible. Not *actually* invisible, but unnoticeable. He'd even been asked to create an employee manual on the subject. But here he was, recognized multiple times by his target. Shit, even the Insigs at the FBI could do better than that.

Sure, she'd passed right by him without seeing him more than once, when he was wearing a disguise. But he couldn't stand the false beards and bulky padding he had to use to evade her. He had been lax, counting on her inattention to keep him hidden. But that damned cat! It was like the animal knew exactly who he was and tried to draw attention to him. Well, he was going to have to be more careful now.

Nico sat in the Liberty Craft House. He was in a corner, far from the door and the bar, but he knew he wasn't being careful. When it came to gluing on that moustache and slicking his hair down with sticky pomade, though, he couldn't do it. It was beneath him, really, all that crap, even if he could ignore the physical irritation. He simply didn't want to do it. Not until he absolutely had to. He checked the time. Tory and Jess shouldn't be here for another half an hour, if they kept to the schedule they'd indicated earlier—and Tory was a stickler for schedules, so he knew they would. In fifteen minutes, he'd head to the toilets and don his disguise.

He lifted his glass and downed the last of his beer. The door opened and a gust of chilly air blew in Tory and Jess, laughing.

"Shit." Nico shrank back in the booth, but it was too late. Jess scanned the room, and her eyes fell on him.

"Nico!" She smiled and waved, striding over to his table and sliding into the seat opposite him. Tory followed, and Nico leaned back as far as possible into his seat, feeling her presence squeezing his lungs.

Jess raised a hand and flagged down a passing waitress. "What have you got on tap?"

They ordered beers, and the waitress asked Nico if he wanted a refill. He swallowed and croaked out, "Yes, please," all the while cursing his stupidity.

"What happened to your family event?" Jess asked, pulling off her coat.

"Ah … change of plans." Nico shrugged. It was impossible to think straight while being strangled like this. Hell, he could barely breathe.

In the middle of taking her jacket off, Tory stopped and gave him a worried look. "If you'd rather we sit elsewhere—"

"No. No, that's fine." He was supposed to stick to Tory like glue, anyway. He'd make the most of this stupid mistake of his. "Please sit." He smiled, though he was certain it didn't fool Tory.

She finished removing her coat and picked up a menu. "Have you had dinner yet?"

"No."

"Have you been here before?" Jess asked as she paged through the menu. "Any suggestions?"

"No, I haven't. I …" How was he going to get

through an entire meal next to this woman?

"Oh! They have shepherd's pie! My mom used to make that." Jess didn't notice his discomfort and settled herself back into her seat with a sigh of pleasure.

Tory appeared as uncomfortable as Nico was. He wondered if she felt the same sort of pressure he did. Did he affect her in the same way she affected him? He knew almost nothing about her condition. Oh, there were stories of powerful Squelchers like her from long ago—people who, it was said, had murdered hundreds of Users, usually in the name of religious fanaticism. But those stories were just that—stories, glorified fairy tales. No one really believed in them.

And yet here he was, face-to-face with an honest-to-goodness monster. What were the odds? What were *his* odds, he wondered as he struggled to breathe. He figured they weren't good. He was glad she had no idea what she was—it improved his chances substantially. No one else in his division could have even sat here and survived.

He straightened in his seat. That's right. He was here because he was the best. This was a once-in-a-lifetime opportunity. He could be the only one in history to learn the secrets of these creatures. He was tasked with learning about her, and he would.

Jess's voice brought Nico out of his reverie. "So since we seem to be running into each other everywhere, tell me a little about yourself." She smiled.

"Oh, well. Not much to tell, really." Nico focused on his menu.

Jess wasn't deterred. "You have family in State College. Did you grow up here?"

"No. I —" Their beers arrived and they ordered their meals. He took a sip of his beer before responding to Jess's raised eyebrows. Part of the truth wouldn't hurt. His childhood was a reasonably safe topic, as long as he steered away from certain details. "I grew up in D.C."

"So who lives in State College?" She certainly was nosey, this friend of Tory's.

"My brother," he lied. "So, what about you? You two went to Penn State?" Better to get them talking. The more he learned, the more easily he could cast his stupid mistake as a daring idea next time he reported to James.

"Yeah, we roomed together, Tory and I." Jess took a sip of her beer.

"Let me guess. You both studied library science." Library science. What a ridiculous degree.

Jess shook her head. "Tory studied English literature. I took a more roundabout path to my current position."

Both Tory and Nico took another swig of beer while Jess rattled on about her Journalism degree and how her first job, in a small community paper writing articles about Aunt Jo's pumpkin pie recipe and the winning hog at the local farm show, ended after she slipped fictional salacious details about Aunt Jo and her pie fetish into an article out of sheer boredom. Nico met Tory's gaze over their beer glasses, and Tory gave a slight shrug, as though to apologize for her overly talkative friend. Or maybe she was saying, *serves you right for asking*. Nico couldn't tell. His eye was drawn to the scar on her cheek. He'd dug around in hospital records—a facial laceration requiring forty-two stitches, caused by a 'falling object' when Tory was ten years old. Must have been one hell of an object to leave that scar.

"So what do you do?"

Nico started as he realized the question was directed at him. "Oh, I work for the government." He waved a hand. "Boring office work. Nothing interesting."

Tory smiled. "You'd be surprised by what we find interesting. We're librarians. We spend all day in a quiet room."

It was an invitation to talk, and Nico itched to impress these women with stories of his work. He hadn't met a woman yet who wasn't awed by spy stories. But these weren't women for him to seduce. This was a target. He couldn't let them know anything about his work.

He laughed. "So do I, but I don't even get to say 'shh' to rowdy kids." He took another swig of beer. It seemed to help. The more he drank, the less he felt the pressure of Tory's presence, the easier he could breathe and think. He quickly downed the rest of his drink.

Their food arrived, and they spent a few minutes eating silently. Nico ordered his third beer. Jess recounted how she and Tory had made fools of themselves their junior year at a reception for a famous author. The male romance author apparently had a reputation for drunken debauchery and did his best to maintain the reputation, as it was great for sales.

"By the time we made it through the throngs of women around him, we'd had so much champagne, we could barely walk." Jess giggled as she took another bite of her meal.

Tory's dark complexion couldn't hide her blush. "*I* wasn't drunk. *You* were the one who got sloshed."

Jess raised her eyebrows. "So what was your excuse for knocking down that table full of wine glasses?" She giggled again.

Tory frowned. "I never even touched the table. You were there—you know I didn't."

Jess laughed. "I was working hard on just staying upright long enough to get an autograph. I have no idea what you did. But face it Tory, you've got a bit of a reputation as a klutz." Jess threw an arm around Tory's shoulder and hugged her, as if to say she meant the insult kindly, but Tory pressed her lips together and didn't smile.

Jess pulled back. "You have to admit it's true. You're

always knocking things over, breaking things, tripping."

Tory shook her head. "When have I ever tripped?"

"That time on the deck of that little café ... what was its name?"

"That deck was broken! I didn't trip—the deck collapsed out from under me. The engineer who came out to inspect it afterward was surprised it hadn't collapsed before."

"Still, you tripped."

Tory rolled her eyes.

Jess excused herself to go to the toilet. Tory focused on her food. Nico felt the embarrassment rolling off her, even over the pressure of her power. He felt ... sorry for her? He shook himself mentally. That was stupid. Sorry for a monster? He took another sip of his beer. "Your friend is talkative." A lame thing to say, but the silence was making him nervous.

Tory huffed. "Too talkative." She looked up at Nico, and her eyes seemed to spear him. Did they concentrate her power? "I'm really not a klutz. She's right, things seem to break or fall down around me more than around other people, but it's never my fault." She shrugged and looked back at her plate. "I guess I'm just unlucky."

"Is that how you got that scar?" Keep her talking. That was good.

Tory ran her fingers along the ridge on her cheek. "The only time Mom ever took me to the Pennsylvania Farm Show. We were walking into this kiddy area—you know, petting zoo, games and stuff. They had a big archway over the entrance, with a plywood pig nailed to it. I guess they'd used nails that were too short or something. It fell right as we walked under. Tore off most of this cheek." She rubbed her face.

"Ouch." Nico winced in sympathy.

"Yeah. I'm lucky to have a scar this small, actually." She smiled. "Broke my wrist once too, when a carnival ride collapsed with me in it. That was the last straw for Mom. She refused to take me anywhere after that. She said stuff for kids was dangerous."

"Must have made for a dull childhood." Nico couldn't help thinking of his own childhood, rich with illusions, games and carnivals. His uncle Jake ran a fun house, and whenever his dad wasn't around to disapprove, Nico would spend his afternoons with Jake, helping him conjure ever more elaborate flights of fancy for his visitors. It was all foolishness—he could see that now—but he'd thrived on it as a kid. What did a Squelcher do as a kid? He'd never considered them as people with real lives before. Something squirmed in his stomach. He frowned and took another sip from his glass.

Tory shrugged. "I had books. My mom owns a bookstore." She smiled. "I was allowed to read any of the books there as long as I didn't damage them, so they could still be sold when I was done with them."

Nico laughed. "You must hate to see all those old dog-eared library books."

"No. I like old books too. And even Mom always said you can tell how good a book is by how tattered it is. 'Don't bother buying used books that are in good shape,' she said. 'They're obviously lousy.' And speaking of old books, how do you like *Silas Marner*?"

"Oh, I've hardly started reading it." He couldn't tell her he'd bought it just yesterday at Beacon Books.

"I have to say, it's unusual for a guy to get into George Eliot. She's usually stuck in with Jane Austen in people's minds—dismissed as chick lit."

Nico felt a need to defend his reading tastes. "Maybe she was writing around the same time as Austen, but her books are totally different—they're intelligent, politically and socially astute—"

Tory leaned forward, elbows on the table. "Exactly!

She really deserves more attention than she gets."

Jess returned from the restroom. "You two are getting cozy."

Tory and Nico both leaned back. Nico took a deep breath. He had hardly noticed the pressure of Tory's presence. He polished off his beer. Yes, it dulled the feeling, but didn't eliminate it. He rubbed his chest.

"We were discussing books," Tory said. "Nico's a fan of George Eliot."

Jess scoffed. "I've no use for her stuff. Too boring. Give me some good old gothic horror if you're going to make me read classics." She opened her mouth to continue, but her phone rang. She pressed her lips together in a tight line and shared a look with Tory.

"That's your sister's ring tone, isn't it?"

Jess nodded.

"Don't answer." Tory shook her head.

The phone continued to ring. Jess pulled it out with a sigh. "She's my sister. I should at least listen to what she has to say. Excuse me." She slipped out of the booth and headed for the door, phone pressed to her ear.

Tory looked after her with a frown.

Nico raised his eyebrows. "I take it she and her sister aren't on good terms?"

Tory rolled her eyes. "Jess recently caught her sister and her boyfriend having sex."

Nico winced. "Ouch."

"Yeah, it was bad. But Jess's relationships always seem to end badly."

"And yours?" What a stupid question. He should be talking politics, not relationships.

Tory focused on her food. "I don't get into relationships."

Served him right, asking a question like that. He chewed a french fry and tried again. "So do you read other books besides the classics?"

This brought her eyes back to his, and he felt a pressure in his chest. He'd almost forgotten about her power after three or four beers, but that squeeze must be it. "There's very little I won't read." Perfect timing. Nico mentioned a popular memoir by a recent president, and it led to a spirited discussion of American politics in which he learned she was remarkably astute. They didn't see eye to eye, but her arguments were so well-considered, he found his own opinions shifting and sliding toward hers. It was her eyes, he decided. The way she looked directly at him when she talked—it *must* be how she used her power. He couldn't resist her words, her ideas, her smile when she looked at him. He wondered if she did it on purpose. Did she know how that pressure in his chest compelled him?

He tore his eyes from hers to break the spell, picking at his now cold dinner. "Well, you've nearly convinced me. That's some power you have." He stole a glance at her face. Would the word power register with her?

She laughed. "I'm just explaining what I believe. You're welcome to your own opinions."

Nothing. The word meant nothing to her.

At that moment, Jess burst back into the restaurant like a tornado. Patrons' heads swiveled toward her, before she self-consciously slowed her steps and eased the scowl off her face. She reached their booth and threw herself into the seat.

Tory's eyebrows rose. "I take it you didn't like what she had to say."

Jess shook her head. "I think I need a new hair color."

Nico's phone buzzed in his pocket. "Excuse me." He glanced at the screen and his stomach lurched. A text from his boss: *Bring T in for questioning. Call me. Discuss procedure.* He quickly shoved the phone back in his pocket.

"Sorry. I've got to go." He stood. "It was nice to meet you two." He nodded at them both and slipped out of the booth.

Five minutes later in a shadowed doorway on the street, Nico held the phone to his ear and spoke softly.

"I can't be the one to bring her in. I can't be the one to interview her."

"What makes you say that?" James asked.

Damn. Nico didn't want to admit his cock-up. He took a deep breath. "I can't bring her in because ..." Because they'd had a nice conversation over a beer? Because he felt sorry for her, growing up as a Squelcher? Because other than her condition, she seemed like just an ordinary person—no threat to anyone? Because he liked her? Nico frowned at that thought. She was a monster; he couldn't possibly like her.

He bit the bullet. "Because she trusts me, and I'd hate to mess up that avenue of gathering information."

"She trusts you? She shouldn't even know you. What's going on?"

Steeling himself, Nico explained how he'd been seen and recognized multiple times, and how he accidentally had dinner with Tory and her friend.

"What the hell? Disguise is your thing. How could you be recognized?"

"Can't exactly pull off my usual tricks around a Squelcher, can I?"

"Oh, come on! You know your appearance is only half the disguise. What happened to your acting skills? Nico, you're the best. How could you mess this up?"

Nico gritted his teeth. Aside from being seen, he'd done exactly what he'd been tasked with. "I have not messed this up. I've gotten the information you want. Does it matter how I've done it? You haven't been close to her. You haven't felt what it's like—the pressure in your chest, the difficulty breathing and thinking. It's like being strangled. Like someone jumping on your chest. I'd like to see you put on an act while you're within range of her."

"I put you on this job because you were the only one who could get close to her without harm. You've said yourself she's powerful. The big boss says bring her in— who do you suggest is going to do that?"

"You could take Davis off the Russia job." Maybe they could switch places after all. Davis didn't deserve the Russia job anyway.

"Nico!" James' tone of voice told Nico he'd stepped too far out of line. Being the best in the Division, he doubted he could push so hard as to be fired, but they would prevent him from being promoted. He'd have to do this.

Nico sighed. "When and where? I assume you've got a list of questions for me?"

10

<hr>

Tory

When Tory and Jess went to pay their bill, they found Nico had already paid for them.

Jess let out a cry. "And we didn't even get his phone number. I wouldn't mind going out with him again."

"It was nice of him to pay after we crashed his quiet meal." Tory wasn't entirely sure Nico would welcome another meal with them, though she wouldn't mind talking books with him again. Their discussion had been cut off too quickly when Jess returned. She smiled. She could learn to like a guy who discussed books. And he'd actually listened when they were talking about politics, instead of dismissing her ideas like so many men did.

As they walked back to the hotel, Jess brought up their plans for the following day. "If we go to the university library in the morning, maybe we can do something fun in the afternoon, like go to that cave ... you remember, the one where you go through in a boat?"

"Penn's Cave? And for the record, going to the library *is* fun," Tory replied with a smile.

"Of course it is, but it's also work. All work and no play makes Tory a dull girl." She scrutinized Tory. "Maybe that's your problem with guys—you can't relax, can't loosen up and have fun."

"I don't have a problem with guys. I just haven't

found the right one yet." But Tory wondered if maybe she did have a problem. Maybe there *was* something wrong with her.

Back at the hotel, Tory pulled out her laptop.

Jess yawned and collapsed onto her bed. "Aren't you tired yet?"

"I want to see what I can find on that Victor Hughes," Tory replied as she typed in a search for him.

"Oh! That's right. I almost forgot about him." Jess sprang up and peered over Tory's shoulder at the screen.

Tory scanned the search results and clicked on a staff page on Boston University's website.

"Professor of Archaeology. Research interests: witchcraft in ancient cultures, evolution of religious beliefs." Then the photograph finally loaded. Tory's shoulders slumped. "Oh."

"Was your dad white?" Jess peered at Tory, scrutinizing her face for signs of Caucasian genes in her dark features.

Tory shrugged. "I guess he could have been." The thought had never occurred to her, but there was no reason he *had* to share her skin color. "But this guy's way too young." The man in the picture couldn't have been older than forty.

"Maybe he was very young when he met your mom," Jess suggested.

"Yeah, like, ten years old?" Tory frowned. She'd been so certain this was her dad. She kept reading. There was no indication what year he'd gotten his PhD, or where. She looked at the photo again. "Maybe it's an old photo?"

Jess shook her head. "I don't know, Tory. Look, his list of professional papers only goes back to 2005. The first paper would have been his PhD work."

"But the list is titled 'Recent Publications', so presumably he's got other papers published before these." She was clutching at straws. She knew that. But she'd been certain this was her father. How could he not be?

"Or he's just trying to make himself look better by implying he's got more publications than these."

Tory grunted. Jess had a point. She clicked back to her search results. "Let's see if we can find out what he was doing before 2005."

An article in *Archaeology Magazine* in 2006 mentioned Victor Hughes. His research even hit the New York Times in 2008 with an article about the Salem Witch Trials and the parallel persecution of witches worldwide in the same time period. There was nothing that pointed to this particular Victor Hughes being old enough to be Tory's father.

"But he's looking for that book. Same as my father was. And his name is Victor, which has to be my father's name. He's got to be my father." Tory rubbed her face. "Am I just seeing a connection because I want there to be one, Jess?"

Jess frowned. "What if …" She hesitated. "What if *this* Victor is your brother? Well, half-brother, I guess."

"You mean, what if my dad …?" Tory couldn't even consider the possibility her father had a son that her mother didn't know about.

"Sorry Tory, but we know he left your mom in a pretty shitty fashion. You can't expect him to be a model of propriety."

"But a *brother*?"

Jess nodded. "A brother. Named after your father. Victor Hughes, Junior."

Tory set aside her feelings about the possibility she had a brother and considered the implications. "So if you're right, then we should be looking for a different Victor Hughes." She clicked into librarian mode. She could figure this out; it was simply a matter of research. She opened a new tab and typed in another search.

Jess laughed. "Hm. I think we can eliminate the

French politician born in 1762—he's a little too old."

"And I doubt he's the retired professional baseball player, though he is the right age. Mom would never fall for a jock, and she *hates* baseball."

"Oh! And look at *this* Victor Hughes." Jess reached around Tory to the keyboard and clicked on a link. "Wow! Nothing left to the imagination in those tights."

Tory rolled her eyes. "My father is not a twenty-year-old ballet dancer." She clicked back to her search.

"Hello! What about this?" Tory flicked to a history site that caught her eye. "A newspaper article from the *Middleton Times*, dated 15 June 1968. Twelve members of the local community arrested during a civil rights protest, including one Victor Hughes." Tory hoped this was her father. She could live with a father who went to jail for civil rights. And it would make sense he might have later married an African American woman, even if he was white. But ... she did the calculations in her head. "Nope. Can't be him unless he's significantly older than Mom. Mom would have been five years old in 1968."

Jess cocked her head. "If he had a son a decade older than you, he *might* be significantly older than your mom. He would only have to be ten years older than her to maybe be at a civil rights rally in 1968. She never mentioned his age to you?"

"No, and I never thought to ask. I guess I just assumed they were the same age." She flung herself back in the chair, nearly head-butting Jess in the stomach. "This is hopeless, isn't it?"

Jess yawned again. "How about we put it away for the night. We can have a crack at it again tomorrow when we're not already tired."

Tory was scanning her Facebook feed, waiting for Jess to be

ready to go to breakfast when there was a knock on the hotel door. She frowned. The cleaning staff wouldn't be starting this early. She peered through the peephole in the door, and her spirits lifted. What was *he* doing here at this hour?

She opened the door and smiled. "Morning Nico."

Nico didn't return her smile. He flashed a badge instead. "Nico Michaelson, FBI. I'd like to ask you a few questions, Miss Williams." He swallowed.

Tory blinked at him. *What?* "FBI? Is this your boring desk job for the government?" Her stomach sank, and she frowned. "Wait. Have you been following me?" Her mind whirled. "You were at the library, then the café, then you show up multiple times here. You *are* following me." Disbelief quickly turned to anger. She crossed her arms and clamped her jaw shut to avoid spitting out the obscenities she wanted to hurl at him.

Nico grimaced. "I'm really sorry. We just want to ask you a few questions."

"About what?" Tory thought of Jess and her inconstant lovers. Is this how she felt? Betrayed? She *had* found it a little odd, running into Nico repeatedly, but he was somehow charming, in an awkward way. She'd enjoyed their conversation last night and had been hoping she and Jess would see him again to thank him for paying for their meal, at least, and maybe for more conversation. But she hadn't expected to run into him like this. And calling her 'Miss Williams'? After they'd had dinner together? She dug her fingernails into her palms.

"It's about your father."

Well! That was unexpected. "My father?" She barked a laugh. "That's easy. I don't know anything about him. There's no need for you to question me. And why are you investigating my father?" Obviously Nico knew more about her dad than she did. Maybe she could get some information about him.

"Still, we'd like to talk to you. It's a matter of … national security."

Tory laughed. This was ridiculous.

Nico frowned and swallowed again. His professional demeanor was wearing thin, and she realized he wasn't enjoying this any more than she was. "Please?"

When Jess finally came out of the shower, Tory was sitting on her bed, staring at the business card Nico had left, the place and time of their meeting written on the back.

"Were you talking to someone out here? I thought I heard voices."

Tory nodded but couldn't meet Jess's gaze. She fingered Nico's business card.

"Tory? Are you okay?"

"It was Nico." Tory turned and handed Jess the card.

"FBI?" Jess's eyes went wide. "He's not much to look at, but FBI? That's sexy."

"He wants to interview me. He's been following me."

Jess's head snapped up. "What?"

"It's about my father, apparently."

Jess sat down hard on her bed. "Holy shit."

11

Nico

Nico paced the small hotel conference room he'd booked for the interview. He'd done dozens of interviews since he started working for the FBI; he shouldn't be nervous. *Was* he nervous? He considered for a moment—sweaty palms, racing heart, pacing—yes, he was nervous. But why? He counted off in his head.

One, this Squelcher's power was a complete unknown. The last recorded Squelcher that he knew of was James Carmichael, who lived during the sixteenth century. He had supposedly been responsible for starting the North Berwick witch trials in Scotland, which ultimately claimed the lives of over seventy Users. Over the centuries, the stories of Carmichael's power had undoubtedly been inflated, but it was said he could kill with a touch. Carmichael had been considered a monster. Of course, as with all monsters, after a few hundred years, some believed in him and some didn't. Some modern scholars thought the whole idea of the existence of Squelchers was bunk. Nico knew it wasn't bunk, but beyond that, Tory's power was mysterious and, frankly, terrifying.

Two, Tory's power might be terrifying, but Tory herself was … not. She was friendly and intelligent. Nico had enjoyed their conversation over dinner, in spite of himself. And after the hotel clerk had mentioned it, he had to admit she wasn't bad-looking, if you could overlook that scar on her face.

And that brought him to number three. The scar, the broken arm, and probably dozens of other accidents Tory had experienced were almost certainly a result of her power. Users took shortcuts all the time—whenever it wouldn't be noticed by Insigs—why spend money on maintenance when you could get away without it? A poorly-affixed wooden pig, a dodgy carnival ride, a rotted café deck—they would never have failed if Tory wasn't a Squelcher. How many other times had she been injured or nearly injured because of a power she knew nothing about? And it had driven off her father—a father who obviously loved her. If she'd really been monstrous, it would have been easy to dismiss her misfortunes, but Nico's stomach turned sour when he thought about adding to those misfortunes.

Nico shook his head. This woman could destroy his whole world if she wanted to. She could bring the U.S. government to its knees if she knew how much they relied on the Users within the FBI. Why was he worried about her little misfortunes when he was dealing with a woman who, he had to remind himself, was a monster?

And then there was number four. The questions James wanted him to ask Tory were misleading. They were meant to turn her against the father she'd never met, a father who loved her. They were meant to discourage her from seeking him out and to mislead her as to who he was. They weren't meant to extract any information at all. The FBI was determined to minimize her threat by keeping her ignorant.

At least they hadn't asked him to kill her. The thought made him squirm.

Nico was all for keeping her ignorant, but her father had already done a fine job of that for the past twenty-eight years. FBI meddling seemed like a bad idea.

He took a deep breath and reminded himself that

it didn't matter what he thought. He was here to do a job. Messing it up could cost him a promotion, and he wasn't going to risk being stuck at the bottom of the ladder for this woman.

A light tapping sounded on the door. Nico jumped, then took a moment to compose himself.

"Treat her like everyone else you've interviewed," he muttered to himself. "It'll be fine." He wiped his hands on his trousers, unconvinced.

He opened the door to find that Jess and Puck had come with Tory.

"Miss Williams. Thank you for coming." He looked at Jess. "I'll have to ask you to wait outside the room."

Jess frowned, but Tory handed Puck to her. "It'll be fine. I can't imagine this will take long."

"I'll be right out here if you need me." Jess shot a look at Nico that told him there'd be hell to pay if he hurt Tory in any way.

Tory entered the room with her arms crossed, and Nico shut the door behind her. "Please sit." He gestured to the chair he'd pulled out for her.

He took his own seat across the table from her and shuffled papers around to buy a moment to adjust to the press of her power. It seemed stronger today. Or maybe that was the glare she was giving him. Again he wondered if her eyes concentrated her power. He cleared his throat.

"Miss Williams, what do you know about your father?"

Tory rolled her eyes. "Nothing. I told you that yesterday."

"Come now, you must know something." Nico tried to meet Tory's gaze, but it made his chest tighten. He dropped his eyes to his papers.

"I have never met my father. I know nothing about him." Her words were tight and clipped.

"Nothing at all? Tell me why you've never met him."

"Why is the FBI interested in my father, anyway?" Tory asked, ignoring Nico's question.

"Do you know why your father left you and your mother, Miss Williams?" This was the key question, really. Did Tory know her father was a User and she was a Squelcher? Nico already knew the answer, but James wanted verification.

"How should I know? I was a baby! You should ask my mom, though I don't think she could tell you either. Honestly, I don't know anything about him. I'm not even sure of his name."

"Miss Williams—"

"Please don't call me that." Tory squeezed her eyes shut.

"Excuse me?" Nico struggled to keep his professional mask on.

"Don't call me Miss Williams. Call me Tory." She rubbed her face. "For God's sake, we had dinner together last night. I thought ..." She laughed. "I thought you might even ... you know ... like me. But no, you were tailing me. Been tailing me for weeks."

Nico pressed a hand to his stomach—he was beginning to feel sick. He *had* been tailing her. It was his job. But he had also enjoyed dinner, and those pained eyes she turned on him hurt more than her strangling power.

He slumped and dropped his gaze to the table. "Tory, I'm sorry. You were never supposed to actually see me. That was my fault."

"Why do you want to know about my father?"

"Your father is a person of interest in a suspected terrorist plot against a federal agency."

"What? He's a terrorist?"

Dammit. He didn't want to tell her these lies. "I really can't say any more than that without compromising our investigation. Now, Tory, if you can provide any information to help us, please do."

Tory's shock showed on her face. She suddenly seemed to deflate and rubbed a hand over her eyes. "Honestly, I don't know much. Only what my mom told me. He left the day I was born. He left a note telling her he needed to look for a book—*Magical Anomalies of the New World*. But he didn't say why the book was important. He implied he'd return when he found it." She paused for a moment, and her lips pressed together in a thin line. "But he never came back. I guess the book was more important than his wife and child."

"Do you know anything about his current whereabouts?" Another question that would hopefully establish her innocuousness.

"Not really. But I think he may have had a son my mom doesn't know about." She told him about the Victor Hughes who had been looking for the same book just last week. "That's his name, isn't it? My dad's name?"

Nico swallowed and forced himself to lie again. "Your father has gone by many names over the years, to cover his tracks."

"To cover his tracks? Nico, what has my father done?"

The pressure in his chest seemed to increase, and Nico found it hard to breathe. The FBI had given him a whole fake criminal history of her father to feed to her, but he found himself unable to speak a word of it. He stood and moved to open the window, hoping the fresh air and extra distance from her would allow him to speak. But when he turned back to her eyes fixed on him, any words he'd thought to say evaporated.

He opened his mouth, and then closed it again.

"You can't tell me, can you? Because of the ongoing investigation." She dropped her head into her hands. "I should have known he wasn't a good person. Who leaves their wife in the hospital with their baby?" She barked a laugh. "I'd always hoped he loved me anyway. When I saw the note he left, I thought it vindicated him. He *had* intended to return. I thought maybe if I found the book ..." She sniffed and raised her head. "Are you done with me?" She blinked furiously.

Nico nodded. "Thank you Tory. And ... I'm sorry." His stomach twisted and his chest felt compressed, and this time he was certain it had nothing to do with her power.

Tory gave a wry smile. "It's not your fault my father's a jerk."

He couldn't tell her that wasn't what he was sorry about. She left the room, and he collapsed into a chair, his head in his hands.

Nico was supposed to report to James immediately after the interview. He knew he should call, but he e-mailed instead. His stomach felt sour, and he didn't want to face James' probing questions about exactly what had been said. The objective had been met. Tory thought her father was a jerk, and he was confident she wouldn't try to contact him.

Then he lay in his hotel room trying to sort out the pressure in his chest and the knot in his stomach. There was no blaming them on Tory's power—she was nowhere near him now. But they were connected to her, to this investigation, to his growing unease at what he was being asked to do.

"Don't listen to your conscience," he remembered his father saying once. "It will only get in the way of the job."

But Nico didn't think it was only his conscience tying his innards in knots.

12

Tory

After relating the whole interview to Jess over lunch and a cup of coffee, Tory retreated to their hotel room and called her mom.

"Terrorism?" Her mother sounded less shocked than Tory expected. "Well, he was never happy with the government—always protesting one thing or another. But you say he's a suspect?"

Tory replayed the conversation in her head. "No, he's a *person of interest.*"

"That makes more sense. Your father was never a violent man, and I can't imagine him condoning terrorism, but he did associate with some strange people. Probably got mixed up with the wrong crowd." She sighed, and the sound carried decades of longing.

Tory hadn't thought of it that way. She'd never heard her mother speak positively of her father before, but of course he wouldn't have been violent. Her mother would never have put up with that. Tory berated herself for immediately jumping to the conclusion he was a suspect.

"And, Mom?" she said, contemplating telling her mother her suspicions about her father's other child.

Her mother interrupted her. "And why did they question *you*? You've never met the man. Why didn't they come to me instead?"

Tory was happy to be sidetracked. "That's what I asked Nico. I told him I didn't even know my father's name."

"You don't?" There was genuine surprise in her mother's voice.

"No, Mom. You always told me it didn't matter because he had left. You told me I had no father."

"I was right, you know. Victor Hughes was a lovely husband for a few years, and I'm blessed that he gave me you, but he was never your father."

Victor Hughes. Tory was right. *But which Victor Hughes?* she thought as she hung up a few minutes later. Her mother had again urged her to forget her father, but Tory didn't think she could. She rubbed her face.

"What now?" Jess asked. "Are you okay? Can't be easy to find out your dad's a terrorist."

"My dad's not a terrorist."

"But Nico said—"

"Nico said he was a *person of interest*. That's all. Mom says Dad would never condone violence."

"She hasn't seen him in nearly thirty years. How does she know?"

"I trust my mom more than Nico."

Jess narrowed her eyes. "So what do you plan to do now?"

"I'm going to meet my dad." Tory pulled out her laptop and opened her e-mail. She'd found the e-mail address of Victor Hughes, Professor of Archaeology.

"Are you sure this is a good idea?" Jess frowned. "He's wanted by the FBI."

"He's not *wanted*. Besides, I'm just e-mailing ... my brother?"

Tory pulled Puck to her lap for comfort, took a deep breath, and began typing.

Dear ...

Dear who? Dear Victor? Dear Dr. Hughes? Oh shit.

Dear Dr. Hughes:
I am searching for a man named Victor Hughes who was once married to Donna Williams. This man is my father and, I believe, might be yours as well? I have lost contact with him, as he left my mother when I was a baby. I would very much like to find him. If you know this man and can help me get in contact with him, it would mean a lot to me.
Thank you,
Tory Williams

She reread the letter. It was awkward. There was no way to make it otherwise. "Well, Puck, here goes." She shut her eyes and hit send.

───୧୨୧───

An hour later, Tory was deep in the stacks at Penn State Library, poring over a pile of ancient books. Jess was somewhere in the library with Puck. No doubt both of them were charming some good-looking librarian somewhere.

The book Tory sought wasn't here; that had been clear after about thirty minutes. But a few other books had intrigued her. Maybe they would give some insight into her father. Why had he wanted a book on magic? She gently turned the pages of a musty tome entitled *Magic and Monsters in New England*. It was full of dark illustrations of amorphous forms lurking behind trees and in cupboards.

Vampire hound. Mainly preys upon deer, but Mr. Cartwright reports having been attacked by a pack of four on the road outside Newport in January of 1823.

Dryad. Tree spirit. Generally benign, but vindictive, with a long memory for transgressions.

Tory closed the book. Fairy tales. She pulled the next book toward her—*Household Spells*. It was as musty as the previous book, and she sneezed. She opened the cover to a blank page. Turning it over revealed another blank page and another and another. The whole book was blank. Was it supposed to be a notebook, for writing your 'household spells' in? Why had it been saved in the library?

She sighed. "This is a waste of my time," she said aloud, though there was no one to hear. Ignoring the rest of the books she'd requested from the librarian, she gathered them all together and took them back to the Special Collections desk.

"Did you find what you were looking for?" the librarian asked.

"No, but thank you for helping," Tory replied.

The librarian picked up the stack of books. "You could try the Smithsonian. They have a huge collection of old documents and books. They might be able to help you."

"That's a good idea. Thanks."

Tory climbed the stairs back to the main floor of the library. She texted Jess. *I'm done. Where are you?*

Front steps. Tory headed out into the autumn sunshine.

"How'd it go?" Jess was sitting on the steps, legs outstretched. Puck was curled on her lap.

"Strike out. You?"

"Same. Puck was charming, and I was having a lovely conversation with a gorgeous pre-med student. Then we were kicked out by a woman with a feather duster and hideously dyed hair."

Tory laughed and raised her eyebrows at Jess, resplendent in her fuchsia locks, the color of the moment.

"No, really, Tory. Hers was hideous."

Tory sat down beside Jess, reaching over to scratch Puck's ears. "I'll take your word for it."

"So what next? Do we get to have some fun?"

Tory shrugged. "Maybe we should just go home." The conversation with Nico had settled like a lump of clay in her stomach, and Tory couldn't muster enthusiasm for anything.

"Are you kidding? We've barely gone anywhere. We've only been away a couple of days. This was supposed to be an adventure!"

"I was supposed to be finding my dad and this book."

Jess waved the statement away. "That was just an excuse to get you out the door. Come on, Tory. You've gone twenty-eight years without your dad and without that book. Forget about finding them and just enjoy a couple of weeks seeing new things."

Well, there was still the chance of locating both Dad and the book. She did her best to smile. "What do you think about heading to D.C. tomorrow?"

Jess nodded. "Perfect!"

13

Nico

"You said she wasn't looking for him anymore. You said she was convinced her father was a jerk." James' voice was hard.

Nico sighed into his phone. "That's what I thought. But you see? She doesn't think Victor Hughes is her father—not *that* Victor Hughes, anyway. She thinks he's her brother."

"Father, brother, what difference does it make? She can't be in contact with him. We can't risk her learning what she is and then being influenced by his politics." He paused, pinching the bridge of his nose, no doubt. "You need to take her out."

Take her out? Maybe to a nice Italian restaurant? But that's not what James meant. Nico gritted his teeth. He'd known the order was coming, but it didn't make it easier to hear. "There's no guarantee he'll respond to her. He's quite effectively avoided her for decades."

"She needs to be eliminated."

"Can we just wait? Wait and see if anything comes of her e-mail to him." The idea of killing Tory twisted his gut even more than her power did. But she was a Squelcher. He had to remember that.

"We can't wait. Once she knows, she'll be on her guard. Once she knows ... hell, we don't even know how Squelchers control their power. But they're rare enough we can be sure they're not trained by others. It must be instinctual. Once she knows she has the power, we'll have to assume she knows how to use it. We can't wait."

"Surely she won't learn that fast. Surely we'll have time." Time for him to figure out how to avoid killing her.

"Kill the monster!" James' voice rose. "Today. That's an order." He hung up.

Nico swore and threw his phone onto the hotel bed. He rubbed his face.

Kill Tory.

Fuck.

It's not that he hadn't discreetly eliminated people for the government before. He could kill criminals and spies. But Tory hadn't done anything wrong. He was being asked to kill her for what she was—something she had no control over, something she didn't even know about.

Kill the monster.

Tory wasn't a monster.

She loved that cat of hers. She put up with her friend Jess—that was a saint's work. She loved literature. She was a fucking *librarian*! How could a librarian be a monster?

An alarm pinged on his phone—the tracking device on Tory's car. Nico started. Tory and Jess were on the move. He snatched up his phone, grabbed his bag, and headed down the steps.

Half an hour later, on the freeway heading east, Nico's phone rang. James. He ignored the call.

When Tory and Jess pulled into a Hardee's somewhere near Harrisburg, Nico kept going. He couldn't risk being seen again, though he would have liked a coffee. Would have liked to drink it with her.

He shook his head. He had to clear those thoughts and focus on the job at hand. He pulled onto the shoulder a few miles beyond the restaurant to wait for Tory.

He checked his phone. James had left a message.

"I'm sending you some information about Squelchers from our files here. It might help you understand the importance of what I've asked you to do." There was a threat in the words.

Nico flicked to his e-mail. James had sent a PDF scan of a document called *The Squelcher Threat*, published in 1917.

A semi roared past, shaking the car. Nico looked up. He should stay alert. He didn't want to miss Tory as she passed. He'd read *The Squelcher Threat* later.

About one o'clock in the afternoon, Nico pulled into the parking lot of a motel on the outskirts of Washington D.C. He thought it was ironic that he'd chased Tory over three hundred miles, only to end up within spitting distance of his office. Tory and Jess had gone into the motel five minutes ago. Nico spent a few minutes in his car donning a moustache and a wig before entering the building himself.

He neither saw nor heard Tory and Jess as he checked in and climbed the stairs to his room. That was fine. He didn't intend to follow Tory everywhere. He didn't have to if his only job was to kill her.

He didn't have to if he convinced James she didn't need to die.

In his room, he quickly hacked into her e-mail. No response from Victor Hughes. He breathed a sigh of relief. If Nico could delay killing Tory long enough, James would have to admit she'd never find out she was a Squelcher, because Victor would never let her find him. She'd never become a threat. He didn't have to kill her.

He turned his attention to the document James had sent him. "So what kind of monster could you be if you knew what you were, Tory?" he muttered aloud. He remembered her apologies for Jess's in-your-face behavior, her shyness, her eagerness to talk about books. He shook his head. Not a monster.

The Squelcher is both an enduring mystery and a deadly foe to Users. The document went on to catalogue Squelchers infamous for their attacks on wizards and witches. A prostitute in about 100 BC who allegedly snuffed out 32 Users in the course of her profession. A soldier in the Roman army who apparently had a hand in the assassination of Julius Caesar in 44 BC. Heinrich Kramer, who published *Malleus Maleficarum* in 1487, which whipped up popular support for the persecution of Users. A blacksmith in Germany who went on a personal crusade to rid the country of Users, killing fifty-four between 1642 and 1657 when he was kicked in the head by a horse and died. And James Carmichael in Scotland, in the 1500s, who Nico already knew about.

Nico shook his head. This made Squelchers a threat? More witches and wizards had been killed by foolish accidents than by Squelchers, if this account was anything to go by. He read on.

Because they lack even the minor power of the average person, Squelchers are incapable of a number of rather ordinary behaviors: religious faith, romantic love, and true excellence in creative pursuits such as art, dance and music. Their inability to love often turns them into loners, cut off from society. Some pretend faith and love in order to fit in to normal human society, but these shams ultimately crumble under the weight of the monster within.

Nico laughed. That would explain her 'problem' with men. He should tell Jess. Then his smile faded and he shook his head. No. He couldn't tell Jess. He couldn't be seen again, now that they knew who he was. A tightness formed in his chest and he plunged back into the document.

Though a Squelcher's ability is not a 'power' as such, it has significant destructive effects on Users and objects imbued with power.

There is strong indication that a Squelcher aware of their condition can manipulate their influence in order to extend its range, focus its effects (on an object or person), and even detect Users (though how this latter is accomplished is unknown).

Kanya Wattana, a User who lived in the first century in what is now Thailand, reported that she once dueled with a Squelcher—power against power. Ultimately, the contest came down to knives, because her power was thoroughly defeated. 'It felt as though the Squelcher had my heart in a vice, squeezing until it could not beat. It squeezed my brain too, until I could barely hold the knife. I am not ashamed to say it was only by luck that I was the victor."

"I know that feeling," Nico muttered. "But how do they control it?" The document gave no information about exactly what a Squelcher could do and how they manipulated their power. Of course, it was something no User could ever know and no Insig would think to ask.

"Unless," Nico said aloud to himself, "unless someone *talked* to a Squelcher." And why not? He knew he could withstand her presence, at least when she wasn't trying to affect him with her power. Why couldn't he ask her about it? Learn valuable information for the benefit of all Users? Wouldn't that be better than killing her and losing the knowledge she unwittingly possessed? He envisioned writing the definitive work on Squelchers, with detailed information on what they were, what they could do, and ultimately how Users could neutralize them. He'd be famous! They'd have to promote him. The idea made him straighten up and lifted the weight in his chest. He slapped the desk.

"Yes. He'll have to agree to it." He quickly fired off an e-mail to James.

14

Tory

It was cool and overcast when Tory and Jess arrived in D.C. At the hotel, they asked the front desk clerk about pets on the National Mall.

"They're allowed on the Mall, but not in the museums and things." The man smiled. "We take our dog down there on the weekends."

Tory frowned. "So if we wanted to go to the Museum of American History Library?"

The man patted Puck's head. "You'd have to leave this guy outside."

Puck seemed happy to stay at the hotel. After a brief inspection of the room, he curled up on a pillow and fell asleep. Tory and Jess caught a bus downtown.

"I'm starving!" Jess cried. "First stop is lunch."

"Sorry to make us push on through without stopping," Tory said. "I just didn't want to have to get off the highway and then get back on, with that horrible traffic."

Jess shrugged. "No problem. I expect the lunch options in downtown D.C. are a lot better than the options along the freeway, anyway."

Stepping off the bus downtown, Tory felt like a starry-eyed country bumpkin. There were so many people! She'd seen the nation's capital plenty of times on television, but she was dumbstruck when they reached the National

Mall, with its iconic buildings and monuments. Grinning, she started into the Mall, but Jess grabbed her arm.

"Lunch?"

Tory laughed. "Right. Lunch."

"There was a nice-looking place back a block." Jess pulled Tory along the street to a little Mexican restaurant where they got burritos and a table at the window.

"So has Victor Hughes has responded to your e-mail yet?" Jess took a bite of her burrito.

"I haven't had a chance to look."

Jess raised her eyebrows. Tory swallowed. "Okay. I've been afraid to look."

"Go on then. Check right now. What are you afraid of?"

Tory rolled her eyes. "Of maybe having a brother I don't know about? Of learning things about my father I don't want to know?" She wiped her hands on her napkin and pulled out her phone.

Glancing at her e-mail, she took a deep breath. "He sent me a reply."

Jess leaned over the table to peer at the screen. Tory pulled the phone to her chest and raised her eyebrows. Jess huffed and slumped back in her chair. "You'd better tell me what he says, at least." She took another bite of her burrito.

Tory opened the e-mail. Holding her breath, she began to read.

My Dearest Tory,

Tory blinked. My dearest Tory?

There is so much to explain. I wish I could tell you in person. But as you will understand soon, it's not possible for me to see you.

What I am about to tell you will be hard to understand. Hard to believe. Please set aside your doubts and know that what I tell

you is absolutely the truth.
I am your father.

Tory sucked in a breath. Jess looked up from her lunch, but said nothing.

I was your beautiful mother's husband. It pains me to say that, for I left you both in such a terrible way. My only defense is that I was terrified.
Terrified of you, my dear child.

"What?" The question came out involuntarily.
"What is it?" Jess asked, unable to contain herself.
Tory waved Jess to silence and read on.

I suspect you don't believe in magic, but the reality is that it exists. All humans contain a spark of magic, and some, like me, have enough power to be able to wield it (yes, I am a wizard; a User, we call ourselves if we might be overheard by ordinary folk (Insigs)). I say all humans have magic, but that's not entirely true. You, Tory, have no magic. In fact, you are what is known as a Squelcher—your very presence destroys magic.
This is why I had to leave. I'm ashamed to say I deceived your mother as to my age. As far as she believes, I am four years older than she is. I am actually old enough to be her father and maintain my ruse as a much younger man through the use of magic.

No. Way. Tory's jaw sagged, and Jess leaned in. "What does it say?"
Tory glanced up. "He says he's my father."
"What? It can't be! He's not even forty years old!"
"Not according to him … but he's a nutcase." Tory took a bite of her burrito and chewed thoughtfully as she read on.

So you see, when you were born, you stripped away my magic, stripped away my disguise. You might have taken my life too—my magic maintains a youthful body, and without it, I would rapidly age. I couldn't remain with you. I paced the maternity ward lobby for an hour after you were born, trying to decide what to do—leave my loving wife and baby, or stay only to have my lies exposed and my life overturned anyway. When I left, it was with a desperate desire to find a cure for your condition so I could return to you and your mother. I loved you both. I still love you both.

I have been searching for the cure for twenty-eight years. The book I mentioned, and which I know you, too, now seek, is the only hope I have. In it is supposedly the only account of the reversal of a case of congenital maleficium, as it was once known.

Congenital maleficium? It sounded like some horrible disease. Tory pressed a hand to her chest and frowned.

Do not be afraid for your own health, my dear. Though Users view Squelchers as defective, being one is not inherently dangerous. I've done a great deal of research on Squelchers since you were born. The only side-effects you might note are a lack of imagination, no interest in religion, and the inability to experience romantic love.

Tory nodded. "That could explain things."

"What?" Jess leaned forward again, not hiding her impatience.

"I'll show it to you after I've finished reading it."

"It's *that* long?"

Tory glanced up. "Oh, yes. And it's … weird."

"Weird? How?"

"Shh!" Tory waved a hand. "Let me finish it first."

Why am I telling you all this now? Because you are in danger. You are being followed by an FBI agent in the Magical Division (yes, the U.S. government relies heavily on magic for espionage and law enforcement). I have been tracking this agent ever since I knew he was interested in you. At first, he was merely gathering information, but his orders have changed. He knows you've contacted me, and the FBI assumes that makes you a threat. He intends to kill you. Please don't ask how I know this. As I said, I've been tracking him as closely as he's been tracking you.

Tory sucked in a breath and hugged herself. Nico was out to kill her?

The FBI fears that I will encourage you to use your power against the U.S. government (it's a long story—please know that while I do have certain anti-government views, I have never and will never resort to violence).

Hm. Mom was right, then.

I struggled with how to reply to your e-mail. By avoiding contact with you for years I've been able to deflect the government's attention from you—as long as you were ignorant of your power, you had little chance of becoming a real threat. But it seems as though the Magical Division is determined to permanently remove you as a threat, regardless.

A threat? When had Tory ever threatened the government? She clutched her phone so hard her knuckles turned white. Her lunch turned sour in her stomach, and her heart knocked against her ribs.

Your ignorance can no longer protect you, and so it's time for you to know who and what you are. Your anti-magic is powerful— incredibly so, if my brief exposure to it is any indication. You must learn to control it. I can't help you with this—Squelchers are extremely rare, and witches and wizards don't know much about them, as you can imagine.

    I will do my best to continue to protect you, but you must be careful. I suggest you go home, have no more correspondence with me, and check your car, apartment and everything else for bugs and tracking devices. Most of all, learn to use your power! Your life may depend upon it.

    Love,
    Victor

Bugs? Tracking devices? Use her power? What power? None of this made sense at all. Magic? Anti-magic? Wizards and witches? They were make-believe. None of that stuff was real. Who was this guy, claiming to be her father and cooking up this outlandish story?

    P.S: In case you don't believe what I've told you—I once gave your mother a little ornate wooden box. I enchanted it to play her favorite song when it was opened. It will, no doubt, have stopped working when she brought you home from the hospital—your anti-magic would have destroyed the enchantment. It is the only proof of your power that I can think to give you that doesn't risk my own life.

"Holy shit." Tory's eyes were wide.

"What *is* it?" Jess was seething on the other side of the table. She'd finished her burrito and had her napkin crumpled tightly in her fist.

    PPS: Please tell your mother none of this. It should be me who tells her. I'm a coward, because I could have gone to her once you were grown, and I haven't. Now that you know the truth, I promise I'll tell her. Just give me a little time to screw up the courage.

Tory huffed out a breath and leaned back in her chair. She raised her eyes to Jess. "You are *not* going to believe this." Then she laughed. "I'm not convinced *I* believe it." Another laugh as she scanned the letter again.

"Tory! What does the letter say?" Jess leaned forward, her fists clenched.

"Sorry." Tory smiled and handed the phone over. "Here. Read it and tell me what you think."

Tory ate her lunch, watching Jess's face as she read. Her eyebrows rose, and rose again. She frowned. She laughed. She gasped. She handed the phone back to Tory, her mouth hanging open.

Tory smiled. "I have never seen you at a loss for words."

"I've never read anything so ... ridiculous. You don't believe any of that, do you?"

Tory glanced at the phone in her hand. "Actually, I think I do."

15

Nico

No. Eliminate her. James' response was terse and uncompromising. Nico slammed a fist on the table.

He talked aloud as he tapped on his keyboard. "She doesn't even know what she is, how can she be a ..." He finally accessed Tory's e-mail and scanned her in-box. "Damn." He read the letter from her father. Well, the cat was out of the bag now. She knew about her power. He frowned. She knew about him too. She knew he was supposed to kill her. His frown deepened. How did Victor know that? He shook his head. He didn't care. He wasn't going to tell James; it would only make things worse. He'd use a different encryption key for his e-mail and hope it would throw Victor off.

It was Tory he was worried about. But they could learn something from her, couldn't they? She wasn't going to instantly try to overthrow the government. She may *never* try to overthrow the government.

He remembered laughing with her over dinner, beer making his perception of her power fuzzy. He remembered her terror when Puck went missing in State College and her relief when she found the cat with him. He remembered that smiling clown-face scar on her cheek. It wasn't really so bad, now he thought about it. And set in that face ... Dammit, what was he thinking? His brain had conjured up her image, and all he could think of was how her hair fell in ringlets around her face.

He dropped his head into his hands. "I can't kill her." It was as simple as that. He'd have to come up with an argument James would accept.

He opened a new e-mail. Staring at the blinking cursor, he considered his tactics.

James was ambitious, almost as ambitious as Nico. He was likely getting pressure from above and wouldn't defy orders unless there was more to be gained by it. Nico couldn't think of a better way to rise through the ranks than to do something as audacious as plumb a Squelcher for the secrets of her power. Of course, Nico had to be the one to do it—James didn't have the magical ability to withstand her—but maybe he could make a deal with James to share the credit for it. He could make it seem like James' idea. With a display of James' cunning and Nico's raw power they could both do quite well out of this. They could both end up written into the history books. They might even be able to weasel their way into those select positions within the Department of Justice that had the ear of the president. Nico smiled at the thought. He'd always aspired to be head of the Magical Division, but this could push him far beyond that position.

Yes. *That* was why he was reluctant to kill Tory. It had nothing to do with dark curls framing liquid brown eyes; it was because she was useful. She would catapult his career. Maybe James had been right to put him on this assignment. Let Davis have Russia.

He rubbed his hands together, formulating the words in his head, and then started typing.

It took the better part of an hour to construct the arguments Nico was sure would sway James. It was a delicate balance, and he had to anticipate James' counter-arguments and overcome his reluctance to defy orders, but he was finally happy with it. He read the message once more, just to be certain it was perfect.

A notification flashed on his screen. An e-mail from James. Had he reconsidered, even without Nico's arguments? He clicked on the message.

I have spoken with the National Security team. We feel your effectiveness has been compromised by your contact with the Squelcher. We're taking you off this job and sending a sniper to finish things. You are hereby requested to return to the office for reassignment. This order is effective immediately and not under discussion.

"Compromised?" Nico snorted. "Because I want to take the opportunity to advance our understanding of anti-magic?" *And maybe have an excuse to talk to Tory again.* Nico refused to acknowledge the thought flashing through his mind.

Return to the office for reassignment. So some sharpshooter could knock Tory off for no reason other than she might possibly someday become a threat?

"Fuck that," Nico said aloud.

He slammed his laptop shut and grabbed his jacket.

16

Tory

"Nico's trying to kill you? That fuckbucket!" Jess's voice rose, and people at neighboring tables turned their way.

"Shh!" Tory smiled at the strangers frowning at them. She shoved her phone into her purse and stood. "Come on."

Tory pulled Jess out of the restaurant and toward the National Mall. Her mind was by turns numb with shock and racing with fear.

Her dad was alive.

He loved her.

He was … a wizard?

And she was … what, exactly? A Squelcher. The opposite of a wizard?

And because of that, the U.S. government wanted to kill her?

"Tory, where are you going?" Jess's gaze darted around them. "If you're really in danger, should we be walking around on the street like this?"

"Surely even the U.S. government can't assassinate someone on the National Mall," Tory argued, picking up her pace.

"But where are we going?"

"The Museum of American History Library."

"But if Nico is trying to kill you—"

"Then I'd better find out more about my ... power ... or whatever it is. I need to find that book." Tory laughed inwardly at Jess's uncertainty. Usually Jess was the one forging ahead, deciding on their path.

"Are you sure of this?" Jess asked, jogging a little to keep up. "You can't possibly believe all that stuff."

Tory stopped mid-stride, and Jess nearly ran into her. "What did he say that didn't make sense? I don't have any imagination, I don't believe in God, and I've never been in love."

Jess rolled her eyes. "Maybe that's true, but it doesn't mean it has anything to do with magic, which, last I checked, was not actually real."

"You're right. If you had told me those things about myself, I wouldn't think anything of it. But Victor Hughes has never met me. How could he know those things? And how could he know that the music box he gave my mother stopped working the day I was brought home from the hospital?"

Jess's eyebrows shot up. "You mean that really happened?"

Tory nodded. "Yes. Besides ..." She scrunched up her face, trying to work out how to explain it. "It *feels* like the truth. It's like this jigsaw puzzle inside me just clicked into place. Victor Hughes was telling the truth. I'm certain of it." She couldn't blame Jess for her incredulous look; her certainty surprised even herself. But whatever this Squelcher thing was, she was it. She didn't doubt it. She swallowed a lump in her throat; she didn't mind not having an imagination or religious faith, but love? She'd always assumed she'd eventually find the right man and fall in love. Now she knew she wouldn't, unless she could find a cure.

She shook her head and said aloud, "At least I have Puck."

"What?"

"Never mind. Let's find that book."

By the time they reached the door of the museum, Jess had recovered somewhat. She laughed. "It does explain a lot about you. Poor Leroy!" She pulled open the door. "I think I need to change my hair color."

Tory smiled. Jess just took what life handed her and ran with it. She was thankful to have her along for this ... adventure? She wasn't quite sure what to call this experience yet.

The entrance foyer bustled with people. Tory and Jess had to stand in line at the information desk.

"Excuse me. We're interested in visiting the library. I don't see it on the map, though."

The woman at the desk smiled. "The library is open by appointment only. Have you made a reservation?"

Tory wished she'd done a little research beforehand. "No."

Jess butted in, taking charge again like her usual self. "Can we make a reservation for now?"

The woman laughed. "I doubt it. The library isn't regularly staffed."

"How about later this afternoon?"

"Is it urgent?" Both Tory and Jess nodded. The woman sighed and picked up the phone. "Let me talk to the library staff." She punched in a number and waited for a moment, doodling on a pad of paper. "Oh. Hey Carla. This is Em, at reception. Hey, I have a pair of women here who want to make an appointment for the library ... This afternoon is what they're asking for ... Yeah ... They're from—" Em raised her eyebrows at Tory and Jess.

"We're researchers from the McKean County Library System," Jess said. Tory forced herself not to smile, and she hoped they wouldn't be asked to prove they still worked for the library.

Em repeated the information. Then she scribbled

on the paper in front of her. "Right. Yep. No, I'll let them know. Thanks." She hung up and raised her eyes to Tory and Jess. "Nine o'clock tomorrow morning is the first available time. The library's closed to all visitors today." She shrugged. "Pest control, apparently. Oh, and Carla suggested you do a search of their online catalogue before you arrive, so you know what you're looking for."

Disappointment settled in Tory's stomach. "Right. Nine o'clock." She forced a smile. "Thanks."

They stepped away from the information desk. "Now what?" Jess asked.

Tory rubbed her face. "I have no idea."

Jess smiled. "I do." Tory raised her eyebrows, and Jess waved a hand around. "We're in D.C. We're at the Smithsonian. Let's enjoy the afternoon!"

"I suppose ..." Now that she wasn't focused on the need to find the book, fear squeezed Tory's chest. She darted her gaze around the bustling foyer.

Jess nodded as though she heard Tory's thoughts. "I think you had it right earlier. Even the government can't just assassinate someone on the National Mall. They'll do it in some shady back alley or in the ladies' room at a nightclub." Her eyes sparkled, and Tory thought she was far too enthusiastic about the drama of an assassination. "As long as we stay in public places, you're completely safe."

"And when the museums close and we have to go back to our hotel?"

Jess's smile faltered, and she shrugged. Tory took a deep breath. They'd have to take this one minute at a time. She forced a smile. "Where to, then?"

"Air and Space Museum!" Jess clapped her hands and did a little hop worthy of a ten-year-old.

Tory laughed. "Air and Space, then."

Neither of them brought up Victor Hughes' e-mail as they walked the exhibit halls. Jess was her usual loud, flirtatious self. Except maybe she was a bit too loud and too flirtatious. Tory could see her trying hard to act like nothing had changed.

Tory tried too, but she spent more time looking over her shoulder than at the exhibits. The text and pictures swam in her vision, and afterwards she couldn't have described half of the things they'd seen. When she wasn't searching for Nico, who she envisioned creeping up on her around every corner, she was poking and prodding her whole body with her mind. Her presence destroyed magic? Victor had called it a power. What did anti-magic feel like? For the first time ever, she wondered if she experienced the world differently than others. What did anti-magic do? As the afternoon wore on, she withdrew further and further into herself. The crowds pressed too close and made her jittery. Jess was too loud, too giddy; Tory had to bite her tongue to avoid snapping at her. She just wanted to be at home, with Puck in her lap and a book to read.

Finally she pulled Jess away from a replica of one of the Wright brothers' planes. "Jess—" she began.

"It's time to go, isn't it?" Jess's brow furrowed. "I've been thinking we should take a taxi back to the hotel, not the bus."

Tory nodded. She pulled out her phone to ring for a cab, and then froze. Her fingers were suddenly cold. "Maybe you should call, Jess. What if he's bugged my phone somehow? He'll know when and where we're waiting for a cab."

Jess's eyes went wide. "You're right." She pulled out her phone and ordered a cab. They waited in the lobby until they saw the vehicle pull up in front, and then they dashed out and jumped in. Tory immediately slouched in her seat, so she wasn't visible from the window. The driver gave her a funny look, then shook his head and pulled away from the curb.

At the hotel, they made another dash from the cab to the building. They hurried up the stairs—Jess decided the elevator was too dangerous. "Bad things happen in elevators in the movies," she declared. When they reached their room, Jess blocked Tory with her arm before she could insert her key card. "Wait! It could be booby trapped."

"And how will we know it's booby trapped without trying it?"

"We don't." Jess peered at the walls and ceiling around the door. "But if it *were* booby trapped, it would fire something at your head or chest, right?" She squatted down in front of the door, and then waved at Tory. "Come on! Get down." Tory squatted, feeling completely ridiculous. Jess took a deep breath. "Here goes." She reached up and inserted her card, shutting her eyes and ducking her head.

Click. A green light flashed on the door.

A man stepped out of a room down the hall. Tory and Jess both started. The man looked at them oddly. Tory blushed. She and Jess stood. Jess waved and smiled. "Just— you know—going in." She pushed open the door and they hurried inside.

Jess burst out laughing as soon as the door was shut behind them. Puck leapt off the bed and trotted to Tory, rubbing against her legs.

"Oh Puck. It's so good to see you." Tory bent and picked the cat up, desperate for the comfort of his soft fur. Jess tumbled into the room's armchair, still giggling, and Tory settled on one of the beds, with Puck on her lap.

"Now what?" Tory asked once Jess's chuckles had subsided.

Jess clapped her hands and leaned forward. "I go out and get takeout for us. I'm safe out there. Then we hunker down in here for the night, go to the museum in the morning, and learn about your power." Her eyes sparkled. "Oh! This is like James Bond meets Harry Potter!"

"I'm glad you're so excited about me being on a government hit-list." But Tory couldn't help smiling a little at her friend's excitement.

"So tell me. Can you feel your power? Is it like a … force or … a *presence?*"

"My power?" Tory closed her eyes for a moment. Jess was serious. She believed. She was trying to help. Tory felt deep inside herself. What would anti-magic feel like? What *was* in there, anyway? She felt the icy remnants of her father's betrayal, melting now, and was surprised how big that betrayal had been to her. She found her love of Puck, warm and furry and purring. She found her friendship with Jess, a thick rope woven of their shared experiences, that held them together in spite of their polar natures. She found her mom, a rock in the middle of the rushing stream of life. She found a vast library, deep and quiet. She sighed and opened her eyes. "No. I can't feel anything."

"Damn." Jess leaned back in her chair. "Hopefully this book will have some information for us."

"Hopefully this book is *in* the library." Tory shifted Puck off her lap and stood to grab her phone. "That woman said there's an online catalogue."

Jess stood. "What do you want to eat? I saw a pizza place and a Chinese place nearby. I'll go get dinner while you look for the book."

"Whatever you want. I'm easy." Tory wondered if she'd even be able to eat. Her stomach was tied in knots.

Jess pulled on her coat and stepped out the door.

17

Nico

He should have known he wasn't going to find Tory amidst the throngs in downtown D.C. He had donned a magical disguise on top of his physical one, turning his baseball cap into a Stetson and losing the Converse high tops in favor of a pair of tooled leather boots. He figured the magic would be a good indication if he got close to her, even if he couldn't see her. But in all his wanderings, his disguise remained intact.

Nico returned to the hotel late in a light drizzle, with aching feet. Streetlights glinted wetly off the pavement, and his hat was frosted with mist. He dropped his magical disguise as he approached the door of the hotel, so he could enter as the same man who had booked a room earlier.

The door swung open and out stepped Jess. She stopped on the sheltered front step and flipped her hood up, frowning at the rain. Nico glanced through the glass door, expecting Tory right behind her. But Jess was alone.

On impulse, Nico jogged up to her. "Jess."

Startled, Jess peered at him. "Do I know you?"

Nico ripped off the false moustache, and Jess sucked in a breath. Her eyes narrowed. "You! You shitwaffle!"

"No. Wait!" Nico grabbed her wrist to keep her from bolting.

"Let go of me!" Jess struggled against his grip.

"Listen. Will you listen to me? Tory's in danger."

"Yes, we know that. From you!" She practically spat in his face.

"No. Not from me," Nico hissed. "From the FBI."

"Of which you are an agent, in case you've forgotten." Jess tugged again at her arm, but Nico held firm.

"Well I'm not working with them. Not anymore." He swallowed, ignoring his misgivings about defying his orders. "I'm no longer assigned to Tory's case."

"Tory's case." Jess sneered at him. "She's done nothing wrong! She's broken no laws. What the *hell* do you think you're doing?"

"I am trying to prevent her death." Nico held Jess's gaze. She blinked and stopped struggling.

"Let go and tell me."

Nico released her, and Jess crossed her arms, waiting.

How could he explain his decision when he didn't even understand it himself? He dropped his gaze to the pavement. "When they told me to kill Tory, I said no. I tried to convince them she was more valuable to us alive. There hasn't been a Squelcher for nearly two hundred years, and we know nothing about them."

"So you wanted to *study* her?"

"No. I mean, yes, but …" Nico sighed. "We—Users—are taught that Squelchers are monsters. The few records that exist of them talk about how they destroyed magic and killed witches and wizards—ordinary witch burnings were nothing by comparison."

"So you think she's a monster."

"No. Not anymore." He flicked his eyes to Jess, still glaring at him with distrust. He couldn't blame her. He shrugged and flashed a weak smile. "I did at first, but then I started following her and decided she was the most boring person ever."

Jess gave a snort, but Nico couldn't tell if it was amusement or derision on her face.

"Then you lost your jobs and went on this crazy road trip, and I thought maybe she'd do something interesting, at least. I put a tracking device on her car and followed you to State College." He scuffed at a stone on the pavement. "Remember the bookstore owners who didn't like you? Beacon Books and that one where the display collapsed? The owners were witches. They knew what Tory was. They were terrified of her, of what she might do to them."

"The lighthouse sign! It broke. That was Tory's anti-magic?"

Nico nodded. Jess's frown was one of concentration now, and he relaxed a little. "The book display too. It had been held up with magic."

Jess laughed. "So Tory *did* knock it down. But she doesn't do it on purpose. She says she can't even feel it or anything. How can she possibly be a threat with it?"

"A couple of months ago, she visited a used bookstore owned by an elderly wizard who kept himself alive magically."

Jess sucked in a breath, and Nico nodded. "He was dead before he knew what happened. Tory never even saw him. She must have thought the store was unattended."

"So how come you're alive? You're a wizard, right? And—" she laughed "—we've had dinner together."

Nico smiled. "I'm actually as young as I look." He shrugged. "And I'm powerful. That's why they put me on this job. Because I could get close to Tory without harm."

"So she's dangerous. But now that she knows about her power, she can avoid witches and wizards, and there should be no problem."

Nico nodded. "After meeting her, I agree. Tory is …" He stopped, alarmed at the descriptive words flitting through his mind. "She's a lovely woman, and …"

Jess sucked in another breath. "You *like* her!" She laughed. "Oh. My. God!"

Nico felt himself blush. "No. It's not like that. I ..."

"Don't try to deny it; I see it written all over your face." She punched him playfully on the arm. "You know she can't love, though, right?"

"Look, I don't like Tory. I mean, I like her, but I don't *like* her, you know?" He huffed, flustered as he struggled to quash the ache in his chest. "I just don't want her to be killed. She needs to learn about her power. *I* need to learn about her power, so I can convince the FBI she's not a threat, so they'll stop trying to kill her."

"Her father says her power can protect her."

"From magical attack, yes. But the FBI knows that. They're sending a sniper who'll use real bullets. Her power's useless against that." He shrugged. "At least, I assume so."

"So what is she supposed to do? Stay locked in her hotel room for the rest of her life?" Jess crossed her arms again. "It's nice of you to tell us she's in danger, which we already knew anyway. If you really wanted her to be safe, you'd tell them to stop—you're part of the frickin' FBI, after all."

"I've *tried*. It's not that easy." This wasn't going well.

"Lovely. Excuse me. I need to pick up something to eat, since *she can't even leave her room*." Jess waved an angry hand toward the building.

"Wait." Nico rummaged in his coat pockets and pulled out a small pouch. "Take these." He pushed the pouch into her hands, and she prodded it.

"Marbles?"

"Glow pods. Squeeze them, and they make light."

"Oh, and this is supposed to protect Tory from a sniper?" Her voice bristled like a porcupine.

Nico struggled to explain. "They're magical. They're an emergency thing. The pouch they're in protects them from magic, so no one can destroy them. A mage that's incapacitated can use them without expending any energy."

"Yeah. An ordinary flashlight can do that too." She made to hand the pouch back to Nico.

Nico pushed it back at her. "The pouch will protect them from Tory's anti-magic until she's ready to use them. Use them to help her understand and gain control of her power—they'll go out when her anti-magic touches them. The only way we're going to convince the FBI to leave her alone is to learn about her power. We have to prove she's not a threat, but unless she understands and controls her anti-magic, she *is* a threat."

"Oh." Jess's expression softened, and she pressed the pouch to her stomach. "Thank you."

"And if it helps her to know, I can feel her anti-magic ten feet away." He nodded at the pouch. "Best not to open that within ten feet of her."

A large group of tourists came out the door, jostling them. Nico nodded to Jess and went inside, wondering if he'd done the right thing. His insides shuddered, and he balled his hands into fists. He'd either lose his job over this, or he'd become a legend.

18

---ᘓᙡᘐ---

Tory

Tory felt a swoop of joy. "They have it!" She scratched Puck's ears. "The Smithsonian has the book!"

She couldn't wait to tell Jess. Her stomach growled and she checked the time. Jess had been gone for a long time. Shouldn't she have been back by now?

Just then she heard a click, and the door opened.

"That took a while." Tory smiled at her friend.

Jess rolled her eyes. "Sorry. Had to make an extra stop. You wouldn't believe how hard it is to find hair dye in this neighborhood!" She pulled a box from the bag she carried. "I had to settle for tangerine instead of cherry red, which I really wanted."

Tory frowned. "What's wrong?"

Jess let out a breath and dropped the bag on the desk. "Am I really that transparent?"

"You gave it away with tangerine."

Jess laughed and pulled out a pair of small pizza boxes. "You are not going to believe this."

They ate pizza while Jess related her meeting with Nico. She tossed the pouch of magic marbles on the bed, and Tory stared at it.

"Well!" was all Tory could manage for a reply. She hardly knew what to think of Nico anymore. Then she remembered. "I found the book. The museum has it."

"Yes!"

In the morning, Tory and Jess, with her now orange hair, took a taxi to the museum. Tory's palms were sweaty as they stepped out of the cab. A sniper? Could they do that? Her heart pounded. Would they do that in a public place like this? Jess seemed nervous too; her head swiveled to take in the already-busy sidewalk. Then she took Tory around the shoulders and hustled her toward the museum.

"Nico's following," she muttered in Tory's ear. "Don't look," she added as Tory turned her head.

"Do you really think he's trying to help me?"

Jess gave a laugh and they ducked into the building. "He's *in love* with you, Tory."

"Oh, stop! He doesn't even know me."

They crossed the lobby to the information desk, their footsteps echoing. Jess whispered, "He's been stalking you for weeks." As though that explained everything.

Tory shook her head. "Whatever. Let's just worry about the book first."

They were directed to the upper floors where a librarian met them and let them into the locked library. She asked them what they were looking for, and then went to retrieve the book while Tory and Jess watched a video on how to handle rare books.

The video finished, and the librarian hadn't returned. Tory tapped her foot impatiently. "What's taking her so long?"

"Relax. A book that old is probably housed in a box in the basement behind filing cabinets full of city ordinances from the nineteenth century—you can't tell me it's in great demand."

She was right, but that didn't make it any easier to wait. Tory stood and paced the room, scanning shelves of books, some old, some new. Her eyes roved over titles like *The March of Democracy*, *America in Crisis* and *The Epic of America*, but she barely saw them. Her heart pounded like she'd run up the stairs, and she nervously played with her necklace.

Half an hour later, the librarian finally returned. "I'm sorry. We don't actually seem to have the book." She frowned. "It came in with a large private collection about a year ago, and many of those books needed repairs. It's possible it hasn't come back from restoration yet. I did find a few others that might be of interest, though." She laid three archival boxes on a table and opened them. *Famous Witches of Massachusetts*, *Wiccan Ways*, and a first-edition copy of *The Scarlet Letter*.

Tory frowned. "No. We're looking for a specific book, not for information on witchcraft. Where do you restore your books—could we go there and look for it?"

The librarian sighed. "I could ring the restoration team and ask if it's there." She looked like she'd really rather not, but Tory nodded.

"That would be great—it's important we find this book."

By the time the librarian returned, Tory was ready to storm down the corridor searching for her. "Did you find it?"

She shook her head. "They don't have it. Their records indicate it was returned to the library in March."

Tory forced herself into the calm she used with troublesome library patrons. "Well, if it's not being restored and it's not in the library, could it be in a different library?"

"No. It's supposed to be here." The librarian shrugged. "Sometimes books get misshelved. Then they're as good as lost until we do a full inventory." She laughed. "And with such a large and varied collection, even then we might not find it."

Tory pressed her lips together to avoid saying something snarky about what sort of librarian would lose a book. She didn't come this close to the book only to have a librarian say she couldn't find it. Her professional pride was piqued. She thought about some of the ways books had been 'lost' at Laurel Glen. "Have you looked among similar call numbers? Could the number have been misread? A one mistaken for an L or something? Could it be an oversized book and shelved in a different area?"

The librarian's eyebrows rose. "Um …"

"We're librarians," said Tory, gesturing between Jess and herself. "Do you think we could take a look ourselves?"

The librarian frowned. "The public isn't generally allowed in the archival area."

"Our library houses a good-sized collection of old and rare books," Jess lied. Laurel Glen had a dusty collection, but only a few could be considered old and rare. "We understand how to handle items like this."

The librarian looked back and forth between them. They outnumbered her, and Tory hoped the bullying stance both she and Jess had unconsciously adopted would sway her. "I'll have to ask my supervisor. You may need some sort of clearance or something."

Another wait taxed Tory's patience, and she paced with her arms crossed, refusing to consider that she might not find the book.

When the librarian returned, she carried two pairs of white gloves, and Tory smiled.

The librarian handed them each a pair. "You have half an hour to search. Many of the volumes in the archives are extremely fragile. We ask that you not disturb more than you need to in your search."

"Thank you," Tory replied.

The librarian led them down a hallway and into a windowless room lined with shelves. A large map cabinet squatted at the end of the room, and an old dinged wooden table sat in the middle. Many of the books on the shelves were encased in archival boxes, but some were unprotected, and the overall visual effect was a motley, haphazard-looking display.

Tory took a deep breath. "Okay."

"If you find it, bring it out to the public room to read. I'll be back in thirty minutes."

The door clicked shut behind the librarian, and Tory shared a glance with Jess. "I suppose we start with the call number, just in case it's there and she missed it."

Jess nodded. "I'll look for it in the oversized section." She pointed to an area with large books lying on their sides.

Tory read out the call number. "GR106 .G5 1844. Good luck." She drifted down the shelves, pleased to see that, in spite of the disorganized look, the books were well-shelved. She quickly found the right section. "*Folk Beliefs of New England, New England Ghosts, Weird Tales from the New World.*" She muttered the titles to herself as she scanned them. *Magical Anomalies of the New World* wasn't there. She widened her search to the neighboring sections and then to the shelves directly above and below, with no luck.

Jess came up behind her. "It's not oversized."

"It's not shelved anywhere near where it should be, either." Tory frowned. "I guess we have to just scan all the shelves."

"We only have half an hour."

Tory ran her eyes over the shelves. "We'll have to be quick, then. You take that side, I'll take this one."

Starting at one end of the room, Tory peered at spines until her eyes swam. Once, she saw the word *Magical* and her hopes soared. But only for an instant. *Magical Thinking and the History of Urban Myths* wasn't what she sought. Ten minutes ticked by. Then fifteen. Tory had only scanned a third of her side of the room, and Jess was no further along on her side. They were never going to be able to finish in thirty minutes.

Absentmindedly, she reached out and pulled a book forward. A small volume, it had been pushed back farther than the others next to it. It bothered her aesthetic sensibility.

Then she froze. "Jess! What if it's a small book and has been shoved behind the others?"

"Misshelved *and* hidden?" Jess whistled. "We'll never find it."

"Look at the tops of the books, not just the spines—you should be able to see it, even if it's shoved into the back."

With renewed hope, Tory continued her scan. Unfortunately, checking both spines and tops was more time-consuming, but she didn't want to miss it if the spine wasn't visible. Ten more fruitless minutes passed, and Tory's spirits sank. Maybe they could get more time. Why were they only allowed half an hour, anyway?

The door opened. "Any luck?" asked the librarian.

Tory frowned. "No. Could we possibly have more time to search?"

"I'm sorry. You really shouldn't be in here at all. It was hard enough for me to get you half an hour."

Tory suppressed a growl of frustration and continued to scan the books.

"You really need to come out now," the librarian said.

Jess crossed the room and touched Tory on the arm. "It's not here, Tory."

"It *has* to be. If we just had more time to—" Tory lunged at the shelf, reaching deep behind two volumes to extract a slim leather-bound book.

She turned the cover upward. *Wheelwrights of New England.* Her shoulders slumped. She thrust the book at the librarian. "This was misshelved."

The librarian frowned and placed the book on the table. "Well, then." She gestured toward the door.

"Wait!" Tory dropped to her hands and knees and pressed a cheek against the floor.

"What are you doing?" Jess asked.

"Remember when *The Lorax* went missing? We found it *under* the shelves." She scanned the dusty, narrow space in front of her face, and then quickly shuffled forward to the next section of shelving.

"Tory, this isn't the children's section of a public library. No one here is going to accidentally kick a rare manuscript under a shelf." Jess's voice was strained. Tory was sure she was embarrassing her, but she didn't care. She *had* to find that book.

The librarian strode toward Tory. "Look here. You really need to leave now."

Tory sucked in a breath. There was something under the shelf. She waved a hand in the air. "I need something long and thin—a yardstick or broom handle."

"I'm quite certain there's nothing under our shelves." The librarian's voice was clipped. "You need to—"

Jess handed Tory a broom, and she slipped it under the shelf, sweeping the object toward her. It was a slim archival box. "Ha!" She lifted the box off the floor and brushed dust off it.

The librarian shook her head. "It must be empty."

Tory sat back on her haunches and opened the box. The title, *Magical Anomalies of the New World*, glittered up at her, gold foil letters pressed into a cracked red leather cover. "This is it!"

Jess shook her head and laughed.

"Well. It *is* here." The librarian's thin lips betrayed her embarrassment, and Tory couldn't help but give her a smug smile.

115

They took the book back to the public library room, where the librarian left them to read. Tory's hands shook with nerves. This was it. The book that might tell her who she was. The book that might bring her father back into her life.

She swallowed and clenched her hands to try to steady them. "Maybe you should handle the book, Jess. I don't think I could manage to turn a page without ripping it."

Jess set the book on a foam book cradle and gently opened the cover. "This makes Laurel Glen's collection look like modern literature," she joked. She turned the first page. "Does this thing have a table of contents?"

It didn't. They peered at each page as Jess turned them, passing headings such as *Spell Sores*, *Dead Spots*, and *Magical Rebound*.

Jess turned a page to reveal a drawing of a scowling man with a crooked nose and missing teeth, arm outstretched toward a woman cowering on the ground. The caption read: *A Squelcher attacks a helpless witch*.

"Clearly all you have to do is point to use your power." Jess grunted. "If that's how they see Squelchers, it's no wonder they're worried about you."

Tory turned her eyes to the facing page. "What does the text say?" She read aloud. "*Squelchers are mysterious creatures resembling humans, but possessing no human magics*."

"*Resembling* humans?" Jess wrinkled her nose. "What? Did they think Squelchers were animals?"

"No. Defects," Tory said, reading further. "It says here they're defective humans who delight in torturing Users. It says they feed on magic, sucking it away from enchanted objects and living witches and wizards." She shook her head. "Who wrote this?"

"Esther Godwit." Jess laughed. "There's a good witch name if I ever heard one." She shook her head. "I'm still struggling with the idea this is all *real*. You know?"

Tory nodded. "Magic is fiction—*Harry Potter* and *The Lion, the Witch and the Wardrobe*."

Jess was scanning the text, and there was no more laughter in her voice. "This is more like *Grimm's Fairy Tales*."

Tory read on.

Their prolonged touch is deadly to most witches and wizards, and some have been known to manipulate their power, casting it out from their bodies to attack Users.

Users can feel the proximity of a Squelcher with a tightness in the chest and shortness of breath, but from a distance, Squelchers are invisible to magical detection, owing to the absence of magic within them. They are also impervious to magical attack.

This condition, known formally as congenital maleficium, is extremely rare. The only Squelcher known in the New World appeared in the town of Ipswich, Massachusetts in 1693. He was detected as a young boy by a local witch, and met with an untimely accident shortly thereafter.

Tory snorted. Accident? Not likely.

A cure for the condition was postulated in 1546 by the renowned witch Xiuying Kwan. Only the most powerful of Users can administer the cure, as it involves close physical contact with the Squelcher. During the cure, the User transfers magical energy from themselves into the body of the Squelcher, infusing the heart with magic. The Squelcher must be a willing participant and must have sufficient control of his power to prevent it from snuffing out the magic. The only attempt at this cure was made in 1602 by Sol Hashemi under questionable circumstances. The Squelcher was partially cured, becoming capable of the full range of human emotions, but remained a danger to Users, as her power remained intact. Sol Hashemi barely escaped with his life, and his magical abilities were permanently impaired by the attempt.

No one since has sought to cure a Squelcher. It appears that the best cure is death.

"The best cure is death." Tory gave a bitter laugh and rubbed her temples. "Great."

"That's it?" Jess flipped a few more pages. "That's all they have to say about it?"

"Victor thought he'd find a cure here. All those years of searching, to find out I'm better off dead. Looks like the FBI had it right."

"Whoa!" Jess held up her hands. "Let's just stop that line of thought right now. You are *not* better off dead. Twenty-four hours ago, you were an ordinary woman with a promising career and awesome friends." Jess pointed at herself. "That hasn't changed."

"An ordinary woman who had no imagination and couldn't love." Tory didn't really care about the lack of religious faith, and the imagination was a minor inconvenience, really. It was the absence of love that had been worming under her skin. And now, apparently, there was no hope of that changing.

"We don't know that for a fact. All this could still be fiction." Jess waved a hand at the book.

"And my father and Nico have the same delusion? What's the chance of that?" Besides, that heavy lump in her stomach was the truth.

"Well, it *could* be. Is that any more far-fetched than the fact you're some weird mutant human without magic, and that all the rest of us *have* magical powers?"

"How am I supposed to sort out the truth? I *know* I have no imagination. I *know* I have no religious faith. I *know* I've never fallen in love. Those line up pretty neatly with Victor's information."

Jess pulled the small pouch from her jacket pocket and waved it in the air. "We have these. Magic marbles!" She smiled and gave a game-show-host flourish of her hand that made Tory laugh.

"So they're supposed to glow, and Nico says I'll be able to snuff them out with my ... anti-magic?"

"That's what he said. And if it works ..." Jess shrugged. "I suppose we'll have to believe that Nico and Victor are right."

"And that the FBI is really trying to kill me." Tory would be more ready to believe she was a Squelcher if it didn't come along with this terrifying threat.

Jess dropped her gaze to the marbles. "That too."

"And what good will it do me to know for certain I'm a freak?"

"Nico says we need to know and understand your power in order to convince the FBI to leave you alone."

Tory arched her eyebrows. "What? He's actually going to go to his boss and tell them I'm harmless?"

Jess shrugged. "That's what he said."

"Hm ..." Tory stood. "Let's see what happens." Nervous again, she rubbed her hands on her pants as she stepped away from Jess along the row of tables in the center of the room.

"Ten feet? Is this about right?"

"Go further." Jess waved her away. "Just to be sure."

Tory took another five steps back. She drew in a breath and held it to try to still her nerves. She let it out in a huff. "Okay. I'm ready."

Jess opened the pouch and took out one of the ordinary-looking marbles. She held it up at eye level and squeezed. "Ah!" She cringed away from the intense light. "He could have warned me how bright they are." She blinked a few times and then straightened again, lowering the marble away from her face. "Okay. Start walking toward me."

Tory clenched her fists at her sides and took a step. Nothing happened. She took another step. And another. Still the marble continued to glow. Maybe this was all a farce after all. The marbles were some clever technology, not magic. She was an ordinary woman. She wasn't being hunted by government assassins. Her hope rose. She took another step. Still nothing happened. She relaxed her hands. Another step. She smiled. Yes. This was all a hoax. She started striding forward, fearless now.

"Oh!" They both cried out as the marble winked out. Tory's hands curled back into fists.

Jess's eyes were wide and for a moment she stared, frozen, at the dark orb. Then she shook her head. "That was just one. We don't know how long these things are supposed to glow for. Let's do another, and this time, start walking right away, and quickly."

Tory nodded and moved back to her starting point. Jess pulled out a second marble, holding it below eye level this time. "Ready? One, two, three, go." She squeezed.

At the flash of light, Tory launched herself forward. One, two, three … she counted her steps. Five, six … the marble went dark.

Jess swore. She and Tory looked at each other in shock for a moment. "Either this is the most elaborate hoax ever …" Jess began.

"Or I'm a Squelcher," Tory finished. She swallowed the fear that formed a lump in her throat. A Squelcher, and better off dead.

Jess let out a long breath, and then snapped into action. "Right. Nico thought you could use these to learn to control your power. The book says you should be able to control it—cast it out like a weapon? So let's try that."

Tory laughed. "Jess, I don't know how! I can't even feel this power I'm supposed to have."

A door opened and the librarian strode in. A quizzical look crossed her face when she saw Tory and Jess standing, facing one another and far from the book they'd requested. "Is everything okay? I thought I'd check on you before I go on break. Do you need any other titles?"

"No thank you. We're fine," Tory said. "Um … Is there anyone else scheduled to use the library today?" She hoped the question wasn't too odd. It occurred to her that if anyone came in, they'd be hard-pressed to explain what they were doing, but Tory was terrified to go back out onto the streets until she understood more about her power. Victor said it could protect her. She felt a desperate need for that protection.

"Not until noon."

"Great. Thanks." Tory nodded. The woman turned and left.

"Two and a half hours," Tory said.

"Let's get cracking."

They had a dozen marbles. They'd already used two, and Tory was no closer to being able to control her power than she had been before.

19

Nico

Nico paced the sidewalk, waiting for Tory and Jess and scanning the rooftops for snipers. How long were they going to spend in the library? They must have found the book.

The book. He needed to know what was in it, but after his encounter with Jess the night before, he didn't think she and Tory would talk to him about it, and he certainly wasn't going to go and read it over their shoulders right now. He ducked into the museum and made a library reservation for the afternoon, then headed back out onto the street. He circled the building but saw nothing. He widened his search area. Maybe the FBI hadn't trailed Tory and Jess to the museum this morning like he assumed they would. Maybe they didn't know where the women were.

Perhaps they'd made the same calculation he had—to kill her here would be too risky. His steps faltered. He should have stayed at the hotel. The sniper could be taking up position there now, waiting for Tory to return.

He raked his fingers through his hair. "Damn! What was I thinking?"

A passing tourist gave him a funny look and a wide berth.

What *had* he been thinking? He shook his head. He'd only thought of staying near Tory.

Staying near her. To learn more. That was it. He

wanted to learn more about her. Make his name as the one who cracked the secrets of Squelchers. Who wouldn't want to be the one to do that? And naturally, he needed to keep her alive and stay near her in order to do that.

He settled on a bench in front of the building, pretending to read a guidebook while he kept an eye on the museum entrance.

As long as he stayed near her, he could protect her.

20

Tory

Tory frowned. "I need to be able to *feel* this power if I'm going to control it."

Jess furrowed her brow in thought. "Did you feel anything when the marbles went out? Your power did *something* at that moment to snuff out the magic. Surely you could feel that?"

"The only thing I felt was surprise. I think."

"Let's try it again. This time, close your eyes and I'll walk toward you. You tell me when the light goes out."

Tory nodded and took up her position again. She shut her eyes. "Go ahead." At first she balled her hands into fists, tense and listening for Jess's footsteps. No. Something told her she needed to relax. Needed to open herself up to ... *feelings* or something. She opened her hands and let her tense shoulders sag. She tried to imagine the space around her, ignoring Jess and the marble. Her power was out there. Extending beyond her body. Where was it?

She felt a twinge in her stomach. "There! Was that it?"

Jess whooped. "Yes! What did you feel?"

Tory opened her eyes. "I don't know. A ... pluck. Like someone just tugged on a tendon." Jess gave her a quizzical look. Tory laughed, absentmindedly rubbing her stomach. "You asked, and that's the best way I can describe it."

"So, your power *twinges* when you encounter magic. That's a start. Now you know how that feels, can you feel it when it's not touching magic?"

Tory shook her head. "No."

"Okay, so let's do another. Turn your back this time. That last time I was about a table length away from you when the marble went out. Let's see how far your power extends behind you."

Tory supposed that made sense. She turned her back and closed her eyes. Again she relaxed her muscles and focused on the space around her. She'd only just relaxed when she felt the twang. "There! Oh! And a second one?" She turned.

Jess was frowning at her. "You felt two twinges?"

"I did." Jess held only one marble in her hand. She held it an arm's length in front of her. Suddenly, Tory understood. She sucked in a breath. "Jess, step back." Jess took three steps back. "Now come forward again." Tory didn't shut her eyes, but she felt it all the same. "Jess, I'm feeling you! I'm feeling *your* magic! You know how my dad said everyone has a little magic? Well I can feel it."

Jess's eyebrows rose. "You're kidding!" Then she frowned. "But, doesn't your power destroy magic? How could you have felt my magic twice? And wouldn't you have destroyed it years ago?"

Tory's mind was racing, and she waved a hand. "Maybe I'm only temporarily suppressing it. You're alive, so your natural magic rebounds when you're out of range of my power."

"Do you know that, or is it a guess?"

Tory laughed. "I'm making this up as I go, Jess." A shiver of frisson washed over her as more pieces of the puzzle of herself fell into place. "I know the feeling of people's magic, though. It's the feeling I get whenever someone gets into my personal space. I thought I was just an introvert." She smiled. "But I was feeling my anti-magic interacting with other people's magic." Then she cocked her head. "Did *you* feel my power?"

Jess shook her head. "Not at all."

"So if I can feel you, we don't necessarily need those marbles. Maybe we should save them for now."

Jess nodded, pocketing the spent marble in her hand along with the pouch. "So, let's see exactly where the edge of your power extends."

"Oh, I can tell you that already. It's like this bubble around me. Eight feet, maybe?" She frowned, thinking. "Although sometimes it's less, and sometimes it's more."

"That's you controlling it!" Jess's voice rose with excitement.

"But I haven't been."

Jess raised her hands. "I know. You haven't been consciously controlling it, but what if your sense of personal space is like an instinctive thing—in situations in which you feel uncomfortable, you instinctively extend anti-magic as a protective barrier." She shrugged. "Of course, that doesn't do you any good against anyone but witches and wizards, but ..."

Tory thought about it for a moment. "I guess it makes some sense."

"And that would mean you already know how to control your power, subconsciously. So it should be simple for you to control it consciously."

"Yeah. Just like that." Tory snapped her fingers and gave Jess a sarcastic look.

"I'm just trying to think positively, here. Come on. Let's do some more. So, you felt me about here. That's no more than five feet." Jess frowned. "Do you really not like me to come any closer?"

Tory laughed. "I was nervous about it, okay?" She

thought for a moment. "No. Ordinarily you don't trigger that feeling until you're quite close."

"Whew! Good. Anyway, I want you to try to make that distance greater. Try to push me away with your power."

"But I don't know how to control it!"

"Just *try*." Jess stepped back. "Okay, extend your power until you touch me with it."

Extend her power. As if it were that easy to manipulate something you couldn't feel or see. Tory pressed her lips into a thin line.

"Just *try*," Jess pleaded.

Tory closed her eyes, focused on the space around her, and pushed. She imagined the bubble around her expanding outward in all directions. She felt a twinge and opened her eyes. "I think I did it!" She relaxed and … was that her power she felt snapping back into place? She blinked, ignoring Jess's congratulations. She pushed again, her eyes tracking where she felt the edge of her power to be. There! Again she felt Jess twinge in her stomach. She let go. The power snapped back into place. Again, more quickly, she pushed and let the anti-magic snap back into place.

"Tory? What are you watching?" Tory raised her eyes to Jess's creased brow.

"I can almost see it."

"Really?" Jess looked at the floor between them.

"No. Not with my eyes." Tory tried to explain but there weren't words for the sense she had, at least no words she knew. "It's a feeling. Like …" she paused, thinking. "It's like when you have your eyes closed, and you still know exactly where the tips of your fingers are."

"Huh?"

"There's a word for that …" Tory snapped her fingers, trying to remember. "Kinesthesia!"

"I still don't entirely understand."

Tory laughed. "Neither do I. But I know where it is

now. I really can feel it." She looked all around her, though she wasn't actually seeing her power with her eyes. "Right now, it's like a globe around me, with a radius of about five feet." She shut her eyes and felt some more. Then she laughed and snapped her eyes open. "It even goes into the floor below." She pushed. "Now I've pushed it out to where you are."

"Can you pull it in smaller?" Jess asked.

Tory pulled until she felt her power close and thick around her—a ball concentrated at her chest. She began to sweat. "Walk toward me."

Jess paced, one step at a time toward Tory until she was just inches away. She felt a twinge and let out the breath she was holding. "Yes. But it's a lot harder to pull it in. Like stuffing something into a too-small container."

Jess's eyes widened and she grinned. Then her brow furrowed in concentration. "Is it always a globe? Can you change the shape?"

"I don't know. I think so, but I'm not sure how I know that. How could we test it?"

"The marbles! We can put a ring of them around you, outside of your 'normal' range. Then you put them out one by one."

Tory nodded and Jess jumped to lay out the marbles. Some were within sight, and others were behind shelves. "These will be a challenge—you'll have to find them."

Tory nodded. "I'll start with the easy ones." She took a deep breath. She envisioned the bubble around her elongating toward the first marble. She stretched out an arm of power, like some strange amoeba, and imagined the cytoplasm of her anti-magic streaming toward the marble. With a twinge, it winked out. She relaxed and smiled.

Jess whooped. "All the others are still lit!"

Tory nodded toward another marble. "That one next." With more confidence this time, she stretched her power out and tapped the marble with it. It went out.

Jess clapped. "Try one of the hidden ones."

Tory nodded. She knew vaguely where one was, and she stretched her power out in that direction. It passed effortlessly through the bookshelf and books between. When she reached as far as she thought the marble was, she slowly envisioned the arm of power sweeping back and forth in widening arcs.

Watching the marble, Jess called out, "You did it!" But Tory already knew. She'd felt it. "Can you reach out behind you?"

"I can try." Tory sent a tendril of power backward, toward a marble behind the shelves on her other side. Jess ran around to watch. Tory felt a twinge and Jess whooped.

"How accurate are you able to be?"

Tory's amoeba arms had been thick and clumsy, now she thought about it. "I don't know. Put two marbles close together on that table. I'll try to get the one on the left without touching the right."

Jess set out the marbles, about a foot apart. Tory sent an arm of power toward the one on the left, letting it narrow as it approached the marbles. It winked out, and the other continued to glow.

"Closer," Tory said.

Jess set a new marble six inches from the first.

When she easily snuffed that one, Jess set another down, three inches away.

They both cheered when Tory snuffed that one too, without touching the other one.

"Wow! That one gave a little pop." Jess dipped her hand into the pouch. "We've only got three left."

Tory tingled all the way to her fingers and toes. She squared her shoulders. "Line them up. Touching. I'll take out the one in the middle."

Jess's eyebrows rose. "Really?"

Tory nodded. "Yeah. Really." She smiled. Concentrating hard, she pulled her anti-magic into a spear shape, narrow and sharp-tipped. She imagined all her power concentrated in that tip as she stretched it out to the marble. As the tip got close, she felt it wobble. She took a breath and held it, focusing and steadying the spear. Then she stabbed.

A loud pop rang out. Jess screamed as the marble exploded into her face. Tory gasped. She heard feet pounding in the corridor outside. She quickly shoved her power at the remaining glowing marbles, which had been tossed off the table by the explosion. They winked out. Ordinary marbles now. She ran to Jess, who had covered her face with her hands.

"Are you alright? Jess?" What if she'd hurt her best friend with her power? Her tingling excitement fizzled, and her heart hammered in her chest.

The door flew open.

"What is going on in here?" The librarian and a tall man in a suit barged into the room, both breathless from running.

Tory turned to them. "Ah ..."

"Sorry! My fault." Jess's voice was falsely light. "I dropped a bag of marbles, and then, silly me, slipped on one as I was trying to gather them up."

The librarian frowned. "You're bleeding."

Tory whipped her head around again. Jess dabbed at her forehead with her fingers. "Yeah. Hit my head on the corner of the table. Not a big deal." She smiled. "Hardly feel it."

"Let me get you a tissue." The librarian scurried out of the room.

The man crossed his arms. "What were you doing with marbles, anyway?"

Tory raised her eyebrows at Jess, wondering what she was going to say. Jess gave her a surreptitious wink. "My son. You know kids. I had to take the marbles away from him this morning, because he and his sister were fighting over them." She rolled her eyes. "I shoved the bag into my pocket and forgot about it. We were collecting our things to leave, and the marbles fell out of my pocket."

The man frowned, but any further questions were cut off by the arrival of the librarian with a handful of tissues. Jess took them and pressed them to her forehead.

"Sit, Jess," Tory said. "I'll pick up the marbles and gather our things." She knelt down to scoop up a marble, hoping the staff didn't notice the scattering of glass fragments on the floor. She glanced up at the disapproving faces. "We'll be leaving in just a minute. Sorry for the disturbance." The pair turned to leave. "Oh, and we're done with the book. Thank you. You can put it away now."

The librarian turned back. "That's fine. Actually the researcher scheduled for noon wants the same book." She laughed. "Fancy that!"

Tory felt blood drain from her face. "Fancy that," she muttered as the pair shut the door behind them. She turned to Jess, whose eyes were wide. "Are you sure you're okay, Jess?"

Jess nodded. "It really is just a scratch." She pulled the tissues away from her forehead and dabbed at it a couple of times. "See? The bleeding's nearly stopped."

Tory swept up the glass and marbles as best she could. "Who do you think is after the book?"

"Either Nico or your dad. Probably Nico."

Tory pressed her lips together and dropped the marbles back into the pouch that Jess held out for her. "Nico." She couldn't shake the sense of betrayal. She was surprised it was stronger for Nico than for her father. Anger flared in her chest. She gathered their coats and purses and handed Jess her things.

Jess gave her forehead one last pat, and then

crumpled the tissues into her pocket. "Ready?"

Tory nodded and they turned to head out the door. It opened as Tory was reaching toward the handle. The librarian, her hand on the door, ushered in Nico. His eyes met hers and she stared daggers at him for a moment. Then she smiled, sharpened her anti-magic and thrust it at him.

He cried out and bent double, clutching his stomach.

Tory gasped and snatched her anti-magic back, furling it tightly around her. She clapped her hand to her mouth and dashed out of the room. As she and Jess strode down the hallway, she heard the librarian behind them.

"Sir? Are you alright sir?"

Please let him be okay! Tory sped up and raced down the steps, Jess struggling to keep up.

"Tory. Tory!"

Tory ignored her. She ran through the lobby and burst out the door into the midday sun. She threw herself onto a bench nearby and put her head in her hands.

"Tory, what happened back there?"

"Oh Jess! I nearly killed him! I could have killed him. Oh please, tell me he's not dead!" She rocked back and forth, shaking from head to toe, terrified of what had just happened, terrified of herself. "I had no idea!"

"Tory."

"Jess, I don't want to be a killer!"

"Tory." Jess wrapped an arm around Tory's shoulders.

"I was so excited. It was like a game, with those marbles, but Jess, I stabbed him with my power, and it was like I stabbed him with a real weapon! I felt it go in! I felt him fight it! And his face!"

"Tory. I'm calling us a cab." She took her arm off Tory's shoulders, but Tory hardly noticed. She didn't hear Jess make the call, and she was barely aware when Jess pushed her into the cab. Wrapped in her own shaking terror, she didn't register anything until the cab pulled up at the hotel.

21

Nico

Pain. Like nothing Nico had ever felt before. It tore at his gut, slicing through flesh and bone and magic. He could almost see the shape of her power. His eyes widened, and he just glimpsed her own shock before he doubled over in agony.

The spear was gone in an instant, though the pain lingered for a few minutes. Nico gradually recovered, and heard the librarian's frantic voice. "Sir! Are you alright?" He peeled his arms away from his stomach, expecting to see a gaping wound. There was nothing. His shirt and jacket were pristine. He prodded. Not even a scratch on his skin. He took a deep breath and straightened. He felt pale and shaky and imagined he looked about the same.

He smiled. "I'm fine. Just a … a medical condition. Comes and goes. It's nothing." He waved a dismissive hand and took another breath. "The book?"

"Oh. Yes. Of course. Right over here." She led him to the book, which was still open to the Squelcher page. Nico scanned the page, turned it over to make sure there was no more, and asked, "May I take photographs?" He *had* to get back out there and follow Tory. He could read the book later from his photos.

"As long as you don't use a flash."

Nico took two snaps—of the drawing and of the

text. He pocketed his phone and nodded to the librarian, who hovered with a concerned look on her face. "Thanks. That's all I need."

He passed a tall man in a suit on his way out and heard the librarian say to him, "We have had the strangest visitors today."

Nico took the stairs two at a time and burst out of the museum just as Tory and Jess ducked into a cab.

He hadn't dared bring his own car downtown—it was a government vehicle, and he really didn't need anyone from the Division noticing him. Damn! He'd never get a cab in time to catch up with them.

He called for one anyway. As soon as he hung up, a taxi pulled up at the curb. Out of the corner of his eye, he saw a young couple jogging over. "Sorry," he muttered, trying to ignore their glares as he jumped into the car and gave the driver the address.

At the first traffic light, his taxi pulled up behind Tory's, and Nico breathed a sigh of relief. He hadn't lost her, and it looked like they were headed to the hotel, which is what he'd expected.

As the vehicle neared the hotel, Nico scanned the roof, the bushes, the fences, for any sign of a sniper. He saw nothing. Then a glint of light caught his eye. There was someone in one of the hotel windows. The barrel of a gun caught the light again. Second floor, third room from the end.

Wait a minute.

That was *his* room.

"Bastards!" he muttered.

Tory's cab had arrived, and Jess was helping her out when the sniper fired. Nico was ready. This was something he'd trained for—deflecting bullets. It was tricky, but he was good at it. As long as he got it before he or the bullet was within range of Tory's anti-magic ... he concentrated, muttering under his breath.

The bullet soared upward, over the cab, over the women's heads, to land harmlessly with a ping on the road.

"Fifteen twenty-three," said the cab driver, and Nico realized by his tone that he'd said it more than once.

Nico rummaged in his wallet and pulled out a twenty. "Keep the change." He lurched out of the car. Tory and Jess were almost to the door now. Jess had her arm around Tory, almost carrying her as they ran. Nico frowned. What had happened? Had she been hit? Impossible. He'd deflected the bullet. He glanced back at the window.

The sniper was gone.

He ran toward the door, but stopped before he reached it. The women had gone inside. He rubbed his stomach, remembering the spear of anti-magic Tory had stabbed him with. Maybe he shouldn't go to her. He glanced again at his window. It was still empty.

He was certain the sniper would have vanished without a trace by the time he arrived in his room. He would have come and gone magically, no doubt—a non-magical sniper whisked in and out by a powerful wizard, avoiding any danger to Users. Nico waited another minute, until he was sure Tory and Jess were out of the lobby, and then made his way to his room.

He locked the door behind him and searched the room. It hadn't been ransacked. Not a single one of his things was out of place. But sitting in the center of the bed, in plain view, was a rifle. A pretty piece of evidence, if the sniper had hit Tory.

Nico ground his teeth together. He pulled out his phone and stabbed out a number. When a man's voice answered, he said, "James. This is Nico. Tell me why the Division is trying to frame me for murder."

22

※

Tory

Tory didn't know where the shot had come from, but when she and Jess heard it, Jess grabbed her and urged her to run for the hotel door. They thundered up the stairs and into their room. Jess rammed the deadbolt home. Tory scanned the room. Puck was curled up in the middle of her bed. She knew that if anyone had been in the room, he would be tagging along behind them, but she prodded the curtains, bent to check under the bed, and then peered into the bathroom, just to make sure. She swept Puck into her arms and took a steadying breath, which did nothing but show her how much she was shaking. She turned to Jess.

Jess's face was white, her orange hair looking like an extension of her alarm. She wrapped her arms protectively around herself, breathing hard. "Hm. That was interesting."

Tory realized she'd pushed her anti-magic out to encompass the entire room, as though to create a sphere of safety around them. Except it wouldn't help against bullets. Well, at least she could protect them all against magic. That was something. She took another breath and felt her heartbeat slow a little. Puck squirmed—she was clutching him too tightly. She released her hold, and he dropped to the bed, tail up and purring.

"They must know we're here," Jess said. "We should have run for the car."

"And left Puck?"

Jess shrugged. "I suppose you're right. But they'll be waiting for us to leave the room, leave the building."

"No, they'll be waiting for *me* to leave. Jess, you should go. Take Puck with you." She fished in her pocket and pulled out the car key. She held it out to her friend.

Color flushed Jess's face and she unwrapped her arms to put her hands on her hips. "Are you kidding?"

"Please. You'll be safe. It's me they want."

Jess scoffed. "Even if you weren't my best friend, even if you didn't need me here, this is the most exciting thing to ever happen to me." She laughed. "I've been an effing librarian for five years. The most interesting thing that's happened in that whole time has been when that ancient guy, Mr. Roth, died in the classics section with a copy of *Lady Chatterley's Lover* on his lap."

"But you could be killed! Puck could be killed. What if a bullet intended for me hits you instead?"

Jess flopped into an armchair. "I've been thinking about my life, Tory. A degree in journalism, but what am I doing with it? I expected to be investigating scandals, crimes, maybe even reporting on wars and humanitarian crises. I expected to be in the thick of things, in mortal danger on a regular basis. Instead I'm shelving books." She barked a laugh. "All those boyfriends—the fuckfaces and the shitbuckets—they've been my way of having a little excitement in my life. A little drama."

"You *do* like drama." Tory sat on the bed, dangling the key in her hand while Puck batted at it. "But this is more than your sister sleeping with your boyfriend."

"I studied journalism because I *like* drama. I like dealing with conflict. I want to feel my heart race. And, frankly, working as a librarian is about as thrilling as eating a plain rice cake."

"But—" Tory's argument was cut short by a rapping at the door.

Tory froze, and her heart leapt to her throat. The rapping came again, insistent, followed by, "Tory! Jess!" in a low, urgent voice.

Jess rose and tiptoed to the door. She peeked through the peephole, then turned and pressed her back against the door. "It's Nico," she hissed.

Tory shot to her feet and, without thinking, pushed her anti-magic through the door.

Nico groaned. "Tory. Tory, stop. I want to help." He gave a pained cry. "Please stop."

Jess frowned. "Are you using your power? Tory?"

Tory gasped. She covered her face with her hands and snatched her anti-magic back. "Oh my god! I've done it again!"

"Tory. Let me in." Nico's voice sounded stronger, but still pleading. "I promise I won't hurt you."

"Tory?" Jess put a hand on Tory's shoulder. "I think he really is trying to help."

Tory nodded, straightened and dropped her hands. She furled her power tightly around herself and wrapped her arms around her stomach, as though to hold the anti-magic in. Jess pulled back the bolt and opened the door.

Nico tumbled in, breathless and pale. Tory's hand flew to her mouth and tears sprang to her eyes. "I'm sorry," she whispered.

Nico stared at her and licked his lips. "Tory." He flushed and dropped his gaze to Puck, who was twining around his ankles. When he looked up, he didn't look directly at her, but scanned the room. "I'm glad you've gained control of your power. Did the glow pods help?"

"Yes. Thank you." Tory swallowed, ashamed. "I really am sorry ... about ... at the library and just now. I ... well, I'm not sure I have as good a control of my power as I should."

Nico shook his head and looked at her again. "No.

I'm ... I'm glad you can use it to protect yourself."

Behind Nico's back, Jess smothered a smile with her hand. Tory raised an eyebrow in a silent question. Nico turned, and Jess dropped her hand and forced her face into a serious expression. "Someone shot at Tory as we came in— we're a little on edge. Why are you here, Nico?"

Nico nodded. "I know. Government sharpshooter. He'd have hit, if I hadn't deflected the bullet." Tory blinked in surprise. "He fired from my room and left the rifle as evidence."

"What?" Tory squeezed herself tighter.

Nico barked a laugh and turned back to Tory. "Apparently, the Magical Division has decided I've been *compromised*, and it would be convenient to dispose of me as well as you."

"By framing you for my murder? Why don't they just shoot you too?"

Nico snorted. "They have a thing about not spilling magical blood."

"Oh, because your blood is so much more valuable than mine. Of course." Tory couldn't keep the anger out of her voice. "You know, in spite of what you might think, I'm actually a human being too. I'm not some monster to—"

Nico held up a hand. "I *know*. That's why I'm here. The Magical Division thinks you are a monster and, frankly, so do most wizards and witches, but—" he ran his hand through his hair and dropped his gaze, "—I don't. Not anymore. I want to help you."

"Well, you can start by explaining what, exactly, is the Magical Division."

"Or maybe start with what is magic, because until yesterday, magic only existed for us in fantasy novels," Jess added.

Nico sighed. "It's a long story."

"I'll order lunch," Jess offered. "Make yourself

comfortable."

"Look, I don't know if we have time."

"You're asking us to believe in fairy tales and in the good intentions of a man who has been stalking us for three hundred miles." Jess pressed a palm flat on Nico's chest and shoved him into a chair. "Sit." Puck instantly jumped onto Nico's lap. Tory frowned.

Jess picked up the room service menu and handed it to Nico. "What do you want?"

"Um ... the ham sandwich?"

They ordered lunch, including a bottle of wine. "I have a feeling I'll need it," Jess said.

Tory sat cross-legged on her bed and Jess lounged on the other. Tory was glad to note that given a choice, Puck gravitated to her, not Nico. He leapt lightly to the bed and rubbed around her back before settling on her lap.

Jess nodded at Nico. "So. Begin with magic."

"We don't need all the details," Tory clarified, seeing Nico's mildly panicked look. "Just enough to explain what the hell is going on."

Nico took a deep breath. "As you've already figured out, or been told by your—by Victor Hughes—magic exists in every living human. Well, except you, Tory. It plays a role in emotions, beliefs like religious faith, and creativity." He faltered for a moment. "A small percentage of people have extra magical ability—enough to manipulate and do things with." He frowned. "It's like synesthesia, or another sense."

"Like people who smell colors or taste sounds?" Tory asked.

"Yeah, except it's more than a sense too. I've never had to explain it to an Insig—a non magic-user. It's something we try to keep quiet. You know, witch hunts and all."

"Oh, come on." Jess laughed. "There hasn't been a witch hunt in America since the eighteen hundreds."

"It's still not something ordinary people are comfortable with. Besides, the government has a vested interest in keeping our existence a secret, since they employ us in espionage."

"So the Magical Division is part of the FBI?" Tory scratched Puck's ears.

Nico nodded. "Most governments have a secret magical division of some sort."

"And this secret magical division believes I'm enough of a threat that they need to kill me?"

Nico nodded. "I tried to convince them not to. But it's like a dragon just landed in the middle of D.C.—the only thing they can think of is to get rid of you before you do any damage."

A knock sounded at the door and they all jumped. Jess hopped up and peered out. "Ah! Lunch."

Jess distributed their lunches and poured wine for all of them. When she sat down again, she asked, "Is Tory really that dangerous? I mean, no offence to Tory, but she's a librarian. It's not like she's a trained ninja or something."

Nico set down his sandwich. "I'm the most powerful wizard in the Division. Tory could kill me without breaking a sweat, without even touching me." He glanced quickly at her and rubbed his chest. "She could probably wipe out most of the Magical Division without even entering our building. If we lose our governmental magic-users, we're up shit creek without a paddle. Russia, China, Germany, hell, even Canada could launch a magical attack against the government and take us over just like that." He snapped his fingers.

"But why would I do that?" Tory asked.

"It's your father. Maybe he wouldn't resort to violence, but he's got links to terrorist groups, anarchist groups, and an organization called MFG—Magic-free Governance—that believes magic-users should refuse to work for governments, because it leads to the abuse of power."

"That's my dad, not me."

"And you've recently made contact with your father." Nico sounded tired.

Jess took a sip of her wine. "You mean, they think Victor Hughes is going to radicalize his daughter?"

Nico nodded and shrugged, chewing.

"And why don't you believe that too?" Tory narrowed her eyes at Nico and felt her power snaking out toward him. She snatched it back. He'd said she could kill him. She wasn't sure she trusted him, but she knew she didn't want to kill him.

Nico dropped his gaze and focused on his food. "I've been following you for weeks. I ..." Jess was smirking. "I guess I feel like I know you." He shrugged. "A little, anyway."

Tory let out a breath, trying not to resent the fact Nico had been stalking her. "So how do we convince them I'm not a threat and they should leave me alone?"

23

Nico

Nico threw himself onto the bed in his room, reviewing the last hour in his head. He'd convinced Tory not to go home—he assumed there would be a trap waiting for her there. He'd also convinced her not to have any more contact with her father. That would help as he tried to worm his way back into favor at the Division and convince them she really was harmless.

She and Jess would stay in D.C., pretending to sightsee and staying in crowded public spaces as much as possible. Nico would surreptitiously escort them to and from the hotel, doing his best to detect and deflect any attacks. While they were safely surrounded by other tourists, Nico would attempt to convince the Magical Division to leave her alone.

He pulled out a letter she'd written to the head of the Division, claiming she had no anti-government sentiments and would not attempt to use her power to attack Users. He scanned it and sighed. They would, of course, think he'd written it. But it might help.

Nico shut his eyes and swore. He had a bad feeling this assignment was going to kill his career. What would his father have said? His father, who despised Insigs and would never have entertained the possibility a Squelcher was anything other than a monster. He had been Head of the

Magical Division for twenty years and had always expected Nico to follow in his footsteps. And Nico had followed eagerly, with the same restless ambition his father had used to climb to the top. Nico had put in his application for Assistant Director for International Operations when crusty old Gladys Barker had finally announced her retirement, but then James had put Davis on the Russia job. That might have been okay (though if his dad had still been alive, he would have pulled strings until Nico was sent to Russia), except now he'd botched this job.

No. He hadn't botched it. He'd done exactly what he'd been asked to do; he'd determined Tory wasn't a threat.

He frowned and spoke to the ceiling. "She did almost kill you today, Nico."

But she *hadn't*. She'd stopped when she realized what she was doing. She wasn't a killer, and she wasn't a terrorist or an anarchist. She was a librarian. A simple, boring librarian.

"Then why are you risking your career to protect her?"

The ceiling provided no answers.

24

Tory

Tory zipped up her bag and clipped a leash onto Puck's collar. "You ready?"

Jess shrugged her coat on. "Are you sure you want to do this? It could be dangerous."

"For twenty-eight years I've wondered who my father is. He avoided me because my anti-magic would kill him, but now I can control that. I'm not going to let some jerk from the FBI prevent me from getting to know him."

"I don't think he's that bad, Tory."

Tory rolled her eyes. "Jess, your ability to distinguish jerks from nice men is on par with my ability to fall in love."

Jess laughed. "Still. Think about this. Are you sure? Maybe he's an asswipe, but Nico *did* deflect one bullet, and it might be nice to have that protection. And the more contact you have with your dad, the more of a threat they'll think you are." She frowned. "It's not like you to take risks."

Tory shrugged. Take risks? She felt she was already in free fall. "It's not like me to stab invisible spears into men, either, but I did that today. Something about finding out I have a superpower, I suppose." She smiled, hoping it would make her feel more confident.

Jess smiled back. "A superpower—I like that. Let's go then." She clapped her hands and shivered. "Oh! This is fun! Give me five minutes to load the car and find that tracking device." She checked the time. "I'll pull up to the door at exactly three twenty-two."

"And I'll make a run for it." Her heart fluttered at the thought. Was there a sniper waiting for her? Maybe this wasn't a good idea. She wavered for only a second. No. She wanted to meet her father. She *would* meet her father.

She'd rung his office from the hotel phone, assuming her own phone was bugged, and had found out he was on sabbatical at Penn State. She and Jess had laughed at that. "We might have passed him on the street."

They'd be back in State College by evening. Tomorrow morning, she'd show up at his office. She didn't know what made her more nervous—the idea of being shot by a sniper, or the idea of meeting her father.

Jess hefted both their bags. Tory handed her Puck's leash, and Jess and the cat crept out the door. Tory paced the room, checking the time every few seconds. A horrible thought occurred to her: what if the sniper shot Jess, thinking she was Tory?

She laughed out loud. No one could mistake Jess's spiky orange locks for her long dark curls.

She checked the time—3:21. Tory stepped out of the room and strode quickly down the hall. She cringed at the noise her feet made when she reached the stairs, but she didn't slow. She pushed open the stairwell door and saw the car through the front doors. She broke into a jog and hit the doors at speed. Jess flung the passenger door open, and Tory dove in. Tires squealed as Jess hit the gas.

"Keep your head down!" Jess barked.

Tory fumbled with the seatbelt while trying to stay below the window. Jess pulled onto the street and into heavy D.C. traffic. After a few minutes, she said, "We're nearly at the freeway. You're probably alright now."

Tory breathed a sigh of relief and sat up. "Did you find the tracker?"

"Yep. Little magnetic thing up under the rear bumper."

"Where'd you leave it?"

Jess grinned. "Chucked it into the flowerpot by the front door."

Meow. Puck stepped gingerly between the seats and perched on Tory's lap. Tory obligingly scratched his ears.

The drive back to State College was uneventful, and they checked into the hotel with no mishaps, though they had to smuggle Puck in under Tory's jacket. It was clearly not a pet-friendly hotel. Tory hoped they'd gotten away cleanly.

Over breakfast the next morning, Jess said, "Do you think Nico's figured out we've slipped him yet?"

Tory checked the time. "If he hasn't, he will soon. We're ten minutes late for our escort to the Natural History Museum."

They'd booked a room in the Nittany Lion Inn. It was more expensive than they would have liked, but it was conveniently located next to the Carpenter Building where Victor Hughes' temporary office *should* be located, and they thought it was wise to stay off the streets, just in case the FBI caught up with them. Tory wasn't too worried this morning—she'd kept an eye out for vehicles following them and hadn't seen anything suspicious. Of course, Nico thought the FBI had magicked the sniper in and out of his hotel room. Could they have followed her by magical means? She had no idea. She wished she knew more about magic; she was sure it was nothing like a fantasy novel.

As they stepped out of the hotel, Tory's heartbeat sped up, and she darted a glance around. A silver minivan passed on the street. Two men in suits got into a car. A trio of students passed on the sidewalk. Puck squirmed under her coat, and she shushed him, promising she'd let him

148

down in a minute.

"Ready?" Jess asked.

Tory nodded. "I wish there were more people around."

"Yeah, me too." She rubbed her hands together. "Nothing for it, though. Come on Supergirl. Let's go meet your dad."

They hurried down the sidewalk to the Carpenter Building. Jess held the door for Tory and Puck, who trotted along on his leash now. "How convenient! A directory." Jess and Tory scanned the names.

"Room one-twenty." They headed down the hallway. Tory's palms were sweating. She slowed as they neared the office. What if he wasn't there? What if he didn't want to see her, even with control of her power? What if *he* thought she was a monster too? What if—?

"Tory?" Jess turned when Tory slowed to a halt. She took a deep breath, dried her hands on her jeans, and pulled her anti-magic close. She nodded to Jess, and they continued down the hall.

The door was ajar. She peeked around the frame to see a man with coppery hair in a tan suit typing at a computer. His back was turned. She knocked. "Um ... Excuse me. Dr. Hughes?"

The man turned. "May I help you?" His face was bland and polite. Then his eyes widened. He opened his mouth.

Tory tried to smile. "I'm Tory. Your ... daughter." It felt weird saying that—the man looked so young. His hair included a wisp of silver—just enough to look distinguished. His face was unlined, and he sported a tidy beard. He swallowed and stood. He was tall and well-built. He wore a bow tie, and his suit was quaintly retro.

"Tory." He took a step toward her, and then stopped.

"I can control it now. My power. I can keep it close around me. I ... I won't hurt you." She shrugged. What did you say to a man who'd abandoned you as an infant? Now that she was here, all the burning questions she wanted answers to flew out of her head. Instead, she stared dumbly.

The silence dragged on, and then Victor huffed out a weak laugh. "I ... I don't know what to say."

Jess cleared her throat.

Tory started. "Oh! This is my friend Jess. And, uh, my cat, Puck."

Jess reached out a hand. "I'm safe. I promise." She smiled and shook his hand. Puck sat down to wash his paws, looking bored.

Victor's eyes snapped back to Tory. She was beginning to remember the questions she had for him, but had no idea where to start. Victor opened his mouth as if to speak, but then closed it. He blinked.

Jess came to their rescue. "Shall we sit down and have a chat?"

Victor shook his head, as if to clear it. "Yes. Please. Sit. Can I get you a coffee or something?"

"No thanks. We're fine. I'm sorry we've come unexpectedly. Is this a bad time?" Tory wondered if she should have tried to contact him beforehand. She hadn't wanted to risk Nico or anyone listening in. The whole idea that her every move, her every conversation was being tracked gave her a crawling feeling.

"No, no, no. This is fine. Just ... unexpected." He waved them into seats and then shut the door behind them. "You weren't followed here?"

"We don't think so. We at least gave Nico the slip."

"Nico?"

"The FBI agent who's been tracking me."

Victor smiled. "Oh, yes. I remember him."

"You've met him?" Tory leaned forward.

Victor nodded. "In a bar. Apparently you'd driven him to drink, you were so boring to follow."

Tory and Jess both laughed.

"Did he come looking for you?" Jess frowned.

Victor waved a hand. "No. It was just coincidence I sat down next to him at the bar. I don't think he even knew who he was talking to."

An awkward silence pooled between them. Twenty-eight years of his absence seemed insurmountable to Tory, now that she faced him in person. She felt all of her mother's anger, but now that she'd seen what her power could do to a wizard, she could hardly blame him for disappearing. And he hadn't abandoned her completely. There was the college fund, and the fact he'd been looking for that book for nearly thirty years.

Victor watched Puck as the cat twined around Tory's legs, purring. "Interesting you have a cat."

"Hm?" Tory reached down to pet Puck.

"Cats are usually well-attuned to magic. They seem to have an affinity for Users. Odd that Puck has taken to you." He smiled and his eyes lingered on the cat. "We really know almost nothing about ... I hate to even call you a Squelcher, because it has such negative connotations."

Puck moved to Victor and rubbed his head against his leg. They all watched the cat in silence, and Tory tried to digest the idea that the only name for her was a derogatory one. She was used to being a minority, but to be an oddity was something altogether different. It made her feel small and alone. The silence stretched out, and she knew she had to get the conversation going again, ask her questions, learn what she came here to learn.

"I found the book," she offered. It seemed a good place to start. The truth was, she didn't want to hear him talk about why he left, or hear him apologize again for leaving. It was her mother he needed to have that conversation with, not her. What she really wanted from him was to learn more about magic, about how the FBI used their magic-users, and why Victor Hughes opposed it.

Victor's eyebrows rose. "*Magical Anomalies*?"

Tory nodded. "It's at the Smithsonian. We read it yesterday."

Victor leaned forward. "I looked for it there years ago and it wasn't there."

Jess nodded. "It's a relatively new acquisition—from some private collection."

"And we almost didn't find it there either," Tory added. "It was badly misshelved."

Victor smiled. "But you two found it because you're librarians. Did it contain the cure?"

"Not really." Tory scratched Puck's ears, trying hard not to look disappointed. "It briefly mentioned a theoretical cure, and then went on to say the only wizard who had ever tried it nearly died in the attempt, and the Squelcher in question wasn't fully cured."

Victor slumped a little. Then he smiled and gave a laugh. "Frankly, seeing you in person, finally—" He waved his hand toward her and blinked. "There's nothing in need of curing. You're beautiful." His voice cracked. "Excuse me. I ..."

Tory found her own eyes misting up in response.

Jess looked uncomfortable. She stood. "How about I go get us some coffee?"

Victor pulled out a handkerchief and wiped his eyes. "There's a coffee machine in the mail room, just down the hall." He nodded his thanks to Jess, and she left the room.

"Tory, I—"

Tory raised a hand to cut him off. "Victor ... Dad ... I understand why you did what you did. And I didn't come here so you could explain or apologize. I came because I'm being hunted by the U.S. government. Because of you.

I need to know what's going on. What is it you've done that they think you'll turn me against the government? What is it about the government that you don't like? I don't know how to deal with this, how to convince the FBI I'm not a threat, if I don't even understand why they're afraid of me."

Victor wrung his hands. "Sorry you've been drawn into this. It's a long story. I'll try to make it short." He leaned back in his chair and pressed a fist against his lips, thinking. "Wizards and witches have always hidden from the general public, as you can imagine, with witch hunts and whatnot. We used to be fiercely independent. We lived within our various countries, but we didn't really consider ourselves part of those nations. The magical community was global, not divided along geopolitical boundaries. That changed during World War II. Adolf Hitler was a minor wizard—just powerful enough to influence Insigs, just powerful enough to threaten to take over Europe. It was the first time in modern history a wizard had attempted to influence global politics, and many of us were outraged by it." He laughed mirthlessly. "I was a boy at the time, and I hated having to hide among normal people. I thought it was great at first—a wizard was out there in public, not afraid to show himself."

Jess returned with coffee. "Is the mushy bit over?" She winked and handed steaming mugs to Victor and Tory. "I didn't know how you like your coffee, so I've just brought it black. Is that okay?"

Victor nodded and accepted the mug. "That's perfect. Thank you." He smiled at Jess—an incongruously fatherly smile from such a young-looking face.

Tory caught Jess up on Victor's narrative and then nodded for him to continue.

Victor took a sip of coffee. "Well, it was soon clear that Hitler was a bad egg. Clear to some of us, anyway. I hate to say it, but there was a group of wizards and witches who gravitated toward him and his politics. They saw the potential of magical dominance over the rest of the population. But most of us just wanted to stop him. Magic-users started to infiltrate governments in order to give them an edge over Hitler. It was supposed to have been a temporary measure, but many stayed on even after Hitler was gone." He sighed. "I can understand it, really. To be able to use your magic to gain influence in the wider world is a big incentive. It didn't take long before governments set up clandestine magical units."

Tory frowned. "So what's wrong with magic-users in government? Why is it any different from someone with unusual intelligence or particular skills in mathematics or law working for the government?"

Victor smiled, but it was a tired gesture. He looked his age for a moment. "Theoretically, there's nothing wrong with it. You're right. Users should be able to use their skills in the wider community. But magic use isn't like being able to do advanced calculus in your head. It's too easy to manipulate people with magic. It's easy for wizards and witches to do terrible things in the pursuit of power, influence, advancement, fame, or even in the pursuit of the greater good."

Jess's eyes narrowed. "The Magical Division is abusing its power."

Victor nodded. "Yes. The intelligence community is always pushing the boundaries of abuse, but the Magical Division has gone way beyond."

"What are they doing?" Tory asked, a sick feeling in her stomach.

"Torture, blackmail, murders—think gangsters in Chicago, and you're not far off their tactics. Except they're doing it all with magic, so their power to inflict pain and suffering is even greater. And they can do it in ways undetectable by Insigs."

"And you've been trying to stop them? Is that why

they're worried about your influence on me?" Tory took a sip of her coffee.

Victor nodded. "There's a whole group of magic-users who believe witches and wizards should stay out of government. We'd love to eliminate the Magical Division entirely." He took a deep breath. "Unfortunately, most national governments have magical branches now, so eliminating the Magical Division would put the United States at a distinct disadvantage, globally, and that would be meddling in politics just as much as the Division does."

"There's no good solution, is there?" Jess frowned.

"Not unless we can convince witches and wizards in all governments to voluntarily leave."

Tory rested her mug on her knee. "Are all magic-users so power-hungry they can't be trusted in government? I mean, there are plenty of ordinary people with great power over others—employers, teachers, parents, everyday politicians—but they don't all abuse their power. Surely the Magical Division could change?"

Victor shook his head. "I wish I could be so hopeful. You're right. Theoretically, maybe it could change. But magic-users have notoriously long lives. The director sets the tone for the organization and largely determines what tactics they use. There have only been two directors in the Magical Division's history. Theo Michaelson had little respect for Insigs and an intense desire for power. His initial resistance against Hitler was redirected toward Insigs after the war." Victor shuddered. "In truth, he was no better than Hitler himself. Rumor is, he died testing a compound meant to induce sterility in Insigs—toxic gases and a faulty fume hood, apparently. Luther Hawkins, who replaced Michaelson after his untimely death, was cut from the same cloth. He could potentially remain in the position for three hundred years."

Jess swore.

Tory set down her cup and slumped in her seat. "So you're saying I have almost no chance of convincing them not to kill me."

Victor looked like he was in pain. "No. Not unless ..." He took a deep breath. "Not unless you join them."

"Join them? After what you told me about them? Why would I want to do that? Why would they let me?"

"You'd be one hell of a weapon against rival nations."

"I've seen what my power can do. I almost killed Nico without thinking. I could have. But even though he's a jerk, I wouldn't want to hurt him. I don't want to be a weapon!"

Victor smiled. "That's my girl."

25

Nico

Nico checked the time—9:15. Tory and Jess were fifteen minutes late. That wasn't like Tory—after tailing her for weeks, he could set his watch by her. Maybe Jess was delaying them. He could imagine that. He hadn't paid a lot of attention to her, but she didn't strike him as the punctual type.

He began to pace the hotel lobby. He'd give them five more minutes, and then he'd go up to their room. His pacing took him to the door, and he glanced out, scanning for snipers. Would they have whisked a sharpshooter into his room again? He hoped not. He'd given James hell for that one, and had tried to convince his boss that he wasn't *compromised*. He couldn't save Tory unless he had credibility. He cringed inwardly at the terrible things he'd said about her to James—nasty, prejudiced things he remembered his dad saying about Insigs. He'd believed those things, too, not long ago. Now? He wasn't sure what he believed. Tory was as non-magical as you could get and yet ...

His train of thought cut off abruptly and he scanned the parking lot again.

"Fuck!"

He pushed open the door and ran out.

He swore again.

Tory's car was gone.

No e-mails, no phone calls—Tory had done nothing to indicate where she was going. Nico had spent an agonizing hour trying to work out where she was headed, but still had nothing concrete to go on. But he had a hunch. He knew it was more than anyone else at the Magical Division would have. They were probably still waiting for her in some shady location outside.

He rang James.

"She's gone. But I know where she is." He tried to sound confident. He hoped he'd guessed right.

"We're not worried. We've got snipers outside her apartment, and at Victor Hughes' office."

Yes, but *which* office. Did they know he was on sabbatical? "You don't think she's gone all the way to Boston, do you?"

"We think it would be best if she didn't see her father."

They *didn't* know he was on sabbatical, then. Good. "She's not headed to either of those places."

"Where's she gone, then?"

"Put me back on the case and call off the snipers."

James snorted. "Are you saying you've decided to kill her yourself? You know, we've talked to that sniper— the one who missed—he claimed it was an easy shot. He assumed he'd hit her. Now why would he think that, when he missed so badly?"

"You'd have to ask him that. If he's not smart enough to wait around to see his target dead, I think you need a new sniper." Nico tried not to think about what James would do if he knew for certain he'd deflected that bullet.

"You've lost your credibility, Nico. I'm not taking the snipers off the job."

"Give me a chance. Let me prove myself. I made a few mistakes; I admit that. But they were mistakes. I won't make them again."

Silence stretched out on the line. James was doing his nose pinch, Nico was sure of it. Finally he spoke. "You'd better get to her before the snipers do." Then he hung up.

Getting to her before the snipers was the easy part. What then? He had no idea.

He left his car behind and magicked himself to State College.

26

Tory

"You need to flee the country."

"What?" Flee? Tory's reaction scared Puck off her lap. He landed on the floor and sat with his back to her, in protest.

Victor nodded. "It's the only way I can think that you'll be safe." Puck washed his face.

"But where would I go? And anyway, surely they'll track me, so what's the point?"

"Oh, they'll keep tabs on you, for sure. But if you're out of the country, you pose less threat to them." He shrugged. "They should leave you alone. Costa Rica's nice. And pretty neutral, politically. Do you speak Spanish?"

Tory waved a hand. "A little. But that's not the point!" The point was, she was terrified. The point was, this road trip was the most adventuresome thing she'd ever done, and the idea of getting on a plane to a foreign country, never to return, was simply unthinkable. She didn't even have a passport!

"I could go with you," Jess offered.

"What? Jess, why would you come with me? You—"

"I'm unemployed and unencumbered by the male sex." She grinned. "Costa Rica! It would be awesome."

"If you stay here, it's only a matter of time before they catch you, Tory." Victor's brow furrowed.

"But Nico is trying to convince them I'm not a threat."

Victor frowned. "Nico? Isn't he the one trying to kill you?"

Jess laughed. "Nico refused. He helped her get control of her power. He deflected a bullet from her. I'm convinced he's in love." Tory shook her head and rolled her eyes.

"Where is Nico now? Does he know you're here? Does anyone else know you're here? Tory, the Magical Division will never believe you're harmless if they know you've been talking to me."

"What exactly have you done that they're so worried about me talking to you?" Tory envisioned acts of terrorism, and her horror must have shown on her face, because Victor rushed to answer.

"It's nothing like you think. Honest. If I condoned violence, I wouldn't have a problem with the Magical Division. Everything I've done has been perfectly legal. But I've been watching Luther Hawkins for decades, gathering evidence, building a case for his removal from the Division and his incarceration by the International Commission of Magical Law Enforcement on a raft of charges relating to his treatment of Insigs. I brought charges against him years ago, but he slithered out of them somehow. It won't happen next time. He knows I'm after him, personally, as the root of the corruption in the Magical Division."

"So why doesn't he try to kill *you*, instead?" Jess asked.

"Because I'm a wizard. For all his corruption and willingness to torture, abuse and kill Insigs, he has a thing about not harming wizards and witches. He believes we're superior to you and, like Hitler, dreams of ultimately creating the perfect race of magic-users to take over the world." He laughed. "And I fathered a Squelcher. Really, Tory, you're my greatest offence to him." Then his eyes clouded. "And he knows that killing you would be the greatest harm he could do to me."

Tory swallowed. "And you think the only solution is for me to flee overseas?" She was shaking, and she bent to scoop Puck back onto her lap for the comfort of his soft fur.

Victor pulled out a sheet of paper and a pen and began writing furiously, talking as he did so. "I use an e-mail encryption service, so no one can track or read my e-mails. If you use the same service, the FBI can't eavesdrop on our conversations." He looked up. "At least in theory. I change encryption methods from time to time, just in case." He handed her the paper. "Here's the information. Get it set up and then contact me. I'll help you with the necessary preparations. I have some contacts in Costa Rica who can meet you there."

Tory took the paper and folded it carefully with jittery hands. She blinked back tears. This wasn't happening, surely? This couldn't be happening. She couldn't just leave everything. She hugged Puck close.

"Now go, before anyone finds out we've spoken."

Jess and Tory stood. Tory met her father's eyes and saw they swam with tears. She nodded, unable to voice the storm of emotions in her head—elation she'd found a loving father warred with the terror of her situation and disbelief she had to flee the country. She hoped her father understood. She turned to go.

"And, Tory?" Victor said as they reached the door. She turned. "Don't trust Nico." She nodded again and stepped out the door.

27

Nico

Magical travel was tricky. You needed to know exactly where you were going, and you needed to be sure no Insigs saw you disappearing or arriving. And it was exhausting—like sprinting.

Nico bent over double in the toilet stall, breathing hard. Three hundred miles was a lot of distance to traverse in one jump. His heart pounded in his ears, and his stomach heaved. Maybe he should have driven, after all. Slowly his breathing and his heart steadied. His stomach settled. He stood, listening.

He'd magicked himself into the restroom at the bar in State College where he'd met Victor. It was the safest place he could think to go. He was surprised he didn't hear sounds coming from the kitchen on the other side of the wall or from the dining area out the door. Then it hit him.

It was ten-thirty in the morning. The bar was closed. He swore, and then donned a magical disguise—gray hair, long beard and a bushy moustache, and a bright pink suit with a wide green tie—easily identifiable, and hopefully unlike anyone else. The police would look long and hard for this man and never find him.

When his disguise was complete, Nico stepped out of the restroom and strode toward the back door. He hoped there was no one in the alley. He pushed the door open, and an alarm went off. He ducked his head and strode quickly away. He passed no one, and half a block later, he slipped behind a dumpster and dropped his disguise. He straightened his jacket and his shoulders, and strolled calmly down the street.

The walk to the Carpenter Building gave him time to consider his next step. What he *wanted* to do was whisk Tory away somewhere safe. But there *was* no safety for her. Not unless she vanished entirely. His steps slowed as an idea came to him. An impatient student brushed past him, and he picked up his pace again. What if he staged her death? He could pretend to kill her, and then smuggle her somewhere safe to lie low while they created a new identity for her. He could do that. He'd created dozens of fake identities for himself. Passports, driver's licenses, fake birth certificates.

But he'd done that all with magic. Magic that would puff to nothing at her touch. He laughed bitterly. He was nothing without his magic. He was useless. He'd never felt like that before Tory. She stripped *wizard* away until he was simply *man*. And he wasn't much of one.

The Carpenter Building was in view now, but Nico sat down on a bench. He still didn't have a plan, and he felt raw and exposed. He crossed his arms and watched the students hurry past, back and forth along the sidewalk.

Who was he without his magic? Nico had always swaggered through life, secure in his superiority—over Insigs and over other Users. He *was* the most powerful wizard in the Division. He knew that. He reveled in it. But what did he do with that power? He spied on, questioned, tortured, and *neutralized* Insigs. He schemed his way to more power and influence within the Division with no thought to how he affected anyone else.

But he was doing it for the good of the nation, right? And he wasn't making the decisions; he was just following orders, so that made it not his responsibility, right?

His stomach squirmed in answer.

A pair of students walked past, holding hands and laughing. He thought about the political activist whose car he'd tampered with last month. He'd watched her walk down the street hand in hand with her husband just before he'd applied the fatal enchantment that made her car drive itself off a bridge.

He had done it without even considering the activist herself, or her family. Did she have kids? He didn't even know. He hadn't bothered to find out—she was just a target, not a person. An Insig—the name said it all—insignificant. Neutralizing an Insig was as easy as swatting a fly, but what he'd been doing was murdering people. And he'd thought *Tory* was a monster.

He buried his face in his hands. He wanted to slink away from himself, shuck off his own skin. What had he been thinking all these years? What had he been doing?

Only what he'd been taught. His very first memory was of his father causing an older man—an Insig—to trip and fall after he'd told Nico to 'pipe down' at his uncle's fun house. The man had broken his nose, and Nico remembered laughing at him. He'd cherished that memory as one of the few times his father took care of him. It had made him feel important, loved. Now it made him physically ill.

What had his father always said? "Magic is power, and the only thing that matters is power."

What had power gotten his dad? A wife he didn't love and an early death, the nature of which the FBI wouldn't disclose, even to Nico. Still, he suspected his dad had been happy—power was all he ever wanted.

Like father like son. Nico had chased power his whole life. He had a great career and opportunity to move up in the organization. He lived in a mansion and, with his power, he could pretty much go anywhere and do anything he liked.

A group of students passed, laughing and discussing their plans for the weekend.

He didn't have that. Friends. How could he, when his magical abilities were unmatched by even his peers within the Magical Division?

Did friendship rely on magic? His mother had always been surrounded by friends—Insigs, mostly. His dad had never bothered to learn their names, and he had even arranged the seating at her funeral so that Insigs had to sit in the back and weren't admitted to the reception afterwards.

It was only by accident Nico had enjoyed a dinner with Tory. An accident he'd gotten to know her. Was it an accident they liked the same books? How could they have anything in common?

Unless there were more important things than magical power. He wished his mother were still around, wished he'd listened to her more when he was a kid.

Nico rubbed his face, scrubbing away useless regrets. Tory was in danger, and whether it made sense or not, he cared. He needed to consider how he could help.

Pretending to kill her, or whisking her away to live in hiding wouldn't work. He'd watched her long enough to know that changing her identity and leaving everything she knew would kill her, figuratively, if not literally. He couldn't let the snipers get to her, either. So what was left? Convince the Division not to kill her. How the hell was he going to do that? James had given in and let him go after her, but he knew he was on trial. If he didn't deliver her, dead, they certainly wouldn't trust his judgment on whether she was dangerous.

Of course, they didn't need to trust his judgment. They could see for themselves.

"That's it," he said aloud. He jumped up and started for the Carpenter Building at a jog. As he rounded the corner, focused on reaching the entrance, a form sprang from a cluster of evergreens at the side of the path. He didn't even have time to call out in surprise before a hand was slapped over his mouth, and a jolt of magic paralyzed him.

28

Tory

Tory paced the hotel room. Staying active was the only way to avoid shaking uncontrollably. Puck watched her, his head tracking back and forth. Jess lay on her bed frowning at the ceiling. Tory stopped suddenly. "I have to go home. I can't make a decision like this in a hotel room. I need my apartment, my stuff ... I need some normalcy before I—" Her breath hitched. Was she really considering doing what her father suggested? "What will I do with Puck? Can I take him with me? I don't even know what the rules are around bringing a cat into another country. And what about visas and—"

Jess sat up. "Tory, stop." She frowned. "I understand your worries, but I'm not sure it's safe for you to go to your place."

"I *have* to, Jess." Tory ached with fear and exhaustion. She never slept well away from home, and right now she didn't care if there were twenty assassins waiting for her outside her door. She'd run the gauntlet to be home.

Jess considered her for a moment. "What if we go back to my apartment? It's a familiar place, at least. And there's plenty of room now that my sister and Michael are gone."

Tory envisioned Jess's apartment—clothes strewn around, dirty dishes in the sink, books piled in disorganized stacks on the floor. "It's not the same as going to my own space."

"But it's a lot safer. Tory, if you're shot," she swallowed. Then she took a deep breath. "You can't go home. We're going to my place. I'm not going to let my best friend be killed."

Tory blinked, her eyes stinging with tears. Her shoulders slumped. "Okay. I guess you're right."

Jess frowned. "We should disguise you, just in case. What do you think about cutting and dying your hair?" She wrinkled her nose. "Though we might have to bleach it first to get the dye to show. That would take too long." Tory was horrified at the thought, and it obviously showed. Jess shrugged. "Okay, then. Maybe a wig?" She clapped her hands. "That's it! We'll dress you as a man. Wouldn't be the first guy I'd taken to my apartment." She jumped up and grabbed Tory's hair, gathering it into a knot on top of her head. "We can tuck your hair into a nice Stetson, and dress you in a suit …" Her eyes dropped to Tory's chest. "Hm. Those will be a problem."

Tory laughed. "We could dress *you* as a man," she offered.

Jess dropped Tory's hair. "It's not me they're after."

"I know." She sighed. "Look, let's just go. Right now, we seem to be ahead of the snipers. I don't think they know where I am, and they don't know where I'm going. They can't be *everywhere*. Once we're at your place, I can hunker down there, and you can bring me food and supplies until …" Until what? "Until I decide what to do."

"I suppose you're right." Jess frowned. "But let's be careful, eh?"

29

Nico

A man pulled Nico into the bushes and pressed a gun against his side. "Morning, Nico," said a terse voice at his left ear. "We're going to go for a little walk, and you're going to be nice and quiet and not get hurt, alright?" The paralysis left him, and he sagged in the man's grip. He nodded.

The man took his hand off Nico's mouth and draped a heavy arm over his shoulder, like they were old pals. The gun was well-hidden, but remained pressed close. The man led him out of the bushes. There were one or two odd looks from passing students, but most didn't even notice them. Nico glanced sidelong at the man as he propelled him around the building to the very door Nico had been aiming for.

"I know who you are, Victor," he said, evincing a bravado he didn't quite feel. A trigger was far quicker than magic. "You won't get away with this."

"Get away with what? We're simply going to have a little chat. Open the door." He jabbed the gun harder into Nico's side. Nico opened the door, and Victor pushed him in and down a hallway to an office. Inside, he kicked the door shut. "Sit." He pushed Nico into a chair.

Victor walked around the chair to his desk. "Nico Michaelson. Agent for the Magical Division and aspiring assassin of my daughter. What do you have to say for yourself?" He tossed the gun and sat.

Nico watched the gun skitter across the desk. His mouth dropped open. "A *squirt gun?*"

Victor smiled. "And I didn't even have to use it to wet your pants. It's actually quite useful for nailing flies, pesky things." He picked it up and gave a squirt into the air. Then he tossed it back on the desk and leaned forward, his eyes hard and dark. "I am not a violent man, Nico, but if you harm a hair on my daughter's head, you will live to regret it."

Nico raised his hands. "I have no intention of harming your daughter. I—"

"Don't lie to me. I know you have orders to kill her, and I'm familiar enough with the sort of wizard who works for the Magical Division to know they have no compunction about killing."

Nico pressed his lips together. He couldn't hold Victor's gaze. The man was right. The Division picked its staff carefully, and the result was a special sort of unsavory. He dropped his eyes to his hands. "I've been trailing your daughter for a while now. I know ..." *I know she's kind and loves books and ...* "She's not a threat to anyone."

"Yet you're still following her." It wasn't a question, but it demanded an answer.

Nico took a deep breath. "I tried to tell the Division she wasn't a threat. They felt I was *compromised.*" Victor's eyebrows rose, and Nico sweated under his scrutiny. "Tory saw me ... more than once, and ... we had dinner together."

There was a moment of silence, and then Victor laughed. "You had *dinner* with her?"

Nico grimaced. "I didn't mean to. It's that friend of hers, Jess. And the cat. The point is—" He rubbed his chin. "I *am* compromised." He looked Victor in the eye. "I'm not going to hurt your daughter." Then he dropped his gaze and fiddled with the hem of his jacket. "The Division has sent a sharpshooter—a couple, I think—to kill her, because I've refused to do it."

Victor stood. "What?"

"I've been following her to keep her safe." He threw up his hands and let his exasperation show. "I was supposed to escort her to a crowded museum today while I tried to convince the Division to back off, but she slipped out from under my nose to come here." For some reason this made Victor chuckle. Then he got serious again. "Nico, where are these sharpshooters?"

"As of this morning, they were stationed outside your office in Boston and her apartment. I assume, since you were waiting for me, that she's here?"

"She was."

"Where is she now?"

Victor frowned. "I don't know. I sent her away, knowing she shouldn't be seen with me. I ... surely she wouldn't go home?"

Nico sprang up. "When did she leave? Do you know where she was staying?"

Victor rubbed his face. "No, I ... I was so overwhelmed by seeing her, I didn't think to—"

"Never mind. I'll go to her apartment." She would have gone home, despite how stupid that would be. She would have wanted her familiar comforts.

"I'm going to get her out of the country. I have contacts," Victor said.

"That won't stop the Division, even if she would agree to go, which she won't." Nico began to pace.

"How would you know?"

"I've been watching her for weeks. You've never met her. She's a creature of habit. I knew the minute she learned her job was being cut, because her daily schedule changed by ten minutes. She's not going to pick up her entire life and flee overseas, even to save it."

Victor looked drained and old. You could disguise

most of time's ravages, but the eyes gave it away, and Victor's eyes didn't look a day under ninety right now. He wasn't a wizard hell-bent on breaking the Division apart; he was simply an old man protecting his daughter. Nico swallowed and put a hand on Victor's shoulder. "I'll keep her safe. I'll convince the FBI to leave her alone." He met Victor's eyes, and the old man nodded.

"Thank you." Then he shrugged apologetically. "I told her not to trust you."

Nico smiled and shook his head. "I don't think she does. I'm hoping I can change that."

"You know she can't love you, don't you?"

Nico stopped breathing for a moment. Had he just implied ...? He shook his head. "That doesn't really concern me. I'm just trying to make sure she's not murdered."

Victor raised an eyebrow. "Uh-huh."

"Look, I know the Division has done some awful stuff. Illegal stuff." Nico's shoulders slumped. "I've done horrible things. I just want to try to set something right for a change. Do what's right, not what suits the Magical Division."

"That's all, huh?" Victor's mouth twitched up at the corners.

"That's *all.*"

Victor gazed at him for another minute, and Nico struggled to meet his eye. Finally, Victor laughed. "Well, at least I don't have to worry about you breaking her heart." He slapped Nico on the back and led him to the door. "Go swiftly and good luck."

30

~~~

Tory

Jess insisted on driving the last leg of the journey. "You're going to keep your head down and put that hood up," she said, referring to the ugly gray sweatshirt she'd picked up along the way, in an attempt to make Tory less obvious. She frowned. "I wish we weren't arriving in your car." Then she shrugged. "Nothing for it, I suppose."

"See? I told you you should have replaced your car after Daniel wrecked it."

Jess shrugged. "Yeah, but the men after Daniel all had such nice cars. Why buy when I could borrow?"

Tory rolled her eyes.

They turned onto her street, and Tory's heart started pounding. She gathered Puck into her arms, squeezing him close for comfort. Jess pulled around to the back of her apartment building, and Tory resisted the urge to peer out the window, looking for snipers. Surely they wouldn't be at Jess's place? She checked the edges of the hood with her fingers and pushed a stray lock out of sight.

"Stay here for a minute." Jess got out and scanned the parking lot and the building. "Let me go in. I'll wave you over once I'm sure the coast is clear."

Tory watched Jess mount the steps and enter the building. She stroked Puck's fur and told him everything was going to be fine, fully knowing the cat wasn't in the least upset. Her hands shook, and she clasped them together around Puck. What was taking Jess so long?

Finally, Jess came to the door and waved her in. Tory shot out of the car and made for the apartment with her head down and Puck tucked inside the sweatshirt.

Inside, Jess slammed and bolted the door and pulled the curtains shut. Tory let Puck down and leaned against the wall.

"Here, sit down." Jess swept a pair of jeans and a bra off an armchair. "You look like you're going to collapse."

Tory sank into the chair, her shaking knees giving out so she landed with a thud and a puff of dust. She sneezed.

Jess went to the kitchen, and Tory heard cabinets open and close. "Coffee?" Jess called.

"Please." Tory's shaking was slowly subsiding, and she cast her eyes around the room. It looked like Jess's dresser had exploded. The clothes Jess had removed from the armchair now lay in a heap with a couple pairs of underwear and a wrinkled shirt on the sofa. A pair of socks was draped over a lampshade. A red silk bathrobe lounged on the television. A pair of high-heeled boots leaned drunkenly against one another on the coffee table next to a purple sheath dress. On top of the dress sat a bowl containing what might have once been curry, but was now a lumpy mass of fuzzy gray mold.

Tory sighed and rubbed her face. Maybe the hotel room would have been better.

Puck leapt to the coffee table, sniffed at the expired curry and recoiled.

Jess came in with two steaming mugs. She smiled. "This is better!" She handed Tory a mug and settled into the couch, ignoring the laundry piled on it. "I've been considering it, and I think you should first take a little time to just relax. Then we can talk about what you should do.

Stay here as long as you want. I can make up a bed for you on the couch." She shoved the pile of clothing aside.

Tory hid her grimace. There would be no relaxing for her until this room was clean and tidy, that was for sure. "At some point, I'm going to need to go to my apartment and get clothes, my birth certificate—"

Jess held up a hand. "Only if leaving the country is what you decide to do. And *you* are not going to your apartment. I'll go there and get whatever you need."

"Jess," Tory began to protest, but Jess cut her off with a raised hand.

"It's not negotiable. It's too dangerous for you to go home."

"And it's not dangerous for you to go there?"

"It's not me they're after."

Tory wasn't convinced Jess would be safe, but she didn't argue. She took a sip of her coffee and cringed. Was that lipstick on the rim of the mug? She squeezed her eyes shut. Jess was great, but her housekeeping was atrocious.

"I'll have to go out and get some groceries—there's nothing in the house." Jess stood and rummaged through her purse. "I'll just pop around the corner right now and get us some lunch. I'm starving." Jess took a swig of coffee and slung her purse over her shoulder. Leaving the half-empty cup on the table, she headed toward the door. "You want your usual?"

The little sandwich place around the corner from Jess's made an amazing BLT that came with pickle spears and coleslaw. Tory's stomach rumbled at the thought. "Yeah. The BLT." She smiled at Jess. "Thanks."

Jess smiled back. "No problem. You just relax for a bit. I won't be long." She frowned. "Bolt the door behind me."

Tory nodded. Jess went out and Tory slid the bolt home behind her. Then she turned and took in the apartment again. It was truly a wreck. She started picking up Jess's clothes. She couldn't tell if they were clean or dirty, but she folded each article and set them all on Jess's bed. As she worked, her mind spun.

Did she really have to leave the country? Maybe she could just leave the state. But no, that wouldn't work. The FBI didn't care about state boundaries. Did the FBI operate overseas too? And what would she do if she fled to, say, Costa Rica? She wasn't even sure she could find Costa Rica on a map. Could she really just pick up and move there? And what if she had to leave Puck behind?

The questions piled up on top of one another, no answers in sight. Her heart raced faster with each question. She picked a leather jacket off the floor and found a pile of crumbled potato chips underneath it. Roaches scattered, and Tory dropped the jacket again.

"I can't stay here!"

Meow? Puck pounced at one of the skittering insects, trapping it beneath a paw, and then bit it with a loud crunch.

Tory whimpered and shut her eyes. She took a deep breath and tried to still her clamoring thoughts, push down the panic that threatened to rise into her throat. Home. The notion bubbled up, urgent, as an answer to all the questions. She needed to be at home. She couldn't possibly make a life-altering decision surrounded by moldy food, cockroaches, and disarray.

"Sorry Jess," she muttered. She found a grocery receipt and scribbled a quick note on the back side, leaving it on the coffee table where Jess would see it. Then she snatched up her car key, hefted Puck into her arms, and let herself out.

—◦◦◦—

Tory's hands started sweating as she pulled up behind her apartment. Maybe this had been a bad idea. Maybe she should have stayed at Jess's place. Maybe she should have accepted Nico's protection while he tried to sort things out with the FBI. She wished she'd called her mom, told her she loved her. It was too late now.

She turned off the car and pulled her hood up. "Well, here goes. You ready?" she asked Puck.

Meow. He stepped onto her lap and rubbed his face against the steering wheel.

Tory considered leaving Puck safely in the car, but she needed the cat's comforting presence; the short walk to the apartment door would take every bit of bravery she could muster.

She peered out the window, searching for any sign of snipers. She saw no one, but that didn't reassure her much—she didn't know anything about being a sniper, but she was sure they wouldn't be lounging around with their rifles in full view.

She huffed out a breath. "Nothing for it but to do it." She lifted her shirt and tucked Puck under it, cradling him in her arms. "Sorry, but if they see you, they'll know it's me." Puck squirmed for a moment, then settled in with a purr.

The rumble of the cat pressed against her body wasn't enough to relax her, but it gave her just enough confidence to open the car door and step out. She focused on the entrance to the apartment and ran.

Tory forgot to breathe as she braced herself for a bullet. What did it feel like to be shot? What if they hit Puck? She cursed her decision to bring him with her. What if—

Something slammed into Tory's side, knocking her sprawling. She hit the pavement with a thud, and Puck dug his claws into her stomach and shot out from under her shirt, leaving stinging tracks in her skin.

When the moment of shock passed, she recognized Nico. She hadn't seen him at all, but suddenly he was there, lying on top of her, pinning her to the ground. She struggled against him, trying to elbow him with her arm stuck between their bodies. He let out a grunt, but only wrapped his arms around her and held tighter.

Don't trust Nico. Her father had been right.

"Let me go!" She kicked him in the shin, but it didn't seem to affect him. She thrashed her whole body.

"Stop! Tory, stop!" Nico's voice was a hoarse whisper. Strained and choked out. "Tory. Your power."

Tory's eyes widened in shock. Her power! Without thinking, she'd been flooding him with it. She snatched it back, for fear of killing him, but then anger surged. "Let go of me!" She pushed her power back at him so it sizzled on his arms and chest. Not enough to kill, she hoped, but enough to hurt and make him release her. She could feel him resisting with his magic. It was like straining against a heavy weight. She found they were both breathing hard.

Nico grimaced, but retained his hold on her. "Tory, please listen. There are three snipers on the roof. I can't deflect three bullets at once." Tory abruptly stopped struggling. "No, keep fighting me. It has to look like you resisted."

"What?"

"Keep struggling, but let me get you back into the car."

"But I want to go home." Tory pushed against Nico, and he winced. Had she pushed with her anti-magic too? She wished she had better control over it.

"You can't. There's someone inside your apartment too. Just trust me."

Don't trust Nico.

She could kill him. All it would take was a stab of anti-magic. "And if I don't?"

"I still won't let them kill you." Before she could react, he deftly rolled her onto her stomach and pulled both hands behind her back. He bound them with something, and then hauled her to her feet. He dragged her to the car, opened the back door and shoved her inside.

31

Nico

Nico slammed the door shut and ran around to the driver's side. He paused for a moment and pressed a hand against his side. It came away red with blood. "Fuck." He knew he hadn't deflected all the bullets. He wasn't sure he had the energy to heal the wound right now.

Meow! Puck came trotting across the pavement toward him, tail up in greeting.

A shot rang out, and the cat collapsed with a howl.

"Puck!" Jess hurtled into the parking lot on a bicycle, screeched to a halt and let the bike fall as she ran to the cat.

Nico tackled them both. "Jess, get the hell out of here!"

Jess struggled. "Where's Tory? Have they shot her?"

"Not yet. She's in the car." He wrenched her arms behind her back, hoping that if he seemed in control the snipers wouldn't take a shot at her.

"Ow! What are you doing with her?" She looked down at the cat again. "Oh, Puck!" Looking back up, she glared at Nico. "This is all your fault!"

"I promise I won't hurt her. You should go."

"Like hell. Where are you taking her?" Jess demanded.

"To the Magical Division."

"What?" Jess's eyes narrowed. "Not happy to let the

lackeys kill her, eh? Want the glory for yourself?" She smiled. "Go on then. Try it."

Nico increased his grip on Jess's arm. "*I* didn't tell you two to come back to Tory's apartment. What the fuck were you thinking?" He hauled her to her feet. "Get in the car, or they'll shoot you too." He pulled her to the vehicle and shoved her in the back.

"But Puck!" Tears sprang into her eyes.

Nico ran back to the cat, lying in a pool of blood, and scooped him up. Shit. The cat didn't deserve this.

He laid the cat in the passenger seat and then ran around to the driver's side. He slipped behind the wheel, glad to see Tory had left the key in the ignition. Then he looked down and swore.

Jess laughed from the back seat. "What? You don't drive stick?"

Tory struggled into a sitting position. "Let us go N—"

The window next to her shattered. Both women screamed and ducked to the floor.

"Jess, you have to come up here and drive. Get us out of here."

Jess folded her arms. "Maybe you should get the hell out of the car and let *us* get out of here."

"I'm the only one who can help you at this point. Don't you understand that?"

"Seems if you wanted to help us, you could stop those guys from shooting at us."

Nico gritted his teeth and bent his thoughts toward the snipers. Two had vanished. He didn't know where to. One was still in position, ready to fire at the sight of Tory. "They'll keep firing at Tory until we get out of here. I can't drive this car. Either you're going to do it, or—" he broke off his words as the sniper fired again. Shit. His vision dimmed as he focused on deflecting the bullet. It pinged off the pavement and clanged against the side of the car. A sweat broke out on his forehead. "I can only deflect so many bullets, Jess."

Jess frowned at him for a moment, and then rolled her eyes. "Get out. I'll drive."

Nico didn't dare get out of the car. He didn't trust Jess not to take off without him, and he wasn't sure he could even stand anymore. His wound throbbed as he shifted awkwardly into the passenger seat, drawing a limp Puck onto his lap.

Jess sucked in a breath. "You've been shot."

"Yeah, I noticed. Don't open the door. Climb between the seats," he warned breathlessly. He shut his eyes.

Jess clambered to the front seat. "Where do I go?" For the first time, she sounded scared.

"Just drive!" He pressed a hand on his wound.

Jess started the car and lurched out of the parking lot. She sped down the street, but Nico didn't pay attention to where she was going. Instead he examined Puck. He had been shot in the hind leg, and he lay limp in Nico's hands, blood still pouring from the wound.

A block or two from her apartment, Tory sat up and saw Puck. "Oh my god! Puck!" She struggled against her restraints, her eyes wild. "Is he badly hurt? Jess, we need to get to a vet right away," Tory sobbed.

Shit. He had so little power left. It was one or the other. Nico shut his eyes against his own pain and wrapped a hand around the cat's leg. He chanted a spell for healing, not knowing whether it would work on cats or not. He felt the magic flowing into the animal, and at the same time felt his blood flowing out of the wound in his side. He opened his eyes. Puck still lay lifeless in his lap. The car lurched to the right, and he winced. Ignoring Tory's sobs and Jess's curses, he poured more power into his spell.

"Nico?" Jess's voice seemed to come from far away.

"Nico?"

He looked up. For an instant, he saw Jess's frowning face in profile as she continued to drive. Then the world went black.

32

※

Tory

Tory's heart pounded and her whole body shook as she struggled against her bonds in the back of the car. She couldn't get a good view of Puck, Jess just kept cursing, and Nico had his eyes closed and was hunched over the cat. Her cat. Her friend. Shot. If only she'd listened to Jess's advice and not gone home! How stupid! It was all her fault and now Puck was going to die.

And she couldn't even hold him while he died. He was going to die in the arms of that ... that ... wizard. What the hell did Nico think he was doing, abducting her like this? Did he really think this was the way to save her life? And what about Puck?

Wait. Nico had been shot too.

Tory tried to pick apart the moment he'd knocked her down. Had there been gunshots? Now she thought about it, yes, she remembered hearing them. They hadn't registered at the time, because she'd been crashing to the ground under Nico's weight. Her surprise and fear at finding herself tackled had overridden her fear of the snipers. Had Nico taken a bullet for her on purpose? Or was it all a ruse to get them to come with him? Her father had warned her not to trust him, and she didn't. One way or another, this was all his fault.

She leaned forward intending to chew out Nico,

but when she saw his gray face and shallow breathing, she paused. Puck lay on his lap, his hind leg matted with blood. But she couldn't see where he'd been shot, and as she watched, he shifted, curling himself into a ball as though nothing was amiss.

"Jess, pull over."

"When we're far away from those snipers." Jess had a determined set to her jaw, and she gripped the wheel so hard her knuckles were white.

Nico didn't respond at all. Not to Tory's order to pull over, and not to Jess when she did finally come to a halt in a small gravel pull-off near the freeway.

Jess jumped out of the car and opened the back door. She helped Tory out. "A zip tie?" She scoffed. "I'll have you out of that in a moment." She rummaged in her purse and brought out a tiny penknife.

Tory grimaced. "Is that thing even sharp?" The zip tie cut into her wrists as Jess sawed at it.

"Well, I only use it for starting orange peels at lunchtime." She continued sawing. "Ha! Got it!" The zip tie sprang off and Tory rubbed the red welts on her wrists.

"Do we go to a vet or a doctor first?" Jess asked.

Tory frowned. "I don't know. Let's have a look at them both."

Jess nodded, and they both went round to the passenger door. Jess opened it, and Puck raised his head with a querying meow. He stood and stretched. He was a little unsteady, but when Jess lifted him so Tory could examine his leg, she found nothing but a pink welt, healed over, in the midst of the blood.

She shook her head. "He seems fine. It's like the wound has healed over already—like it happened weeks ago." Jess deposited Puck into the back seat where he proceeded to clean his fur.

Tory crouched down beside Nico, who hadn't

moved. She pulled her anti-magic tight around herself and gently pulled away his jacket. She sucked in a breath. His shirt was soaked in blood and sticking to his side. She reached out to check his pulse, and then snatched her hand back. "I don't think I should touch him."

"Huh?" Jess frowned.

"My anti-magic. I think it ..." She cast around for the right word. "I think it burns him, even if I pull it in tight." She looked up at Jess.

"Let me in there, then." Jess pressed her fingers against Nico's neck and checked for a pulse. "He's not dead. I suppose we need to try to stop the bleeding and then get him to a hospital."

With no-nonsense efficiency, Jess unbuttoned Nico's shirt.

"I have a first-aid kit in the back." Tory ran to grab it, hoping it was still there. She'd never used it. It had been a gift from her mother. *Because you never know when you might need it.*

By the time she'd found the kit and brought it back, Jess had Nico's shirt open and pushed away from his side. She grimaced at the sight of the long track the bullet had left in his flesh.

"At least it's not too deep. Looks like it just grazed him," Jess said. She took the first-aid kit from Tory. "It's bleeding pretty heavily, though."

She winced as she pressed a gauze pad to his side. "Get me another one. And some tape." Tory jumped to give her what she needed. She covered the gauze pad with an awkward mess of tape. "Too bad we don't have a razor; that's gonna hurt when he pulls that tape off." Jess grinned.

"Serves him right." Tory wasn't sure how she felt about Nico at the moment, but anger was high on the list. She rubbed her wrists.

Jess stood, looking down at Nico. "So why is he

unconscious?"

Tory shrugged. "I don't know. Blood loss?"

Jess shook her head. "The stain looks big, but surely that's not enough blood loss to knock him out."

"Maybe we should get him to the hospital." Tory held out her hand. "Key? I'll drive."

Nico remained unconscious all the way to the hospital. As they turned off the street, Tory said, "I suppose we take him right up to the emergency room door? Will they bring out a stretcher for him?"

"No." Nico's voice was a croak, and it made Tory start. "No hospital. Not needed."

Jess laughed. "You've been out cold for twenty minutes. I think you need a hospital."

"No." Nico shook his head and opened his eyes. "I'm fine."

Tory pulled into a parking space instead of the drive-up emergency room door. "Are you sure? You don't look fine." Her eyes dropped to Nico's side.

His eyes dropped with hers. He twitched his shirt closed and began to button it. "I'm fine. I can heal the wound with magic."

"It was bleeding pretty badly when we bandaged it up. If that's the best you can do, you need a hospital."

Nico shook his head. "I've just overdone it today. Used too much magic. It's like getting dehydrated or something."

"Do you need some water?" Jess asked.

Nico waved a hand. "No. It's not dehydration. I just need to rest, let my magic regenerate."

"You sure you don't need water? You look like hell."

Nico rubbed his face. "Actually, something to eat would be great." Then his head jolted up. "How's Puck? He'll need water—he lost a lot of blood before I could heal him."

"You healed him?" That explained Puck's miraculous recovery. "But if you healed him, why not yourself?"

"A little food and some rest, and I'll be able to deal with my wound." He frowned. "You've gotten out of your bonds."

"You noticed, eh?" Tory pressed her lips together. "Would you like to explain what game you're playing here?"

Nico closed his eyes again. He really did look awful. It made it hard to be angry at him. "I'm keeping you alive. Bringing you to the FBI so you can convince them you're not a threat."

"Why the zip tie, then?"

"Those snipers had orders to kill unless I got to you first. They had to think I was apprehending you, not rescuing you, or they would have kept firing."

Tory raised her eyebrows. "They *did* keep firing."

Nico shrugged. "It was either that or fake your death, but that would have required you being in on the plan. And since you chose to run off to your father and then—like a complete idiot—go to your apartment, I didn't think I could count on your help. Fuck! Did you not think there would be snipers waiting for you?"

Tory's anger deflated. "I had to talk to my dad. I just wanted to go home. Why should I have trusted you?"

Maybe because he saved your life. Twice.

But he was supposed to kill me!

Yes, and he didn't.

"I'm sorry." Tory sighed. "Thank you."

Jess leaned forward. "What now?"

"Now I take you to headquarters and introduce a completely harmless Tory to the Magical Division."

"And what makes you think they won't just kill me when we get there? If it wasn't safe to go home, how would it possibly be safe to waltz into the FBI headquarters?"

"Because you're with me."

Jess wrinkled her nose. "Didn't they decide you were *compromised*? Why will they believe you?"

"Because you'll both arrive in handcuffs."

"What?" Tory and Jess both frowned at Nico. Further outrage was cut off by Nico's phone ringing in his pocket.

He looked tired. "That'll be James. Those snipers will have told him what they saw. Excuse me." He dug into his pocket and pulled out a phone. "Nico here," he said as he pressed it to his ear. "Yep ... Yes, I did ... No, I didn't think it necessary, nor did I consider it legal ... No, that's not my job ... Yes, I understand how this makes you look." There was a long pause in which Nico pulled the phone away from his ear, and Tory heard a man's voice shouting on the other end of the line. He rolled his eyes and then said, "Save your breath, James. I'm bringing her in, and you can judge for yourself." Another long pause. "I promise she won't pull anything funny." He glanced at Jess. "I've got her best friend too."

33

Nico

"And just what makes you think we're going to come along quietly in handcuffs?" Jess poked Nico in the shoulder as she talked.

Why did this have to be so difficult?

"Because we're going to sit down and plan it all out, so that you both get to walk away unharmed, and I get to keep my job."

Jess snorted. "And who, exactly, is going to make us do this?"

He rubbed his face. "Please? Can we talk about it? Preferably over lunch." He was in no shape to fight with these women—his side screamed in pain and his stomach felt like a yawning cavern. Magical overextension did that— burned through calories like an Olympic workout. There was a reason you didn't see overweight witches and wizards. Nico glanced up to see concern on Tory's face. Did he look that bad?

Tory turned on the car and drove them to a nearby diner where both she and Puck were known. They all ordered grilled cheese sandwiches and fries. Puck trotted to a booth where he leapt deftly to the window sill and made himself at home, with no sign of just having been shot. Nico moved stiffly, his jacket zipped to cover his bloody shirt. He winced as he sank into his seat and closed his eyes for a moment, listening to the ice clinking dully in their water glasses.

He opened his eyes, but couldn't meet Tory or Jess's gaze. He swirled the ice in his glass, trying to figure out how to begin, how to explain himself when *he* hardly understood what he was doing. Thinking he would never be able to convince Tory he meant no harm.

He glanced up to find Tory watching him. Her hair was tangled, tumbling over her shoulders. Her eyes were deep brown and troubled. He felt a tightness in his chest, and for a moment he thought she was attacking him with her anti-magic.

But no. That wasn't it.

He took a breath. "Thank you." He responded to Tory's furrowed brow with, "For keeping your power contained. It makes it easier. When you weren't ... when you couldn't control it, it was draining."

Tory shrugged and dropped her gaze to the table. "Thanks for those marble things. They helped."

Nico nodded and took a bite of his sandwich.

"So what's your plan?" Jess popped a French fry into her mouth and eyed Nico.

What the hell was his plan? He swallowed and tried to muster his confidence. "We force the head honchos of the Magical Division to meet with Tory and clear up their misconception of her." He shrugged. "I suppose we could still fake her death if we had to." He frowned. He'd already told James he was bringing Tory in. If he then appeared to kill her, how would that make him look? Like he made a mistake thinking he could bring her in? No. James would be thrilled if Nico killed her. It would be fine.

"If we fake her death, that would mean she'd ... what, take on a new identity? Leave the country?" Jess frowned.

Nico nodded. "She'd have to have a new identity and leave everything and everyone she knows behind. It wouldn't necessarily mean moving overseas, but that would certainly make things easier."

"We are not faking my death." Tory stirred the ice in her glass. "I'm not leaving my home, my friends, my family, just because the FBI has mistaken me for a terrorist." She put her face in her hands. "I can't do that. I've already lost my job, and I've just found my dad—" her voice hitched, "—and I've only just found out I'm a ... some sort of monster."

Jess wrapped an arm around Tory's shoulders. "You are not a monster, Tory."

"Then I'm defective." Tory's voice was muffled by her hands. Nico's chest tightened again. He had done this. He had confirmed what she was for the FBI, and then failed to convince them she was harmless. He tried to open his mouth, to tell her she wasn't defective, but ... well, in a way she was. Defective in a way that he'd begun to think was critical. That cure the book had hinted of—could he make it work for her? Would she want a cure? Would she ... No. He couldn't let his mind wander in that direction.

"There is nothing wrong with you." Jess laughed. "Watching you with those marbles? That was a superpower, not a defect."

A superpower alright—what was she doing to him? If that wasn't her anti-magic he was feeling in his chest, what was it? He shook his head and forced himself to stop staring at her. "I agree with you, Tory, that faking your death isn't a good option. I have plenty of experience creating false identities, but only magically. Any false documents I'd create for you would revert to blank paper the minute you touched them."

"So that leaves meeting with the Magical Division, then?" Jess's eyes narrowed. "Given that they're hell-bent on killing Tory, how do you plan on arranging a meeting?"

"They'll need assurance that she's not going to attack them." He raised his eyebrows. "That's where you come in, Jess. We'll need you to come with us."

Jess took a sip of her drink. "In handcuffs."

Nico nodded.

"As a hostage." Jess's eyes were hard, and her glass hit the table with a thunk.

Tory looked up. "Jess, you don't have to do it." She straightened in her seat. "In fact, Nico can't make either of us do anything." He felt the pressure of her anti-magic in his chest as she made her point.

"I'm not trying to *make* you do anything, Tory. I'm trying to save your life."

The pressure on his chest eased. At least the anti-magic did. His chest still felt tight, and the wound in his side throbbed again. He couldn't look her in the face. He wondered if a Squelcher could read emotions in people's eyes. What would she see in his? He focused on dipping a fry into the ketchup on his plate.

They ate in silence for a minute. Puck rose from the windowsill with a lazy meow and dropped into Nico's lap, purring loudly. Nico was thankful for the excuse to focus on petting the cat.

"I'm game," Jess finally declared.

Nico relaxed fractionally and nodded his thanks to her. His eyes went to Tory and she met his gaze. "What do we need to do?"

———

Tory pulled out onto the freeway, but hadn't been going for more than two minutes when a siren started up behind them.

Nico looked back. A police car, lights flashing, was coming up behind them. "Shit."

Tory pulled over, and the cruiser followed.

"I'm guessing this has to do with that little altercation outside your apartment," Nico said.

"Then you can explain it to him if he asks." Tory

rolled down her window and a young policeman came up.

"Can I see your driver's license?"

Tory handed it over. "Is there a problem, officer?"

The man looked at Tory's license and bent to peer into the car. Jess smiled and waved at him. Nico nodded. "This your car?"

"Yes it is. Do you want the registration?"

He shook his head. "We're following a report of a possible abduction and shooting. Your car was seen leaving the scene." He frowned. "The report was of a man forcing two women into a vehicle and driving off."

Nico leaned over, holding out his badge. "Nico Michaelson, FBI. We were those three people, sir. The incident in question was an FBI training exercise. Your office would have gotten a notification about that?"

The officer's eyebrows rose as he scanned Nico's ID. "Nope. Wasn't told a thing about it."

"Maybe you just missed it?"

The man frowned and spoke into his radio. "Davis to Suarez, do you read me? Over."

Nico didn't catch the scratchy response, but obviously Suarez did read him. He continued. "Hey, did you know anything about an FBI operation today? On Linden Street? Over."

Again, Nico didn't catch everything. "… Why the hell … here? … heard anything. Over."

"S'what I thought. Over and out." He raised an eyebrow at Nico. "Nothing. You want to explain now, or should I take you three in?"

"Let me ring the office." Nico figured he could talk his way out of this, but he got pleasure in forcing James to do it—it was his responsibility, after all, to be in touch with the local authorities. He knew exactly why James had kept his operation secret—the Magical Division worked in a gray area outside of the law. Until very recently, Nico had shrugged it off, but he saw now that it had led to abuses of their power. He was happy to see James take the heat.

James picked up quickly. "Nico, what the hell is going on? Did you kill her?"

Nico didn't answer the questions. "I have a police officer here who would like to speak to you about the training exercise the FBI conducted this morning in Laurel Glen. It seems the local authorities weren't alerted to the operation. I'm sure the information simply got lost, but they're eager to arrest us, unless I can produce that documentation." He passed the phone to the officer.

"Hello?" There was a long silence, and Nico imagined James arguing that the paperwork had been sent, while quickly firing it off to the tech team who would ensure it appeared to have dropped into someone's in-box three days ago. "Thank you. I'll check with him." The officer handed the phone back to Nico. "Give me a minute to verify this." He retreated to his car.

"I take it the paperwork wasn't actually sent?" Tory's voice had an accusatory note that made Nico squirm.

"No."

"Because what you're doing is illegal."

Nico frowned. "What the *Magical Division* is doing is illegal."

Tory looked at him and raised an eyebrow that said, *Last I checked, you worked for the Magical Division.*

Nico dropped his gaze from her silent accusation. "I'm going against orders. What I'm doing now, I'm doing for ... for you."

Jess leaned forward in the back seat. "And what happens if they decide to arrest us because the FBI hasn't done the paperwork for their little illegal operation?"

"James will sort everything out." Of that, Nico was confident.

"Here he comes," Tory warned, looking in the side

mirror. They fell silent.

The officer approached the window. He handed Nico's badge and Tory's license back. "All checks out." He rolled his eyes. "Turns out my supervisor forgot to forward the information to the team. Sorry about the trouble."

"No problem," Nico said.

The officer nodded a farewell to all three of them. Tory nodded back. Jess waved and smiled.

Tory rolled up her window. "Well, it's good to know this was just a training exercise, and not a real assassination attempt."

Jess poked Nico in the shoulder. "And you just covered for them. Whose side are you on, anyway?"

Nico rubbed his face. Whose side was he on? He didn't want to see Tory die, and he was determined to protect her, but he also couldn't imagine losing his job, or worse, over this. The FBI was his life. His co-workers were his family. His job defined who he was as much as his magic did. How could he abandon that for a Squelcher? No. A woman.

"I'm trying to do what is right."

Tory looked dubious. "My dad said the Magical Division thinks it's above the law. He says what you do is illegal and abusive."

Nico nodded. "It is. I didn't realize it until … until they ordered me to kill you."

"So why are you defending them by making up lies?" Jess asked.

How could he possibly explain without coming across as an ass? "Having powerful witches and wizards in the government is critical to national security. All other countries are using them, and anyone who doesn't is at a serious disadvantage. So we can't get rid of the Magical Division. Unfortunately, it attracts witches and wizards eager to throw their weight around." Tory and Jess both raised eyebrows at him. He shifted uncomfortably and dropped his eyes. "Yes, I'm one of them. I like using my power in the pursuit of national security. It feels more important than the other career options open to magic-users—careers where we get to use our magic—the circus or maybe marketing." He shrugged. "I never questioned our methods before. But now that I've questioned once, I see corruption in everything they do."

"Again, why do you defend them?" Tory asked.

"Because I think I can change the Division for the better. I'm powerful. I have influence." And someday he might be in charge, but he wasn't even certain that's what he wanted anymore. "But I can't change anything if I'm fired. It has to be done from the inside. And so I have to look like I'm working for the Division."

Tory started up the car and pulled back onto the highway. "So you get to keep your job, and I get to keep my life?"

Nico nodded. "And hopefully I can change the way the Magical Division works."

34

⚬⚬⚬

Tory

As Tory drove them toward D.C., they went over their plan again. It was simple enough. For the sake of Nico's credibility, she and Jess agreed to show up handcuffed—it wouldn't do for them to be seen to come willingly. Nico would demonstrate how unwilling Tory was to cause harm with her power, and make the case for her to be an ally, not an enemy.

Tory wrinkled her nose. "I'm not sure I want to be an ally of the Magical Division, after all I've heard."

"They just have to believe you're not going to turn on them. You have to understand, they're terrified of you."

Tory laughed. "Of me?" Then her smile evaporated. "How did I end up like this, anyway? My dad's a wizard—you'd think I'd have *some* magical power."

Nico shrugged. "Some sort of genetic mutation, I suppose. No one really understands Squelchers."

"Great. I'm a mutant." Tory blinked back tears. She was tired, she was scared. This *wasn't* in her life plans. All she wanted was to go back to her normal life. "Why can't I just be normal?"

Nico took a deep breath and blew it out. "There is …" He hesitated and ran his fingers through his hair. "There is the possibility of a cure."

Tory raised her eyebrows. "I read that book. The

only attempt failed. The wizard lost his magic, and the Squelcher wasn't *cured* at all."

Nico raised a finger. "The Squelcher was *partly* cured. She could … experience the full range of human emotions."

"And what wizard would risk his magic for me to be able to be creative, believe in God and fall in love?"

"I would." Nico's whisper was barely loud enough for her to hear.

Tory stopped breathing. She stared at Nico and almost drove off the road. "Are you insane?"

Jess laughed. "He is. He's in *love*."

She whipped her eyes back to the road, but Tory could still see Nico's face turn bright red. "What are you talking about, Jess?"

"You really are oblivious, aren't you?"

"Look, I'm not in love with you, Tory. I just …"

There was glee in Jess's voice. "He just likes you a *lot* and would probably like to go out with you and, you know—"

"Jess!" Now Tory was blushing too. How could she believe this near-stranger was in love with her? "He's been following me because it's his job, not because he's in love."

"If you say so."

Tory gave an exasperated sigh. "Never mind her," she said to Nico. "Sometimes she can be a bit—" she glared at Jess in the rear-view mirror "—annoying."

Jess smiled innocently at Tory. "Me, annoying? Never! You have to admit, he's gone above and beyond the call of duty."

"Jess!"

Nico cleared his throat. "Regardless of my motivations, I'm willing to try, Tory. I've been thinking about it, and I believe there's a way to do it without losing my magic."

"I'm sure that's what that other wizard thought too." Was this about proving his magical prowess? To be the first wizard to 'cure' a Squelcher and survive the process would be quite the bragging point.

A cure.

She wasn't entirely certain how she felt about that idea. Until a few days ago, she didn't even know there was anything different about her. And in spite of her own worries, when he mentioned a cure she balked at the idea that something was wrong with her. Was being a Squelcher a disorder to be cured or was it simply who she was? Had she ever been harmed by it? Not that she knew. Not until the FBI took an interest in her.

Except there was the love thing.

She had to admit, she'd noticed that part of being a Squelcher. She had often thought there was something wrong with her when it came to romance.

But did she want a cure?

It was like asking someone if they wanted a lobotomy. How can you decide to fundamentally change who you are?

What would a creative, romantic Tory look like? Would she start acting like Jess, coloring her hair and falling in love with jerks? She liked Jess, but she didn't think she could stand becoming her.

Jess and her mom had both fallen in love and they'd both been hurt by it. Tory, on the other hand, had gone on plenty of dates and had a great time—no drama, no betrayal.

No excitement either.

An expectant silence had fallen in the car. Nico and Jess were both waiting for her to say something.

"So how, exactly, would this cure work? What would you do?"

Nico cleared his throat. "Well, the book mentioned the need for close physical contact."

Tory remembered the sizzling feeling when Nico had tackled her. It had been unpleasant for her, and it was obviously excruciating for him. "Wouldn't that hurt you?"

Nico nodded. "Probably, but pouring magic into you, which is what I'll need to do, is going to hurt more."

Jess leaned forward. "When you say 'close physical contact', what do you mean? Are you talking holding hands?"

Nico blushed again. "Not exactly. Holding hands wouldn't be enough contact."

Tory raised her eyebrows. "Hm?"

Nico squirmed in his seat. "There are almost no records of Users purposely transferring magic to someone else, so I can't guarantee it would work, but ..."

"But what?" Tory didn't think she wanted to hear, but she had to ask.

"Sometimes, when a witch and wizard have ... been together ... their magic ... mingles. Afterwards you can feel how their magic has changed."

"By 'been together' do you mean had sex?" Jess's voice was full of laughter.

Tory didn't think Nico's face could get redder, and her own ears flamed. "You're propositioning me?"

"No, not like that. I—" He let out a huff. "I think it's the only way. The only way to get enough physical contact to transfer the magic effectively and safely."

Jess positively cackled in the back seat. Tory didn't know whether to be more offended that Nico had asked her for sex, or that he'd only offered as a sort of last resort, as a 'treatment'. "So, you think that having sex with you would suddenly make me able to love." Tory scoffed. "You're a bit full of yourself, aren't you? I can't imagine you're that good."

"No, that's not it. You don't understand magic."

"Then explain it to me." Tory didn't try to disguise the irritation in her voice.

Nico rubbed his chin. "Magic is in every cell of

the body—it's produced as part of the metabolic processes within the cell. When you call on your magic, when you try to manipulate it, you concentrate the magic from each cell. It's the concentration of magic that takes energy—metabolic energy, like you use when you go to the gym. Permanently transferring magical power to another person is probably the most difficult thing a witch or wizard could attempt. If I were to try that through the surface of my palm alone, the concentration of that much magical power into such a small space would probably kill me. It would simply take too much energy—it would basically burn away my body. Increase the surface area, and you decrease the metabolic cost of performing the magic."

"And you think it would take *that* much surface area to cure me?" It sounded like a bunch of baloney to Tory. "That's the worst pick-up line ever."

"It's not a pick-up line," Nico said through gritted teeth. "It's just the truth. I'm offering you a cure. That's what it will take. You can decide if you want it or not."

They lapsed into an uncomfortable silence. Even Jess said nothing. Tory's stomach churned. She dug her fingernails into the steering wheel as she bit back more sharp comments about Nico's audacity to proposition her. As though she wasn't actually a person with feelings. Just a monster. A mutant.

She took a long, slow breath. She should be grateful he was willing to try to help her, in spite of the potential cost to himself, that he cared enough to even suggest it. But she wondered if either one of them would actually be willing to go through with it.

It wasn't the sex that put her off. She'd had sex before, and she hadn't known her other partners much better than she knew Nico, if she was honest about it.

No, the sex wasn't the problem.

It was the idea of changing who she was.

It was the idea of losing this power she'd only just discovered.

She was a Squelcher, but she hadn't yet had a chance to find out exactly what that meant.

Who *was* she?

And what, exactly, did Nico hope to get out of 'curing' her?

She gave him a sidelong glance. He sat with his head in his hands, his eyes closed. Was that pain on his face? She remembered he'd taken a bullet for her less than two hours ago, and he'd used his energy to heal her cat instead of himself. Her anger drained away, leaving her fingernails feeling bruised as she eased her grip on the steering wheel.

"Thank you for the offer, Nico." He opened his eyes. "I don't think I'll take you up on it. Not right now, at least. It's not really a decision to be made lightly."

Nico pulled his hands away from his face. He spoke quietly. "No. I suppose it's not. The offer stands. Let me know if you decide you want to try it."

They didn't say much the rest of the way to D.C. Puck moved from his favorite spot on the dashboard to Nico's lap.

Nico's phone rang at some point. He mostly listened; his side of the conversation was composed of a few terse affirmatives. When he hung up he said, "We're expected at headquarters at nine tomorrow morning."

"Cool." Jess pulled out her phone. "Seeing as we're your captives, I assume the FBI will be picking up our tab for hotel and dinner? We should find an expensive place."

Nico laughed, and somehow the ice was broken. Tory rolled her shoulders to shake off the tension.

"Too bad they won't pay for this shirt." Nico pulled the bloodied garment away from his skin and stuck a finger through the hole in the side.

"How is that wound?" Tory glanced briefly at Nico.

"You're looking a bit better."

"Mostly healed. It's taking a while, because I used so much magic following you two this morning. Lunch helped."

Was it only this morning they'd left D.C.? "Sorry." Tory shrugged. She didn't regret seeing her father. And where else could she have gone but home?

Nico waved a hand dismissively.

Jess leaned forward. "You must live in D.C. We could take you to your place to get a change of clothes."

Nico fidgeted. "No. That's fine. I'm fine."

Jess raised an eyebrow. "I'm not going to dinner with a guy covered in blood. Nor am I loaning you my toothbrush."

He smiled. "You're right. I guess it would be nice to pick up a few things."

Nico directed them to an opulent house on a street of homes ranging from obscenely big to palatial on the outskirts of D.C. Tory pulled into a sweeping drive and turned the car off.

Peering out the window, Jess whistled. "The FBI must pay well. Maybe we could just stay at your place tonight."

Nico laughed and shook his head. "I didn't buy it— this house has been in the family for four generations. And no, we can't stay here tonight."

"Ah! You live with your parents?" Jess asked.

"No. It's just me." He glanced at the house and frowned. "It's a bit big isn't it?"

"But you said it was in your family for generations."

Nico shrugged. "I'm the only generation left." He opened the door and got out. He went to shut the door, but paused, a worried look on his face. "Please don't run off again. I'll only be a minute."

Tory drummed her fingers on the steering wheel while they waited. She wanted this over. She wanted her normal life back.

"Thinking about bolting?" Jess asked.

Tory dropped her hands. "No." *Yes.* But it wouldn't help. The only way to get her life back would be to convince the FBI to stop hunting her.

Jess patted her shoulder. "It'll be fine. We'll sort everything out tomorrow, and then we can go home. Meanwhile, let's enjoy a night in D.C. on the U.S. government's tab." She tapped at her phone. "I found this place—Japanese food, live music every night."

Tory wrinkled her nose. "I don't know. I've never eaten Japanese food."

"Neither have I. That's why I thought it would be great." Jess tapped again at her phone. "How about this one? French. Très chic!"

"Tiny portions and snooty French waiters," Tory said dismissively. She wanted to go home and have mac and cheese or open a can of tuna and share it with Puck on the couch. She wanted routine and comfort, not fancy meals and new foods.

Jess ran through half a dozen other restaurants before Nico returned in a blood-free shirt. He threw an overnight bag into the back, and then climbed in.

"Thanks for waiting. Sorry it took a few minutes. I made us reservations for this evening."

"Where?" Jess asked.

"The Ritz."

35

❀

Nico

They sat at a small candlelit table, and Nico glanced warily at Tory. Jess had been rapturous when he mentioned where they'd be staying and having dinner. Nico told himself he'd chosen it because it was conveniently located, but the truth was, he'd hoped to impress Tory.

She was clearly unimpressed.

Not that she didn't seem to enjoy the meal or appreciate the large apartment suite they were staying in. But she left most of the talking to Jess.

"Oh my god! This is the best abduction ever," Jess said before stuffing a forkful of salad into her mouth. "I should get kidnapped by the FBI more often."

Nico laughed. "I hate to tell you, but this isn't generally the treatment people get from us when we apprehend them."

Jess smiled. "Yeah. I bet your targets don't usually drive themselves back to headquarters either, do they?" She took a sip of wine. "This is excellent." She turned to Tory. "Better than that fancy bottle I stole from Michael. You sure you don't want another glass?" She raised the near-empty bottle.

"No thanks." Tory shook her head, and Jess shrugged, pouring the remainder of the bottle into her own glass.

Tory raised her eyes to Nico and gave him a little shrug, as if to say, *Sorry about her.*

She wasn't having fun. That bothered him even more than Jess's lewd giddiness.

Jess sighed and leaned back in her chair. "That was lovely. Shall we have dessert? I'll see if we can get a dessert menu." She looked around for the waiter.

"I'm stuffed," Tory said, rising. "I think I'll just go back to the room."

Nico would have ordered dessert, but he rose along with Tory. "Me too."

"Party poopers! It's only nine o'clock! I thought we'd move to the bar." Jess rose, wobbling a little.

Tory steadied her. "I think it's time we left. Big day tomorrow."

"Big day playing hostage to this bad boy! Oh, now there's a fun game!" Jess squeezed Nico's arm, and he cleared his throat and glanced around to make sure no one was watching.

Tory rolled her eyes, and gave Nico another apologetic look. "Come on. Back to the room." She took Jess's arm and pulled her off Nico.

Jess shrugged out of Tory's grip. "You go. I'm going to enjoy my night." She started toward the bar.

Nico frowned. "Should we let her do that?"

"Don't let her fool you. She makes a big show of being tipsy, but I've never seen her really drunk. My guess is she'll switch to lime and soda for the rest of the night. Besides, she's got a mean right hook and isn't shy about using it." She looked at him. "But it's up to you—we're supposedly in your custody."

"You're the important one." *In more ways than one.*

Tory waved a hand. "Let her go then. She'll be fine."

Tory led the way to the elevator. They stood against opposite walls, silent as the elevator lurched upward. Nico wasn't sure if that swooping feeling in his stomach was the elevator or his nerves. He tried not to meet Tory's eyes. He wished he knew what she was thinking. He wished he hadn't said anything about the possible cure.

The elevator dinged when it reached their floor. Nico ducked out first, happy to not have to look at Tory. He reached their suite and held the door open for her.

"Thanks." She smiled at him as she went in. Puck leapt down from the back of the couch and padded over to them, tail up, to twine around Tory's legs. She picked him up and he clambered to his favorite spot on her shoulder.

The main room of the suite included a lounge area with overstuffed leather armchairs and a couch facing a large-screen television. A small round table on the other side of the room flanked a kitchenette. Tory made for the kitchenette and turned on the electric kettle.

"Cup of tea?" she asked, turning back to Nico.

He was halfway to his room. He stopped and turned. "Um ... I'm more of a coffee guy."

"Oh. There's a French press here. And coffee. I could make a pot." She smiled. "I prefer coffee myself, but if I drink it this late I'll be up all night." She laughed. "Who am I kidding? I'll be up all night anyway. May as well make coffee. Would you like a cup?"

Nico returned her smile. "Yeah. Thanks."

He sat down on the couch and picked up the remote. Then he put it down again. Tory wouldn't want the TV on. She didn't seem like the television type. Instead, he picked up the *Explore D.C.* magazine on the coffee table and flicked through it, not really seeing anything. Puck dropped with a thump from Tory's shoulder and joined Nico on the couch. He wormed his way onto Nico's lap, shoving the magazine aside and demanding to be petted. Nico obliged absentmindedly.

Why had Tory asked him to have coffee? Did she

want to talk to him about the cure? Would she want to try it tonight? The thought brought on a cold sweat. He'd been dangerously low on magic this afternoon. He didn't think he could muster the power to try. And even if he could manage magically, the idea of having sex with Tory in a sort of clinical way made him sick. Not for fear he'd end up losing his magical abilities or die in the process, but because ... Well, if he was going to have sex with Tory, he wanted it to *mean* something.

Nico shook his head. She was a *Squelcher*, for God's sake! Squelchers and wizards didn't have *relationships*. It simply wasn't possible.

"How do you take your coffee?" Tory's voice pulled him out of his thoughts. He hoped they didn't show on his face as he turned to her.

"Just black."

Tory brought over two steaming mugs and set them on the coffee table. She sat down beside him on the couch, curling her legs under her and drawing Puck away from Nico's lap. Without thinking, he cringed away from her. Tory sucked in a breath and her eyes widened. "I'm sorry. Am I too close? Is my anti-magic hurting you?"

Nico relaxed his shoulders. "No. No. It's fine."

"I still sometimes don't notice how wide it spreads. I actually have to think about keeping it furled close."

"You've been doing a good job of it. I haven't felt it all day. Well, not since we got in the car." He ran a hand through his hair nervously, thinking about how he'd tackled her, and the sizzling pain that seared every point of contact. Pain he'd almost enjoyed. "Thanks for the coffee." He picked up his cup and took a sip to try to hide his embarrassment.

36

Tory

Tory should have gone to bed, but instead she made coffee. Her brain was racing. She was terrified for tomorrow, homesick, and not even sure anymore who or what she was. She knew she wouldn't sleep and, well, Nico was a curiosity. A wizard, like her dad, but young and …

"Are you really as young as you look?" She thought about her dad's forty-year-old face.

Nico nodded. "I'm thirty-two. No magical assistance needed yet."

Tory laughed and shook her head. "It's so strange to me to think about magic being real. It's crazy. How many wizards and witches are there? And how do you stay hidden? It must be frustrating, not being able to use your power openly."

Nico nodded. "That's why it's nice working for the Magical Division. We're secret, of course, even from other branches of the FBI, but within our offices, we can just be who we are."

"Is it hard to turn it off when you leave work?"

Nico smiled. "If you're discreet, you don't have to completely turn it off."

Tory was intrigued. "Go on."

"Well, you'd be surprised how often I get my favorite table at a restaurant. And oddly enough, there's never a line at the grocery store checkout when I arrive." His smile was impish.

"You don't! Do you kick people out? That's so rude!" Rude, but sort of funny too, she thought.

"I don't really kick them out, but I can nudge people into a different line, or make someone wish they had a table by the toilets instead of the prime spot by the window." He shrugged. "I suppose it is rude."

"So the next time I find myself in the longest checkout line, I'll know it's a wizard's fault."

"Oh, no. It wouldn't work on you."

"Really?"

"Nope. You are impervious to magical manipulation. No suggestion, illusion, or spell of any type would work on you."

"Hm."

"Have you ever seen a magic show?"

Tory nodded. "Once. This guy came to my school. He was lousy, though. The 'live rabbit' he pulled out of his hat was an old sock, he couldn't get that interlocking ring trick to even work, and when he tried to saw the lady in half, he *actually cut her*. They had to bring in the ambulance and everything." She saw Nico nodding, and her eyes went wide. "Did *I* do that?"

"Obviously, he was using real magic to create his tricks. Your anti-magic cancelled it out."

Tory slapped a hand to her mouth, horrified. "I hurt that poor woman!"

Nico shook his head. "It wasn't your fault. All those tricks can be done legitimately, without magic. Your magician was a second-rate wizard who found an easy way to make a dime. It was his fault for not learning the tricks properly."

"But if I hadn't been there—"

Nico waved away her words. "It's not your fault. You didn't even know you were a Squelcher."

Tory's shoulders slumped. "Jess called this a superpower, but I think it's a supercurse."

Nico set down his cup and looked at Tory. "When I was eight, I accidentally lit my dog on fire. I didn't have control of my power, and he'd peed on my bed. I was angry, and without even knowing what I was doing, I set him alight." He pressed his lips together and swallowed hard.

"Your dog died?"

Nico nodded.

"I'm so sorry."

Nico shrugged. "I'm just saying I know how you feel. And it isn't your fault." He smiled weakly. "Of course, that's what my parents told me too, but it didn't help much at the time."

"So your parents were ... magic-users too?"

Nico nodded. "My dad worked for the FBI. Mom was a surgeon."

Tory laughed. "A magical surgeon?"

"She was one of the best, apparently. She worked at Georgetown University Hospital."

"Oh! She didn't just operate on witches and wizards?"

Nico laughed. "Users rarely need surgery."

Tory remembered Nico's bullet wound. "Oh. I suppose not."

Nico took a sip of his coffee. Tory hesitated to ask any more questions—his mother was dead, and she didn't want to pry into what might be a sensitive topic.

He talked anyway. "Mom believed witches and wizards should use their power for the greater good. She lived for her work." He stared into his coffee. "She died for it too."

"Oh." Tory didn't know what to say.

"She'd gone off to volunteer for Doctors Without Borders—to some military conflict in Africa, I think. I was twelve years old, so I didn't know much about it." He took a sip of his coffee. "Someone blew up her hospital."

"Oh, Nico. I'm so sorry. That must have been hard for you and your father."

Nico's laugh was bitter. "Not for my dad." Tory raised her eyebrows. Again, she was curious, but she hated to pry.

But Nico didn't need encouragement. Had he had too much to drink? The words poured out. "Mom and Dad didn't really get along. Well, it was more like Dad had no use for Mom. Honestly, I don't know why they got married. All I remember is two people who never spoke to one another."

Tory gently nudged Puck off her lap; Nico looked like he needed a cat. Puck obliged, sprawling between them on the couch. Nico reached out to scratch his head.

"I really don't know how Mom felt about Dad, but after she was gone, he made no secret of his contempt for her work. As far as he was concerned, she had wasted her time and talent on Insigs when she should have been working to liberate Users from Insig oppression." He glanced up at her, and Tory raised her eyebrows. "Yeah, Dad was a bit of a magical supremacist."

"And he worked for the FBI?" Tory frowned, thinking back to her conversation with her father. She sucked in a breath. "He was Director of the Magical Division— Theo Michaelson." She gripped her coffee cup so hard her knuckles whitened. Nico was the son of the man her father said encouraged torture and murder, who wanted to wipe out Insigs.

And he was sitting next to her on the couch.

Nico didn't seem to notice her fear. He stared into his coffee. "Yeah. Dad was like God. I believed every word he said. He wanted me to be like him. Follow in his footsteps. Even after he died, I kept measuring myself by his yardstick." He looked up at Tory, a smile on his lips. "He'd roll over in his grave if he knew I was sitting here telling you all this."

"What? Instead of killing me?" Tory played with Puck's tail, concentrating on keeping her power furled. It wanted to leap out and stab Nico.

Nico nodded.

She let her anti-magic concentrate into a point, aimed at Nico's chest. "So, what made you change?"

"You." He shrugged.

Tory froze. "You mean …"

"When I started trailing you, I was annoyed they'd put me on this job. It was beneath me—I was the darling of the FBI, the most powerful wizard ever to work for the Magical Division. I was headed straight for the top, and then the world would hear me roar. I'd have real power then." Nico had a fierce look in his eye, and Tory honed the tip of her power. She could almost see it quivering like her nerves, inches from Nico's chest.

Then he deflated and smiled. "You were the most boring target I'd ever had to follow. The same routine every day—the same coffee at the same café, the same walk in the park with Puck."

Tory felt her face flush. "I have a good life, I enjoy my daily coffee and my daily walk with Puck," she said defensively.

Nico raised a hand. "I'm not saying it isn't good for you. I'm just saying it was boring from a spectator's perspective."

Was it boring from a participant's perspective too? Tory frowned at the idea. She loved her routine. Of course it wasn't boring.

Nico continued. "I could see how much your ordered life meant to you when the library closed. I saw you cared about the library patrons and that they cared about you." He barked a laugh. "You don't get that as an FBI agent. Moving around all the time, a different assignment every couple of weeks, never really interacting with the same people from day to day." He shrugged. "There's not really anyone who cares about me. Not the way they do about you." He frowned. "I'd never really thought about someone's value before in anything other than magical terms. More magical power equaled higher value—that's what my dad had taught me. Then the library closed, and all those library patrons came to say goodbye to you because you had taken the time to care about them. And I thought maybe Mom had it right—Insigs are every bit as valuable as Users. Maybe more. And you ... you don't even have the magic of an Insig, and yet ..." He smiled ruefully. "Well, it's clear you're a greater asset to the world than I am."

Tory withdrew her spear of anti-magic and loosened her death-grip on her coffee cup. She sipped thoughtfully. She supposed that she should be flattered that she'd changed Nico's mind about Insigs. Then again, the idea that he'd previously believed Insigs to be inferior made her uncomfortable.

"Is this—prejudice—against Insigs common among the magical community?"

Nico shrugged. "That's the terrible thing. I don't even know. It's rife within the Magical Division of the FBI, for sure, but ..." He trailed off and shook his head. "I wish I'd spent more time talking to Mom when she was alive. Maybe I'd know what to do now."

"What to do now?"

"If we manage to convince the Magical Division you're not a threat, and assuming they buy the ruse that it was my cunning and skill that brought you in—" Tory snorted a laugh, and Nico gave an embarrassed smile and shrug. "Assuming that it all goes well tomorrow—you're freed and I'm shown to be competent and reliable—I'll have an excellent chance at the Assistant Director for International

Operations job I've applied for. That would put me one step below the Assistant Director of the Magical Division."

"Is that Luther Hawkins?"

Nico's eyebrows shot up. "You know Luther?"

"Not personally, but my dad mentioned him. Mentioned that he's the root of the abuses of power he feels the Magical Division commits."

"He's not wrong there. Luther's not going anywhere for a long time, but if I am just one step below him, I'll have more power to influence the agents and others in the Magical Division. Maybe I can change things. Maybe ... Well, maybe I'm overestimating my influence, but it's either that or quit the FBI entirely, and that ..."

Nico took a deep breath, as though fortifying himself against something, and Tory knew without him saying it that he was as much a creature of habit as she was. He didn't know what to do, who to be, if he wasn't in the FBI. "I know how you feel. I'm almost dreading this being over, because then I'll have to start searching for a new job, probably a new home ... and I don't even know what I *want* anymore." She forced a smile. "Maybe I should get a job with the FBI. You could become a librarian."

Nico chuckled.

"Oh, speaking of books, how did you become interested in George Eliot's work?" Tory thought the heavy conversation had gone a bit too far. Books, however, were always fun to talk about.

"It's unusual, isn't it?" Nico laughed. "I have my uncle to blame for my love of classic literature, and not just George Eliot's work."

They talked books for almost two hours, comparing notes about their favorites, arguing about who was the best Victorian-era author, and discussing how social and political factors shaped each author's work. Eventually, they switched from coffee to wine. They both settled comfortably into the couch, Tory curled like a cat, Nico with his feet up on the coffee table. Puck sprawled between them, demanding both their attention.

When Jess finally returned long after midnight, they were laughing at a story Tory had told about a little old lady who, after accidentally checking out *Fifty Shades of Grey*, had returned to ask for more books like it, saying she and her husband had read it to each other, and it was 'better than the little blue pills.'

"You two are cozy here." Jess's eyes twinkled. "No, don't let me disturb you," she added as Tory and Nico both rose, exclaiming about the lateness of the hour.

"It *is* late," said Tory.

"And tomorrow won't necessarily be easy," Nico warned. "I'm off to bed."

They said their goodnights, and as Tory undressed for bed, she smiled to herself. She still wasn't entirely sure she trusted Nico, but she liked him. He was easy to talk to and he loved books. She wondered if he'd be able to change the Magical Division. Then she wondered if he'd have a chance to. She hoped tomorrow would go smoothly, but something told her it was going to be more difficult than either of them imagined.

37

❦

Nico

The suite was silent when Nico opened his eyes. For a moment, he worried that Tory and Jess had vanished again. *Damn*, he thought. He'd meant to set a trap on the outer door overnight—he thought he'd magically suspend a few water glasses from the ceiling over the door. If Tory got close to them, her anti-magic would break the spell and cause the glasses to fall noisily to the floor.

But after spending half the night in cozy conversation with her, he'd forgotten all about setting a trap. And the silence in the room worried him. He jumped out of bed and dressed quickly, envisioning another mad chase as he tried to track Tory down again.

He burst out of the room and sighed in relief. Tory and Jess sat at the little table, both staring silently at their phones, steaming coffee mugs in front of them. Tory looked up. "Morning. There's coffee." Nico stepped into the kitchenette and poured himself a cup.

Tory frowned and waved her phone. "I've been trying to learn more about the FBI online. I feel pretty unprepared to make a case for being harmless. I thought if I knew more about the organization, it might help me."

"I'm sorry." Nico ran a hand through his sleep-tossed hair. "I meant to discuss that last night." He took a sip of coffee. "I expect what they'll want is some sort of written statement saying you won't target them with an anti-magical attack or use your power to assist a foreign government or criminal organization, blah, blah, blah. James probably has a document written up and ready for you to sign in triplicate."

Jess looked up. "Then why do you want me there? And why do we have to go handcuffed?"

To make me look good.

"Nico wants to change the Magical Division from the inside. He thinks he might be able to negate Luther Hawkins' influence. But he can't do that if they think he's 'compromised' by me, which is why it needs to look like we're coming unwillingly. Your job is to keep me calm and remind me not to use my anti-magic."

Nico could have kissed Tory for her flattering explanation. Even without it, he could have kissed her. Except he couldn't. Wouldn't. He checked the time. "We should get breakfast and get moving."

They checked out of the hotel and headed to breakfast at a café near headquarters where they could grab a quick muffin. If all went well this morning, Tory would be on her way home, and Nico would be able to call this case closed.

He wouldn't have to trail her anymore.

He'd have no excuse to ever see her again.

"Are you okay?" Jess's brow was wrinkled, and she peered at him over her chocolate croissant.

Nico wrenched his frown into a smile. "Fine. Just thinking."

"About?"

"Worrying about this morning, I guess."

"But you said it should just be a matter of paperwork, right?" Now it was Tory's turn to frown.

Nico nodded reassuringly. "It is, I'm sure. It'll all go smoothly." He refused to consider the alternative. They knew he was showing up with her this morning. They knew he had Jess in tow to ensure Tory behaved. It would go fine. He took a deep breath and drained his coffee cup.

"Ready?" He noticed Tory had barely eaten half her muffin. He didn't blame her. This *should* work out fine, but he had a bad feeling about it, and he didn't know why. His phone buzzed in his pocket, and he jumped nervously.

It was a text from James.

Bring the Squelcher to Conference Room C. Hawkins, Clairmont and Payton will be there along with me. Still have the friend as security?

Nico winced at how impersonal and cold the message was. He typed his response.

Yes. I'm bringing her friend, Jess, and her cat with us. Tory won't harm anyone. Be there soon.

James' response was quick. *We're ready.*

Nico took a deep breath. "They're ready for us. Shall we go?"

The women nodded.

There was the embarrassing issue of driving. They were still traveling in Tory's car, and Nico had to let one of them drive. They parked across the street from the building, and Nico snapped handcuffs on both women, apologizing as he did so and trying not to wrench the cuffs too tight.

"What about Puck?" Tory asked.

"He's coming with us." Nico clipped the cat's leash onto his collar and lifted him out of the car. Tory smiled gratefully at him. He knew the cat would comfort her. It was bad enough to bring her in handcuffed—as if that did any good anyway, since it did nothing to contain her power—but he knew there would be some intense interrogation, and she'd need all the support she could get.

Nico looped Puck's leash over his wrist and took Tory and Jess by the arms to lead them across the street.

"Tell me, Nico, is this how you treat all your women?" Jess asked playfully. "Maybe we could do this again on Friday night at your place."

Nico raised his eyebrows. Tory rolled her eyes. "Jess!" But they all smiled. She *did* know how to lighten the mood. The smiles didn't last long, though. They were all nervous.

Just before they ducked into the shadow of the building, Nico saw movement on the roof out of the corner of his eye. He looked up, but saw nothing. Must have been a pigeon or something. He'd been so keyed up to spot snipers, he was seeing them everywhere.

Besides, this was headquarters. There were armed guards everywhere. Three met them now as they neared the door—Insigs, he noted. Nico flashed his badge, and the guards nodded. The shortest took Tory's arm. "We've got orders to bring you to Conference Room C." Another took Jess's arm, and the third grabbed Nico.

He tried to wrench his arm away from the guard's grip. "I know where Conference Room C is."

"I'm sure you do," said the guard, tightening his grip. "But we have orders to escort you there."

Shit. His heart beat faster. This wasn't starting out well. He shared a worried look with Tory and Jess before they were hauled into the building.

They took the elevator to the third floor and stepped out into a nondescript corridor lined with offices. Toward the end of the corridor, they stopped outside a door marked Conference C. One of the guards knocked.

Luther Hawkins opened the door—tall, clean-shaven and impeccably dressed in a dark blue suit. The last time Nico had seen Luther, he thought him a role model—he was a family friend, after all, and held the job Nico eventually hoped to take. Now Nico was ashamed he'd ever looked up to Luther, and he struggled not to let his distaste show.

Luther flashed a smile that went no further than his

lips. "Ah. Our visitors."

Puck hissed and puffed up his tail. Luther looked down with an amused smile. "Interesting. It has a familiar."

The use of *it* to refer to Tory wasn't lost on Nico. He only hoped she hadn't noticed. A quick glance at her lips pressed into a tight line told him she had.

Luther addressed the guards. "Take the companion and the familiar away. Guard them. If I signal, or if *anything* strange happens, kill them both." Jess's eyes went wide.

"Wait!" Tory struggled against the guard. "You can't do that. Jess and Puck stay with me."

Luther raised his eyebrows at Tory. "You are not in a position to demand anything. Rest assured that if you behave, your friends will be released unharmed."

A despairing look passed between Tory and Jess. A guard took Puck's leash from Nico, and the three led Jess and the cat away.

"Please, come in." Luther stepped back from the door and waved them inside.

38

Tory

A heavy weight settled in the pit of Tory's stomach, seeing the guards lead Jess and Puck down the corridor. What had she gotten them into? Would she ever see them again? She looked to Nico. Wouldn't he protest? His mouth was shut, but his eyes shot daggers at the guards. He met her eyes and gave a slight shake of his head. *Don't do anything.*

Tory swallowed, took a deep breath, and stepped into the room.

"Please, sit." It wasn't a request, it was a demand. Tory and Nico perched on hard wooden chairs. The tall man who had opened the door circled around to the opposite side of a long table where three others sat.

"Welcome to the Magical Division of the FBI." The man's tone was everything except welcoming. "I am the Assistant Director, Luther Hawkins." He gestured as he introduced the others. "This is Arlen Clairmont." A corpulent little man with two chins and a handlebar moustache. "Vanessa Payton." A petite, sharp-faced woman with eyes like laser beams. "And James Bateson." Looking like he stepped straight out of a *GQ* magazine, with a five-o'clock shadow hazing an angular jaw.

Tory forced her face to a bland expression and furled her anti-magic tightly around herself.

"Thank you for joining us this morning," Luther

continued as he settled into the empty chair beside Arlen Clairmont.

Tory raised her eyebrows. "It's not like I had a choice, is it?" Of course, she had been given a choice, and this had seemed like a good idea yesterday. Now she wasn't so sure. Handcuffed and sitting before this group of Users who oozed malice, her pulse quickened and her palms grew sweaty. She felt like a mouse that had accidentally taken shelter in a fox den. She kept having to remind herself of her own power, but since she had hardly ever used it except by mistake, she wasn't at all confident it would do her any good. She set her jaw, clenched her fists, and refused to let her fear show. "What do you want from me?"

Luther shook his head and tsked. "Not even any small talk? I suppose manners can't be expected from one of you."

He was baiting her. She knew that. But anger was easier to handle than fear. Anger gave her strength. She let it build inside, but kept her face bland, trying to match Luther's nonchalance. "I have more important things to do than sit around and soothe your fears that I'll overthrow the government."

That's right. She was here because they were afraid of her. She couldn't forget that. If they were afraid of her, maybe she didn't need to be afraid of them. Maybe? Her fingernails dug into her palms, and she wished Puck and Jess were with her.

"Right, then. We'll get down to business, so we don't waste any more of your time." He shuffled a few papers in front of him on the table. "Can you start by describing the nature of your power?"

"My power?"

Arlen leaned his elbows heavily on the table. "Come now, Miss Williams. We know you are a Squelcher. Young Nico has confirmed it."

Tory felt a burning on her skin. Someone was probing her with magic. She scanned the wizards in front of her. Ah. It was the witch doing it—Vanessa—poking at her to see what she was made of. For a moment, she thought of poking right back—a nice little needle of anti-magic in the witch's left eye. Then she remembered Jess and Puck, and her reason for being here. She needed to appear harmless. She needed to prove she wasn't a threat.

She pulled her anti-magic tighter around her and glared at the witch. The magical finger-poking stopped.

"You said it. I'm a Squelcher. What more do you need to know? Surely if Nico has told you that, he's been able to describe the nature of my power." She laughed without humor. "He's known what I am longer than I have."

Vanessa narrowed her eyes. "Nico doesn't seem to be willing to discuss the nature of your power with us."

Nico held up a hand. "I've told you everything I know. She has broken simple spells from a distance of about ten feet and doesn't appear to have much control over her power." He shot Tory a quick glance that begged her not to contradict his lie.

James spoke up. "You forget that she killed Arthur Grayson."

Tory sat up straighter. "I haven't killed anyone." She glanced at Nico, and his look made her suck in her breath. "Nico, have I killed someone?"

Nico shut his eyes and grimaced.

Vanessa leaned forward. "Oh! She doesn't even know?"

"Know what?" Tory looked wildly between Nico and Vanessa.

James cleared his throat. "On the afternoon of August twenty-third, you entered the Farmer Street Bookstore in Smithville, owned by Mr. Arthur Grayson."

Tory frowned. Yes. She remembered that bookstore.

"But there was no one in the store. It was empty. I even rang the little bell on the counter, and no one came out."

Luther smiled. "Had you looked over the counter, you would have seen Arthur Grayson dead on the floor."

"But I didn't kill him. He must have been dead already when I came in. All I did was walk around and then leave when no one came out to help me."

"Arthur Grayson was a wizard." Vanessa smiled as understanding dawned on Tory's face.

"You mean?" Tears came to her eyes, and she wanted desperately to cover her face. "But I didn't mean to. I didn't know. I ..." She turned to Nico. "You knew this?" He nodded. She almost asked him why he hadn't told her, but then remembered they weren't supposed to have talked, become friends and allies. Were they friends?

She turned her face away, trying to hide her anguish. She'd killed someone, without even knowing it. A yawning pit opened in her stomach and she wanted to crawl away and vanish.

"At least we see you're no killer," Luther said.

Vanessa narrowed her eyes. "Maybe she's just a good actor."

"I am not a killer!" Tears ran down Tory's face, and she lowered her head. She didn't want to show these people any weakness. She felt they were simply waiting to pounce on her.

"Look, will you just get on with it?" Nico sounded exasperated. "You can see she's upset. She didn't mean to kill Arthur Grayson. She didn't even know she was a Squelcher at that point, and she certainly didn't have control of her power."

"But she does know now, and I assume, from the fact she's got her power wrapped tight around her, that she's gained control of it." Vanessa's eyes bored into Tory, as if they could drill in and extract all her secrets.

Tory sniffed and straightened. Vanessa made her want to lash out. She didn't, but her flaring anger gave her strength. "I've learned enough that I'm no longer a danger to people like Arthur Grayson. I can keep my power furled."

Arlen sneered. "Surely you can do more than that?"

Tory remembered the spear of anti-magic she'd thrust into Nico's chest. She resisted glancing at him. "That's all I can do."

She felt Nico's tension relax somewhat. "You see? I've been trying to tell you she's not a threat."

"Perhaps not at the moment," Luther said, his eyes narrow. "But we have to take a long view of the situation. What will it learn to do, in time? Killers are made, not born."

There was that use of *it* again. Tory glared and struggled to keep control of her anti-magic. "I will never use my power to kill someone. You all have power. Do you go around killing people every day?" The instant the words were out, she realized that yes, these people *did* kill others with their power. They had no compunction about that and assumed Tory would be the same.

The thought brought her fear flooding back. These people wouldn't bat an eye at killing her, Jess, or Puck. Her left knee began to shake, and she pressed her foot hard against the floor to try to still it. "What do you want from me? I can't tell you about my power, because I don't know anything about it. Whatever other Squelchers have done in the past, I'm not a killer and I have no intention of becoming one, or of overthrowing the government, or anything else you think me capable of doing."

Luther raised his eyebrows and glanced at Nico. "It seems to know a lot about what we're thinking. You haven't been spilling our secrets have you, Nico?"

A muscle tightened in Nico's jaw. "Tory is a *she*, not an *it*. And I told her only enough to impress upon her the importance of cooperating."

"Well, since *she* can't tell us anything about her power, and *she* seems to know more than is good for her, I'm afraid we'll have to keep her here."

Nico straightened. "You can't do that. She's done nothing wrong."

Luther shook his head. "She killed a wizard, Nico. We'll do what we want with her. There will be others of her kind. This is an opportunity to learn what Squelchers are capable of, what their weaknesses are."

"What do you intend to do? Keep her locked up? Experiment on her?"

Luther smiled.

Nico shot to his feet. "You can't do this. It's against the law."

Vanessa laughed. "And who's going to stop us? You?"

James shook his head. "I told you he was compromised. I didn't think it was this bad."

Arlen leered at Tory. "What did you promise the boy? Sex?" He looked her up and down. It made her skin crawl. "I can see the temptation." He turned to Nico. "I'm curious how you managed to keep it up with antimagic flowing through you. We might have to repeat that experiment with other wizards."

The horror of what Arlen was suggesting stunned Tory into silence. Nico's face went white with anger. "Lay a hand on her, and I'll kill you."

"Oh, defending your piece of ass." Vanessa arched an eyebrow, but her expression didn't last.

"Shut up, Vanessa!" Nico thrashed a hand toward her and sparks flew as Vanessa raised her own hand to block whatever spell it was Nico had thrown.

James stood, tipping his chair to the floor. "Nico! That's enough."

Nico answered by throwing a spell at James.

James' eyes widened in surprise, and he ducked. Something exploded against the wall behind him in a blast of light.

The other wizards surged to their feet. Nico sank into a fighter's crouch, glaring at the others.

"Nico, you don't think you can take on all four of us at once, do you?" Luther's voice was still relaxed, but Tory could see he was ready to spring.

"You think I can't? You've always underestimated me, Luther. James, you too. I'm twice the wizard any of you are."

Arlen chuckled. "But there are *four* of us."

And then they were fighting. Throwing spells back and forth, sparks flying when the spells were blocked, plaster exploding out of the walls when they weren't. It was mayhem, and Tory's first instinct was to dive to the floor out of the line of fire.

She ducked under the table. They all seemed to have forgotten her.

"Give it up, Nico. You can't win against us," Luther said. He threw a spell at Nico which ricocheted off his upraised hand and exploded against the wall.

Nico smiled grimly. "Why don't you give it up? You know I could kill you." He threw a spell back at Luther, but then cried out as a bolt of something from Vanessa struck him in the side and skittered in blue sparks across his chest. He doubled over, and Arlen chuckled as he flung a spell that set the seat of Nico's pants on fire.

Nico swore and doused his pants with a word before hurling a spell at Arlen. The spell bounced off Arlen's arm and right into Vanessa's unsuspecting face. Vanessa yelped and the skin on her face blistered. She snarled and slung something at Nico that he seemed to catch and throw back at her. She ducked, and whatever it was blasted a hole in the wall behind her.

Tory closed her eyes against the bright explosions.

She wondered if she could make it to the door and escape while they fought. She should find Jess and Puck and get out of here. But she was afraid to leave the shelter of the table. Her heart pounded in her chest, and she wished she could block out the sounds.

More grunts, cries and explosions rang out. She peeked out to see Nico set James' shirt on fire while Luther sizzled him with some sort of electric shock that made him cry out in pain. She shut her eyes again, trembling.

Another spell exploded against the wall, and Luther laughed. "Surrender now and we'll let you live, Nico."

Nico laughed. "You wish."

The pace of explosions increased, and with her eyes shut, Tory couldn't tell what was happening. She only knew that she didn't want to be here. She didn't want to watch.

Someone jumped over the table she cowered under, and she opened her eyes. The four wizards had Nico pinned against the wall. He was breathing hard trying to keep up with their barrage. His shirt was blackened and smoking and he held one arm close to his stomach, as though it was injured. Maybe he was twice the wizard the others were, but he wouldn't last much longer. Luther threw a spell at him, and he cried out as a gash opened up on the side of his face. Vanessa cast one immediately after Luther's, and Nico deflected it. It rebounded toward Tory and splintered into sparks inches from her face.

Tory shook herself. What was she thinking? She was a *Squelcher*. She thrust out her anti-magic, throwing up a shield between Nico and the others. Then she wrapped her power around the four wizards and squeezed. They gasped and staggered. Luther clutched at his chest with hands suddenly wrinkled with age. Vanessa's hair turned stark white. Tory scrambled out from under the table and onto her feet.

Nico gasped. "Tory?"

"I'm not going to kill them. Find something to tie them up with."

"They'll just get out magically as soon as you let up your anti-magic."

"Then find some way to incapacitate them," Tory barked.

Nico pressed at the wound on his face and winced. He stepped over to Tory and unlocked her handcuffs. He moved to Luther, gasping on the floor, and cuffed his hands together. "Let him go." Tory eased her anti-magic away from Luther, and Nico cast a spell on him the minute her anti-magic was gone.

"Did you kill him?"

Nico shook his head. "He's asleep." He pulled off Luther's tie and moved to Vanessa. She, too, was near-collapsed on the floor. He bound her and then put her to sleep as Tory pulled her anti-magic away.

Arlen raced for the door. Tory beat him to it and blocked his way out. "Oh no you don't." She pressed hard on him with anti-magic, and beads of sweat broke out on his forehead. "You're younger than the others, aren't you? But I could still kill you." Let him think she might. She kept a close eye on him, terrified she might do so accidentally.

"Out of my way!" Arlen reached out to push Tory aside, but the moment his fingers touched her arm, he screamed and jerked his hand back.

Nico grabbed the hand and wrenched it behind his back. "You're not going anywhere."

Then James leapt at Nico, knocking both him and Arlen to the floor. Tory took a breath and concentrated on James. She honed her anti-magic into a spear and stabbed him, just like she'd stabbed Nico in the library. He cried out and doubled over. "Tie him up, Nico! I can't hold him long like this without killing him." Nico whipped off his own belt and used it to bind James' hands. Tory withdrew the spear

232

and turned her focus to Arlen. He was on all fours, panting like a dog, his chins wobbling. He was obviously spent. She pressed her anti-magic around him, but she hardly needed to. When Nico came to him with James' tie, he simply collapsed onto his stomach and presented his hands to be tied.

When the wizards were all sleeping peacefully on the floor, Tory looked at Nico. His face was awash in blood. She pulled a tissue from her pocket and reached out toward him, then snatched her hand back. "I suppose I should let you heal that instead."

He was still breathing hard. He shook his head. "Don't want to waste the magic right now. This commotion will bring others."

Tory gasped. "Jess!"

Nico's eyes widened, and they both lunged for the door.

39

Nico

Nico led Tory down the corridor to the elevator, headed toward the fourth-floor interrogation rooms where he hoped they'd find Jess and Puck. Just as he reached the elevator, the door opened and half a dozen concerned-looking people tried to surge out.

"Nico!" one of them called in surprise, drawing up short and stopping everyone else. "What's happened?"

Nico didn't skip a beat. "Level one. Magical intrusion. Luther wants everyone down there now!" He pressed the down button and the door closed on the confused and chattering staff. "The stairs!" He pushed open the stairwell door and pounded up to the fourth floor, with Tory close on his heels. He sprinted halfway down the corridor and then slowed, peering into the windows of each room.

"Is this where they brought her?" Tory whispered.

"I don't know. It might be. I hope it is." As they neared the end of the corridor, a piercing alarm began wailing. *If anything strange happens, kill them both.* "Dammit. Where is she?"

Doors opened in the hall and frowning people emerged, peering up and down the corridor. Their eyes lit on Nico and Tory.

"Nico?" Tory's voice shook. They were hemmed in

on either side by Users.

"Pull your anti-magic in," he muttered. "Don't let them know what you are." Then he raised his voice. "Magical intrusion on the first floor. Luther wants everyone down there now." He grabbed Tory's arm, ignoring the sizzle of anti-magic on his hand, and pulled her past his colleagues and into the stairwell.

"Up!" He and Tory raced to the fifth floor. Behind him, others entered the stairwell, a cacophony of confused voices echoing up and down the steps. He thought he heard the word *Squelcher*, and he hoped they had time to find Jess and get out before the confusion turned to action. The siren continued to wail.

The fifth floor was home to the Counterterrorism Division. There were two holding cells on the floor which were occasionally used by the Magical Division. If Jess wasn't in one of them, he didn't know where she could be.

They reached the fire door, and Nico came to a halt. "There are no Users on this floor. Act normal, and no one will know we don't belong here."

Tory looked him up and down and raised her eyebrows. He looked down at his shirt, still smoking slightly, and remembered the gash on his face and the singed seat of his pants. "Okay, maybe we should just move quickly and hope we're not seen."

No alarm sounded on this floor, and the corridor was empty. They hurried down the hall to the first holding cell, and Nico tried the door. It was locked. Damn. He didn't want to waste any magic on simply getting through a door, but it had to be done. He placed a hand on the lock and took a breath.

"Wait." Tory laid a hand on his arm and then snatched it back. She pressed her ear to the door. "If Jess is in there with guards, she'll be talking." A moment later she straightened up and shook her head.

"There's another holding cell." Nico jogged down the hall, Tory on his heels.

There was no need to press an ear against the door—Nico heard Jess's laugh as they approached. A low rumble afterwards must have been the voice of one of the guards.

"There are three guards, assuming they've all stayed with her," Nico whispered. "I'll unlock the door and disarm them magically. You stay back."

"Are you kidding? You'll need me."

"The guards aren't wizards. They're well-trained fighters. You don't stand a chance against them."

"Then neither do you. I'm going with you. That makes it three against three." She responded to Nico's frown with, "I'll keep my anti-magic away from you, don't worry."

There wasn't time to argue. Nico nodded. He turned and pressed a hand against the lock. A simple spell and it clicked. He shouldered open the door, his magical attack already in motion.

One guard stood by the door. A second was in the center of the room, and the third sat on a chair facing Jess, smiling at her. Clearly she'd been charming them—guards weren't supposed to sit on duty.

The guards cried out as their guns sailed out of their hands and clattered into the corner. Jess whooped and, to Nico's surprise, whipped her hands out to thwack the guard nearest her across the face with her handcuffs. Good thing he hadn't tightened them down.

Tory tackled the guard by the door, knocking him off his feet. The one in the middle of the room turned on Nico. Surprised by Jess and exhausted from magic use, Nico wasn't fast enough, and the guard's first punch landed square on his jaw, snapping his head to the side and making him stagger.

Damn. A spell. He needed to cast a spell and take

this guy out. He couldn't think. There was a tightness in his chest, and he struggled to breathe.

Another punch threw him to his knees.

Tory snarled as she rolled along the floor with the door guard. Tory. That was it. She'd lost control of her anti-magic.

A kick to his stomach flattened him. "Tory!" he rasped. "Tory! Your power!"

The guard put a booted foot on Nico's back and wrenched his arm into a position that made his eyes water. "Shut up."

Tory scrambled clear of the guard on her and grabbed a chair. With a great sweep, she cracked him across the head with it. He collapsed to the floor. She gasped and dropped the chair, staring at the guard's crumpled form.

Then she looked up and saw Nico. She swore, and her anti-magic suddenly retreated.

"Don't make a move, or the girl's dead."

Nico and Tory snapped their eyes to Jess, held by the third guard, with a knife at her throat.

"I can kill her before any of your spells hit me," the guard warned. He glanced at Tory. "And whatever you do, it doesn't work on me."

Tory looked down at the guard she'd clobbered, and Nico suppressed a crazy urge to laugh. A chair would work on him alright.

But the man was right. Casting a spell would require moving, and he'd see the movement, and Jess would be dead. He sighed in defeat, and Tory raised her hands. "Please don't hurt her."

Jess swallowed, her eyes fixed pleadingly on Tory.

"I'll do whatever you want. Just let Jess go."

Footsteps thundered down the hallway. Shit. The other wizards were on the way. Nico was in no state to fight them all. He was powerless. Powerless to help Jess and Tory, powerless to save his own reputation, his own career, and powerless to change the Magical Division. The wizards would come in, take control, find Luther and the others unconscious, and that would be that. It was over for all of them.

Funny, the part that worried him least was the end of his career. He watched Tory, her eyes darting from Jess to him. She frowned, and Nico knew she was thinking how he'd failed. How he'd betrayed her trust, bringing her here, into the midst of her enemies, sure in his ability to fix everything. Sure in his own power.

He'd been so arrogant.

He'd underestimated the rest of the Magical Division. He'd underestimated Luther's influence, his power.

They would kill Jess and Tory. He knew it. That's what they'd intended all along. They'd spare him, because he was a wizard, but that was cold comfort—he'd be cast out of the Magical Division and magical society. He'd be shunned. He'd never be able to openly use his magic again.

Damn. Damn. Damn!

The footsteps reached the door, but the instant before it was flung open, the guard holding Jess bellowed in pain and dropped his knife. Jess turned and kneed the man hard in the groin. Nico winced in sympathy. The man doubled over, and Nico saw what had happened. Puck clung to his back, his jaws clamped on the man's neck.

Nico shifted his weight and fired a spell at the man holding him. The guard folded gently to the floor, half on top of Nico.

Then the door burst open, and Nico's colleagues swarmed into the room. It was too late to escape. Nico shut his eyes. He didn't want to watch Tory and Jess die.

The footsteps abruptly stopped, and a gasp made him open his eyes again. His colleagues crowded the door, but no one had advanced into the room. Those at the back pushed the ones in the front forward, and they cried out, clutching their chests.

Nico turned to see Tory glaring at the intruders. She was keeping them back with her anti-magic. Manipulating it around him to concentrate it at the door. It seems he'd underestimated her too.

Jess cried out, dragging his gaze back to her. The third guard had recovered and was grappling with her. Nico shook himself out of his stupor and quickly stunned him.

Jess stepped away from the guard. "About time, wizard. I could have used you a few minutes ago."

"I don't know. You and Puck seemed to have it in hand." He gave her a wry smile.

"Good old Puck." Jess petted the cat, now cleaning his paws as though bringing down an armed guard was nothing.

"Nico Michaelson! Explain!" It was the Assistant Director for International Operations. The woman he hoped to replace.

How could he explain this to her? He'd attacked multiple colleagues, including Luther Hawkins. He'd refused to kill a dangerous Squelcher. In fact, he'd helped her gain control of her power. Control that was currently keeping the entire Magical Division at bay. *Fuck.* He was screwed. There was no way to explain this. And seeing the strength of what Tory was doing, he began to worry for himself. If she turned on him …

"Nico?"

He shoved the guard off him and looked up at Tory. She reached down and offered him a hand. She flashed him the briefest of smiles.

He took her hand. It sizzled as she pulled him to his feet, but he didn't let go immediately. He looked her in the eyes. There was confidence there. She was luminous with it, and it stunned him as much as her power did.

She gave his hand a quick squeeze and let go. He turned to face the Users and she stepped up beside him, standing shoulder to shoulder. Wizard and Squelcher. Who would have thought?

"Nico. Perhaps you can introduce me to your colleagues, and then explain to them what's been going on within the Magical Division and why it needs to stop." Her voice was steel, and he glanced at her. Was this really Tory?

He rubbed his aching shoulder and then straightened himself. "This is Tory Williams. She's a librarian." He saw Tory's smile from the corner of his eye. "She likes cats, classic literature and black coffee. She's a little bit shy, but once you get to know her, she's friendly and easy to talk to." Tory jabbed him with an elbow, and Nico smiled. "Oh. She's also a Squelcher."

There was an audible gasp from the gathered witches and wizards. The ones closest to them took a step backward.

"Yes. I'm a librarian. You should be afraid." Tory stepped forward slightly. "Until recently, I didn't know I was a Squelcher. Unbeknownst to me, my power caused damage." She lowered her eyes for a moment. "Killed a man." Looking back up, she continued. "Nico helped me understand my power. Helped me control it." Again there was a gasp from the crowd, and angry muttering. "It is because of him that I'm able to manipulate my power in such a way as to deter you from entering without killing you and without harming Nico."

Nico nodded. "Tory is fully capable of killing with her power. She chooses not to. And today she trusted me enough to enter this building in handcuffs with her best friend in order to prove to the FBI that she is no danger to the U.S. government."

"And how was my trust repaid? With deception and attempted murder." Tory glared at the assembled crowd. "Is this the mode of operation of the Magical Division? To eliminate all problems with murder? To ignore evidence in favor of age-old prejudice against anyone who isn't a witch or wizard? To illegally target American citizens who haven't committed a crime?"

"You said yourself you killed a wizard." The voice came from the back of the crowd.

Nico rolled his eyes. "It was completely unintentional, and the wizard in question was two hundred and thirty-five years old. The point is that this *is* the modus operandi of the Magical Division. You all know it. We've all done things we know are illegal, immoral. The FBI is supposed to make American citizens safer, but tell me— when was the last time you considered the safety of Insigs in your operations? How many Insigs have you harmed or killed as simply the cost of doing business? We've lost sight of our mission. We've lost sight of what we should be doing with our power."

"If you expect us to protect Insigs, who have done nothing but persecute Users throughout history—"

"When was the last time you, personally, were persecuted?" Nico asked. "Have you really been harmed by Insigs? The last witch hunt in America happened almost two hundred years ago." Nico pointed at the tall African American wizard toward the back. "Bill—have you been persecuted, personally, for your magical abilities?"

"Well … no." Bill shook his head.

"Have you experienced racism within the magical community?"

Bill snorted and nodded.

"Yet I don't see you disregarding the human rights

of Caucasian witches and wizards. Why do you ignore the rights of Insigs?"

Bill frowned, as did a number of others.

"But they don't even know about us," argued someone near the back. "Of course they don't persecute us."

"Your prejudice is based on two-hundred-year-old events. Insigs have moved on—racism, sexism, homophobia—they're all on the decline. Insigs have embraced diversity. Are we really so close-minded we can't? Are we really so much better than them?" He raised his eyebrows at his colleagues. "For all our power, do we use it for the greater good? Or do we use it to reinforce outdated prejudice, and only for our own gain?"

"Well your own father—"

Nico cut off the speaker with his hand. "My father was as misguided as Luther Hawkins. I don't know if any of you remember my mother, Celia Constantine." A number of people nodded and smiled. "She spent her life, and gave her life, in service for the good of everyone, Insig and User alike. Countless Insigs owe her their lives. Countless Insigs are living full, successful lives because of her skill. What a legacy to leave behind! I ask you all—what will your legacy be? A trail of bodies and ruined lives? Oh, you might have your lovely mansion and everything you want at your fingertips, but at what price? When you die, who will mourn your loss?"

This wasn't the speech he intended to give, but the words spilled out. They were what he had been pondering for the past few days. His own legacy. His own life.

Tory stepped in. "Today, you have a choice. Luther Hawkins is handcuffed and sleeping peacefully in Conference Room C right now. My father, Victor Hughes, is a wizard." Eyebrows rose, and Tory smiled wearily. "Yes. I never met him before I had control of my power, as you can imagine. You see, my power has hurt me more than anyone else." She paused, and Nico saw one or two faces soften. "Victor has been compiling evidence against Luther for years. Evidence of illegal activity here in the Magical Division." This was news to Nico. He raised an eyebrow at Tory. "One way or another, you all need to choose. Will you follow Luther's ancient, small-minded prejudice, or will you join the twenty-first century with the rest of us?" She glanced at Nico. "I think Nico has some ideas for changes to the Magical Division. Changes you can be genuinely proud of."

Silence descended among Nico's colleagues. Feet shifted uncomfortably, and it was a minute before Nico realized that Tory had withdrawn her power.

40

Tory

Tory stood between the two wizards in the parking lot, Puck perched in his usual spot on her shoulder.

Victor handed her a fat manila envelope. "Here are the maps. Danilo will meet you at the airport in Guatemala City." Tory took the envelope and smiled at her father. "How did your talk with Mom go yesterday?"

Victor's gaze dropped. He shrugged. "Could have been worse. She only threw one plate at me."

"It's a lot for her to process. It's a lot of years to make up for. Give her time. I know she loved you."

Victor nodded and smiled. He turned back toward the apartment. "Where is that friend of yours?"

Tory laughed. "Jess is always late. She'll be here."

"There she is now." Nico pointed to a bright pink head bobbing toward them. He jogged over, took her suitcase from her and tossed it into the car.

Tory took a deep breath. This was it. She was on her way to Guatemala. She didn't need to flee the country; Nico's speech and Victor's evidence had done their work. Luther Hawkins was out, and Nico had rocketed right to the top of the Magical Division, sweeping in a host of changes in the organization. New checks and balances on all agents' actions, an entirely new upper management, new rules about the treatment of Insigs, and sensitivity training for everyone in the Division—it was an entirely different organization. One that would never persecute a Squelcher.

She wasn't fleeing; she'd chosen this trip. That didn't mean she wasn't terrified, but it was a good terrified. And it would give her a chance to use her own power—the idea gave her goose bumps. Victor had asked her to join one of his archaeological teams in Guatemala. A series of magically-protected temples defied entry and exploration—dozens of researchers and hundreds of curious locals had been killed attempting to enter them over the past century—and he thought her skills might be handy.

Jess had insisted on joining her. She had started a PhD program with Victor, focusing on psycho-social magical understanding, whatever that was.

"Sorry I'm late." Jess hurried up to the group.

Nico checked his watch. "We should get going."

Jess gave a little whoop and hopped into the car.

Tory resisted the urge to hug her father. She'd found she could touch younger Users with care, but the older ones were simply too susceptible to her power, particularly if they kept themselves alive magically beyond their years. She smiled at him. "See you, Dad."

Meow!

Victor chuckled and patted Puck on the head. "Text me when you get there."

Tory nodded and slipped into the passenger seat. Puck leapt to the dashboard and flopped down. Nico followed after shaking Victor's hand. He started the car and pulled away from the curb.

"So how'd you swing a swank FBI car to take us to the airport?" Jess asked.

Nico smiled. "I get a permanent company car now."

Tory shook her head. So much had changed in the past month, she still sometimes wondered if this was really her life, or if she'd wake up from this crazy dream to find she was still a librarian at Laurel Glen Public Library. She sometimes found it hard to remember that librarian. And then there were times when she longed for that life back. She resisted the longing. It did no good to wish for it, and it was time for her to step beyond her comfort zone and do something different.

When they arrived at the airport, Nico accompanied them to the check-in counter. The woman eyed Tory suspiciously. "The cat needs to be in a carrier."

"Oh, he's not traveling with us." She shrugged. "He's just here to send me off."

The woman's eyes said, *Well, aren't you the crazy cat lady?* She said nothing, though, and printed out their luggage tags and handed them their boarding passes. "Gate twenty-two. Upstairs."

At security, Jess farewelled Nico. "Thanks for a wild ride, cowboy." She winked. "Anytime you want to handcuff me and take me to the Ritz, you just give me a call, eh?"

Nico shook his head.

Tory rolled her eyes. "You go on. I'd like a word with Nico. I'll meet you at the gate."

Jess blew a kiss to Nico and headed through security.

Tory fiddled nervously with the strap of her bag, avoiding Nico's eyes. She and Nico hadn't spoken directly of his offer to 'cure' her since the day before the altercation at the FBI, but he'd danced around the topic several times in the weeks since. She knew he wanted to help her, and she also knew his motivation was partly that somehow, he'd fallen in love with her.

She liked Nico. Liked him a lot. Of course she didn't—couldn't—love him. Not romantically. He wanted her to be able to. If the cure worked, she would be capable. But *would* she?

And if she did, would she still be herself? Who was she, anyway? A month ago, she would never have considered heading off to a remote patch of rainforest in Guatemala to help unravel the story behind a set of ancient ruins. A month ago, the thought of leaving Puck with someone else for two months would have terrified her. A month ago, she didn't know she had a power that could stop a dozen powerful wizards in their tracks. Hell, a month ago, she thought wizards were fictional characters in books.

"Nico." She glanced up to find him fidgeting with the zipper on his jacket. He met her gaze. "A while ago, you offered to try to … cure me." He nodded, and she saw hope in his eyes. "Thank you. I appreciate the offer, and I appreciate what it might cost you to try. But …"

His shoulders slumped. "But you're not interested."

"I'm not interested *now*. It's just too much change. Too many new things. I need to work through what it means to be me all over again. I hardly know what it is to be a Squelcher; I don't even know if there's anything to cure, because I don't know what my condition is." She frowned. "Sorry, I'm not expressing myself well."

Nico nodded. "It's okay. I understand. You need to explore the new you. You're right. It's probably best not to throw away a power you haven't even explored." He dropped his gaze. "I guess I just … well, if you change your mind, let me know. The offer stands, and I don't want to pressure you into it."

"Thanks." They stood awkwardly, not quite looking at each other for a minute. Then Tory sighed. "I guess I should go. They'll be boarding soon." She lifted Puck from her shoulder and gave him a kiss. "Be good for Nico. No tearing apart his couch, eh?"

Meow!

Nico reached out for the cat, and Puck happily clambered onto his shoulder. Tory smiled. She would miss him, but Puck was in good hands. She would miss Nico too.

"Stay in touch. Let me know how things go with the

Magical Division."

Nico nodded. "And you. I'll be waiting to hear how your power does against those ancient spells." He pulled a paperback from his jacket pocket. "Oh, I thought you might like to read this." He handed it to her—a used copy of *The Red and the Black*. "I hope you haven't read it already. I got a copy for myself too. I'll want to compare notes."

Tory smiled. "Thanks. No, I haven't read it." She didn't know what else to say. Her conflicted emotions and his frustrated hopes made everything awkward. She held out a hand. Nico took it and pulled her into a brief hug that sizzled on Tory's skin.

"Bye."

"See you." Tory turned and hurried toward security.

Acknowledgements

Thanks to my early readers: Amy, Catherine, Emily, Hayley, Ian and Nikky. Thanks also goes to my editor, Belinda, who saved me from many embarrassing mistakes and leads the way in the conservation of commas.

As always, special thanks goes to my husband, who initiated the idea for this book many years ago and suffered through a very different and much longer version of the story before I wrote this one.

About the Author

⸻

Robinne is an entomologist and educator by training, but she has never been able to control her writing habit. She has been publishing poetry and short stories since the 1970s, and has been known to answer exam questions in verse. Her short stories have won multiple awards for science fiction and fantasy writing.

Robinne's other books include several fantasy/adventure novels for ages 8-13 and two non-fiction books about insects.

Robinne is blessed to live in New Zealand, where even ordinary life is magical.

Visit her online at www.robinneweiss.com.

Other Books by Robinne Weiss

Fantasy and Adventure For ages 8-13:

The Dragon Slayer's Son
The Dragon Slayer's Daughter
The Dragon Defence League
The Ipswich Witch
A Glint of Exoskeleton

Non-Fiction:

Insects in the Classroom
Backyard Bugwatcher

Coming Soon!
Dragon Homecoming

Something fearsome lurks in the mountains. A legend of ice and snow, threatened by a changing climate.

The Dragon Defence League embarks on its most audacious mission yet. A mission that will take them to the ends of the earth and require the help of a nation. Can they pull it off before it's too late?